AN ILLUMINATED HISTORY
OF THE FUTURE

Edited by

CURTIS WHITE

ILLINOIS STATE UNIVERSITY

FICTION COLLECTIVE TWO

Boulder · Normal
Brooklyn

AN ILLUMINATED HISTORY
OF THE FUTURE

Illinois State University / Fiction Collective Two

Curtis White, Series Editor

TABLE OF CONTENTS

This publication is the 1989 winner of the Illinois State
University/Fiction Collective Two award, jointly sponsored by the
Illinois State University Fine Arts Festival and Fiction Collective
Two.

Published by Fiction Collective Two with assistance from the
Illinois State University Foundation; the support of the Publications
Center, University of Colorado, Boulder; and the cooperation of
Brooklyn College, and Teachers and Writers Collaborative.

White, Curtis.
  An Illuminated History of the Future.

ISBN: 0-932511-25-2
ISBN: 0-932511-26-0 (pbk.)

Manufactured in the United States of America.

Special thanks to Paul Auster for his help in the selection of these
stories.

AN ILLUMINATED HISTORY OF THE FUTURE

Curtis White

In Thailand: a Prefatory Parable

In the stories which follow, the future is no longer merely one of the usual suspects to be rounded up. These fictions reconstruct the future. As in *Blade Runner*, beneath the high-tech gloss of a future Los Angeles or Bangkok, down where animal fat has made the concrete soft, that same rag and bone shop simmers, truly, the very casserole of history.

I was welcomed to Thailand by Coca-Cola: an enormous billboard featuring a popular Thai rock band relaxing with cans of Coke. Later, at the Impala Hotel in Bangkok, I was given a more authentic Thai greeting by mosquitoes. I found one or two, but others were small, silent and smart enough to elude and survive. Silent, that is, until I turned the lights out, at which point they buzzed in with all of the subtlety displayed by Japanese businessmen reaping Thai baht over coffee and cigarettes. When I awoke the next morning, there was a set of bites in the shape of a lotus leaf on my pale chest. The bites looked like the perforations on a customs document.

Let me tell you a story. It didn't happen to me while I was in Thailand, but never mind that. I was down in

Songkhla staying in a 100 baht room at the Holland Bar. Fat Dutch guy owned the place. He catered to an upscale gay clientele and their native boys. He owned a VCR and nice color TV but only one tape, a Madonna concert tape live in Italy. (Prime Minister Chatichai ousted ex-Prime Minister Prem on the strength of his commitment to "Material Girl" as the new Thai national anthem.) For my part, I grew to know the muscles in Madonna's arms. By the end of my stay, I was convinced she had fallen for me. I think we could have worked something out, but I was damned busy with the boys. I was straight as a string till I found myself in Thailand. It started out with suck jobs with fellows on the beach. It was all good fun for the boys, although none forgot the service charge. By the end of my stay, I was balling four boys per day, none of them a bit better than they needed to be. It only took two weeks for my disease to depopulate most of southern Thailand even to the Burma mountains that look like angular camels. Only a few women remained in scattered, stubborn rural pockets, places where JELLO still causes a stir. I was asked to leave and agreed it was probably best for all concerned. New boys are being smuggled back into southern Thailand in the flat woven baskets traditionally used for growing silkworms. Damndest thing, the boys take on some of the worm's identity in the process, wriggling over each other and lifting themselves to be fed. When I learned of this strategy, my fatigue and distress became extreme because I knew it would all just have to be done again. That's the misery of mastery here in post-imperial, new colonial Thailand, where the tourist is sahib.

I am tired. I think of being in Thailand and my eyes get heavy. I sleep. On the morning of my second day in Thailand I wake feeling special. I go downstairs for breakfast with the *Bangkok Post* and read that the Panchen Lama has died. The search for his reincarnate successor has begun. For a moment, I feel quite pleased with myself.

The official purpose of my visit to Thailand was to lecture at campuses of Sri Nakarinwirot University on modern American literature. They wanted to know about the short story. When they said the words "short story," I almost believed that such a thing existed. They're so innocent. They wept when I told them that American literature was dead. No time lost grieving in America, I'll tell you. The undergraduate students wear uniforms here, the girls white blouses and blue skirts. I was lecturing one day on postmodernism and the critique of the structure of reference in Saussure when I realized that they weren't understanding a word I said. I informed them that in fact I was speaking in tongues, glossolalia. We were having a religious experience. Oh! They were pleased. So that's what this was! A light blue sexual pall descended upon us. We were in love. I fell upon a young girl whose brown legs I'd been admiring. To my surprise, she was wearing edible panties, prawn flavored. I took my first nibble and the class began to giggle. I asked if I was doing something wrong. Apparently, in Thailand, the head of the professor should never be below the heads of the students. I'd made quite a mistake. But they forgave me because I was a *farang* (foreigner) and was expected to make humiliating errors of custom. Needless to say, I immediately returned to my august position at the front of the class, head above the throng, and continued with my probings at enlightenment.

After the lecture, I was taken to lunch by my Thai colleagues at which meal devastating evidence was presented that I was not human, thus placing the status of my grant in grave question. The wife of one of the Foreign Affairs administrators asked me if I liked Thailand.

"Yes, of course, very much."

"And what do you like most?"

"The food is wonderful. I like the spices."

"And have you tried a Thai girl yet?"

Were Thai girls like potato chips? "No I haven't. I'm afraid that if I have one, I'll need to have another. Next thing you know, the bag will be empty."

"Bag?" she inquired.

I smiled enigmatically, trying to out inscrutable her. My hosts talked among themselves until they reached a conclusion.

"What are you all talking about?" I asked.

"My wife says you are not human."

"Not human?"

"Yes, yes! Not human! Our friends agree."

I didn't know their friends. One was an accountant for a Thai-Texas oil concern. He'd been to Dallas. That seemed to make him objective. That seemed to make his opinion count for a lot.

"Tell her that I am human. Still human. Human anyway. I am human in spite of the facts."

He thought about it and then declared, "This can not be said in Thai."

I wanted to argue that it sure as bloody hell could (I'd read it in the Abhidharma, their own sacred commentary on the teachings of Lord Buddha), but I didn't want to start a row. So I conceded that it was possible that I was not human. I was mortified. If I had confessed to my mortification, perhaps they would have agreed that I was a dead human at least.

Speaking of dead people, I had dinner at the Oriental Hotel, below its famed Joseph Conrad suite, with a Fulbright scholar about to return to the States. Actually, to Knoxville, Tennessee. He told me that he had written an essay for delivery to the Rotary Club called "Thailand: Land of Contrasts."

His little title infuriated me. "Don't be stupid," I scolded. "Say what you mean. Thailand is not a land of contrasts, it is a land of contradictions. There's a difference, you know."

He didn't care for my tone and before you knew it (certainly before I knew it) we were in one hell of an argument over whether or not Orlando, Florida was vulgar. I don't believe in vulgarity, but I was more than happy to take up its cause if that meant that I could attack Disney World. We parted feeling like father and son.

One night I was offered one of Thailand's contradictions for dinner. We guests were offered "Chicken Lolita." What should I have made of this delicacy? It made me think as much of Jonathan Swift's "Modest Proposal" as of Nabokov's kindly classic about "nymphets." Then I thought of Greek myth in which revenge is acquired by serving your child to you, her head under a platter, her thin lips buzzing their last childish tune. I chose the vegetarian fried rice, drank a weak cup of tepid Chinese tea, left a generous tip, and crept back to my room feeling that I had been damned lucky that time.

One last story in Thailand. Night before I left. Cruising Patpong with boys and girls rippling behind me, clutching to my arms like holiday streamers. A largish crowd ahead, being offered something for sale. But too excited. It's a squarish woman with a shoe box, the contents of which is for sale for 2,000 baht. It's a kitty. 2,000 baht for a kitty? No, it's a tiger cub, and not more than a week or two old. Was it stolen from its den? Was the mother killed? Was this woman right to speculate that she could sell it to the gathered *farang*?

I returned to my hotel to pack for the long return trip to Normal, Illinois, flying back across the international date line into last night. I rubbed some aloe vera into the still sanguine lotus leaf of mosquito bites. Thailand had left its mark on me. I determined that when I was asked, "How was Thailand?" I would answer by lifting my shirt to show the inflamed scar leeching to my translucent breast like a bloodsucking annelid worm. (Of course, my friends would take it for a hickey from some nipple-sucking Ganymede. Because I'm not human, I'm doomed to be misunderstood.) My fear was that even though I had resisted the urge to smuggle out one of Thailand's treasures—ivory, sapphires, exotic birds, opium, antiquities, a Buddha image, a tiger, a fifteen year old girl—I sported this bloody badge which might attract the suspicion of a customs agent, who might conclude that it was the mark of a criminal understanding.

Yes, I took a risk penetrating the line of custom's police, my chest and its angry badge itching, my hand not daring to scratch. But it was a risk I took willingly because I'm a big fan of the future. I want one. The authors collected here want one too. They have a plan: to liberate the possible from the dictatorship of the present. So, help them out, won't you? Support the future. Give to the criminal understanding of your choice.

14

R. M. Berry

The Anatomy of Marcantonio Della Torre

(excerpt from: *Leonardo da Vinci Is Dying*)

The young anatomist Marcantonio della Torre had stopped breathing. Of course, that might have been because the air in the little room was so ripe you could have written your name in it. Leonardo sniffed at the candle-flame, let the heat clean out his nose and throat. He always marveled at his young friend's capacity to disregard rot, almost as if he'd handled death so often it bored him. Leonardo had watched della Torre work night after night with midges crawling into his ears, the candles hissing out, and gasses that brought Leonardo's gorge up enveloping his face—and never a blink. His was a kind of anti-soul, thriving on blood, shit, dirt, bones. All his life Leonardo had tried to understand appearances, to live simultaneously within his senses and beside them, and by the time he met della Torre he'd already come to regard his eyes and ears as tools, but odors would always dismay him. A breeze dank with plant mold or the waft of musk from his own arm could smear him across past and future, annihilate everything nearby, make the darkness surrounding the table, the carrion basket at his feet, even his own hands, unimaginable. How could anyone ignore corruption? A moth flapped into the flame, caught spattering fire, burst.

Della Torre's fingers made little sucking noises as they slithered about in the meat. Only if you murdered longing, crammed your life into the tips of your fingers and heard childhood, if at all, like conversation across cold water—no, della Torre had little use for breathing.

"I'm sure it was revenge."

The voice brought Leonardo's head up.

"I know that sounds harsh," della Torre said. "There was virtue in it too, I suppose—duty or honor. I may be incapable of fidelity, but that doesn't mean I can't recognize it."

Leonardo looked over the candle into della Torre's face. They were discussing the anatomist's former schoolmaster, one Guido da Forli, a man della Torre had never decided whether to revere or to despise. The tutor's story had become a regular squabbling point between them, provoking all manner of oratory, proverbs, authoritative allusions, even insults, but in the past della Torre had always walked away laughing. His arrogance was so pure only a petty mind would begrudge it. But tonight he seemed to be straining. One hand picked at a lump of tissue on the table, let it drop. He leaned forward as if unsure whether to say more. Leonardo watched.

"Of course I carved the body he gave me—from nostril to knee. what would you expect? I was the pupil. I spent two entire days up to my wrists in the viscera. When it came time for the university, I was ready."

"Guido da Forli was a teacher," Leonardo said. "He could wait."

"He hated me."

"I don't see that it makes any difference."

Della Torre smirked. "Perhaps not, but disappointment can be a harsh master." Then laying his probe down on the cadaver's navel, della Torre smiled the quizzical smile of a man who'd never been lighthearted a day in his life, mouth turned up, brows turned down, and glancing at the darkness eating their heads, he told Leonardo the story of Matteo da Rimini.

The League of Cambrai of 1509 had proven no more noteworthy than any other Renaissance political entanglement, thrown together as it was to acquire momentarily within the spider web of plots and counterplots pieces of a few virtually ungovernable dominions for the purpose of ceding or obliterating them immediately afterwards, its one memorable difference being the way the Italians made the French look like chumps. Hardly four years later Machiavelli would codify the principle at work here—betray utterly, annihilate completely, bribe lavishly, but never do anything just a little bit—and the French, suspecting everyone for a liar but no one for an extravagant liar, ended up defeating themselves by defeating Venice by believing in the Pope. Specifically, they spread the body parts of 20,000 foot-soldiers across Italy from Cassano to Peschiera before Pope Julius made it up with the Doge, linked elbows with the Emperor, bought up a slew of Swiss mercenaries, appealed to Italian patriotism, and chased the bewildered Louis Douze back across the Alps. Renaissance politics as usual. Nor was there anything extraordinary about the accompanying chaos in Venetian university towns like Padua, the students having long grown accustomed to running riot whenever the government did and the townspeople having always despised the little snotwads in the first place. Any ripple sufficed to start the accusations flying, the students rampaging, the militia banging on the doors at night. And that one of these accusations would mention an anatomist or that the militia would eventually end up banging on an anatomist's door would have struck no one as surprising. Even in Padua where as many as a hundred of the swankiest citizens might appear in the dissecting theater to watch a nameless prosector run his cleaver across a dead prostitute's sternum and where cadavers were officially if parsimoniously supplied to the medical faculty by the Venetian state, even here the circle of tolerance was narrow, fragile. Before every dissection the Pope's indulgence had to be read, the inquisition's authority acknowledged, the cadaver's pardon begged, the university seal flourished, the local rulers invoked, the head lopped off, the eyes poked out and all manner of spooks and hobgoblins shooed away. No, the only unusual thing about all this was the way it converged on Marcantonio della Torre.

Della Torre in 1509 was professor of the philosophy of medicine at Padua, and though only twenty-eight years old, already a notorious figure. Having been appointed university lecturer in ordinary while still a teenager, he'd immediately terrified and offended the entire faculty by dismissing the barber-surgeons from his public readings and taking up the dissecting knife himself, a practice made possible by his ability to recite from memory whole chapters of Galen, thus enabling him to come down from the podium and speak from the table. Moreover, he was rumored to continue his anatomical studies in his own chambers at night. This last had something especially racy and delicious about it. Aside from being strictly illegal, cutting up a human body alone in the dark looked a lot more diabolical than scientific and, given the absolute unavailability of cadavers, assuredly meant grave-robbing, if not murder. Needless to say, the students considered della Torre the hottest show in town. The townsfolk, on the other hand, would've liked to roast him. Even the prosperous burghers who attended his dissections, subsidized the scholars, and prided themselves on having one foot in the new learning—usually the same one they'd gotten into the door of the Medici bank—even these acknowledged that he was uncouth, and no sooner had the French handed the Venetian army its fanny at

Agnadello than the city fathers started tossing around della Torre's name as a possible scapegoat. The students who at the moment were drinking themselves blind, looting and virtually bringing Padua to a standstill would've been a likelier choice, but since they were more numerous and a good deal braver than the depleted constabulary, the authorities preferred to go after their professor. Exactly what, everyone suddenly wanted to know, was an impious subverter of civic virtue who was known to be lacking in human decency, not to mention plain old squeamishness, doing up alone all night during a political crisis as everyone else in town prepared to resist a hostile invasion and practiced their French? The question's impossible syntax should've been its own answer, but it wasn't, which brings up Matteo da Rimini.

Matteo had been a colleague and close friend of Marcantonio's deceased father, Girolamo, and so, unlike everyone else on the faculty, had no personal basis for disliking the young anatomist. Instead, Matteo hated him with the pure and selfless hatred with which only the finest minds of a dying age can hate the future. He did not desire to see Marcantonio stumble; he longed to see him erased, or failing that, to see him quashed, squalidly humiliated, forced to recant his every living breath. This wish was acid in Matteo's bowels, a spike through his dreams. He sucked it, wept it, washed and fondled it, woke each morning praying: Let it happen today! For fourteen years he'd suffered the boy's disdain. The adolescent Marcantonio had simply appeared in the piazza one grimy August afternoon, possessed not so much of a powerful name or patrimony as of a sublime confidence that he was judge of the world. Professors old enough to be his grandsires competed shamelessly for his attention, descended to tricks and pratfalls, whispered their rivals' foibles in his ear, as if this child's admiration could redeem mistaken lives. Marcantonio submitted to their worship, but whenever he deigned to

speak, the men knew they were no better than plumb-
lines in his hands, chisels, rusty saws. Matteo who'd set
out to guide him for Girolamo's sake felt puzzled that,
when addressed, Marcantonio always turned his face
away, and so concluded that his friend's son had grown
up indolent and simple. But then one evening when, at
the end of his patience, Matteo seized Marcantonio's
neck and spun his head around, he saw in the vacant gaze
an insolence so vast it left him giddy. The muscles of
Marcantonio's face remained motionless. His eyelids
never lowered. He peered back at the older man as if,
instead of being reproved, it were he, this fifteen-year-
old simpleton, who was examining Matteo da Rimini.
Matteo blinked his eyes. No one would ever be this
child's teacher. And stepping backwards he heard his
soul ask for the first time the question he'd later hear
whispered in cafes, shops, hallways, the piazza: Was it
really possible, could the son of their beloved Girolamo
possess Satan's own knowledge, was this the evil they'd
always feared would come from seeking the truth?

And so Matteo swore to have nothing further to do
with the boy. He would watch, wait for the reckoning.
But on the day Girolamo della Torre yielded his ghost to
heaven, Matteo had been standing beside his friend's
bed, and bending down to witness the cracked, salty lips
kiss the spirit away, Matteo heard his friend lisp a last
word—Marcantonio! And thinking he recognized in this
sound a father's dying request, Matteo assured him, yes,
he would look to the boy's education, watch over him as
a father, intending of course to do nothing of the kind, no
sensible man ever being bound by deathbed extortion,
but then his friend had grinned, given his head the
slightest shake, and lifting his withered hand, had laid a
finger on Matteo's chest, and Matteo had understood—
it wasn't the boy for whom Girolamo was concerned.

For already Matteo was infected. The taunting
voice—But have you *seen* the septum's pores? Have you

touched them with your finger?—already it filled his mind, took him over at night, and as the years passed and Marcantonio became master, lecturer, instructor, doctor, on and on—still a child!—Matteo saw his own life transformed into something fantastic. His lectures dwindled; his thoughts drifted; the scholars dozed in their seats, passed missives, slipped their hands under one another's gowns. In the street he listened as they murmured della Torre's name in the rapturous tones reserved for burghers' daughters. What had the young master with the sulphurous eyes, the voice like a cleaver, the hands that ventured where the heart recoiled, what had he disclosed, averred, implied, reviled? And, yes, after scolding his credulous proteges, after scoffing when they claimed that respectable citizens, Venetian physicians, even a philosopher from Tuscany had attended the hellion's lectures, Matteo had himself gone. With the coppery bile flooding his throat, despising his mendacity every step of the way, he'd slipped into the furthest row of the dissecting theater, concealed himself behind a tall youth in a green riding habit, and swearing he'd stay just long enough to glimpse Satan's play, watched as the devil squeezed blue liquor into a charred pedophile's aorta, saw him map the veins, trace the thin vessels branching like olive trees down the cadaver's crushed arms, from trunk to toes, held his breath as the reprobate drove his own fingers into rot's orifices and peeled back the tissue, laid bare what Matteo had read about his entire life and witnessed countless times, had even supervised in auditoriums much like this one, had bled, bandaged, cauterized but until this moment had never actually seen. He held his breath, craning forward until a jolt and peremptory snort beside his ear made him realize that in his excitement he'd climbed up the back of the tall youth in front of him, was at that moment digging his nails into the green riding cloak, and—Would God not spare him any indignity?—was actually drooling.

Drooling! Matteo threw his hood over his face, slithered home like a viper, and flinging himself on his cellar floor, shrieked himself to sleep.

Year in, year out. It was as close to hell as a righteous man comes, and some months later in another city, after the League of Cambrai's collapse, as the panic receded and silence returned to the streets, whenever Marcantonio della Torre paused late at night over the transverse section of an arm or thigh, still as enamored of flesh as in Padua but now far less cocky about it, now beginning to feel his first uncertainty about his own powers and their place in the world, as he thought back again and again to his Paduan success, his colleague's astonishment, the hissing of his name in the piazza, trying now to end once and for all the pounding that each morning invaded his dreams, della Torre would understand perfectly the hatred in which Matteo da Rimini had lived, his lechery to see his young rival boiled and quartered, stretched upon a rack of his own presumption. Dull minds might content themselves with cheap jokes and private mutterings, for they'd never glimpsed the possibility of their own souls' extinction. But Matteo was rich earth. Understanding rooted in him quickly. Having witnessed the brilliance that would cast him in the shade, he couldn't return to daily tasks in which he no longer believed. Shut out of the future, disgusted with the past, all he possessed was fury. Marcantonio della Torre had stolen Matteo's education, transformed his memory into a slough of folly and lies, erased forty years of labor, made him into a historical mistake. You could hardly expect him to be a good sport about it.

So when back in Padua a student informed Marcantonio della Torre that his colleague Matteo da Rimini had taken to abusing him noisily in prayers each morning at the Church of the Hermits, or when Marcantonio learned that Matteo was compiling a list of

Galenist anatomical heresies to submit to the Dominicans or later that he'd harangued the Venetian Signoria for nearly two hours about the noxious spirits released into the community via public autopsy, Marcantonio hadn't been taken aback. Even the afternoon when Matteo appeared at della Torre's anatomy lecture in a white robe with a smoldering buckthorn branch intoning exorcisms from Albertus Magnus in ecclesiastical Latin and scattering coriander seeds in the air, Marcantonio had remained unperturbed, refusing to mystify anything as ordinary as an animal with its foot caught in a trap. Obsolete minds were noisy, and good sense taught you to ignore them. Granted, the spectacle had something pathetic about it, but there was nothing Marcantonio could do. The only aspect of the whole messy business that continued to surprise him in Padua as he daily grew more astonished by his own success, by the sight of necks craning toward him in the dissecting theater, nature's infuriating proximity, was how long it seemed to be taking Matteo da Rimini to realize his life was over.

Whether or not Matteo's yammerings actually provoked the writ against della Torre, the result of which would have been—had the militia gotten its halberds on him—a trial far more agonizing than any punishment meted out just for being guilty; whether or not Matteo really could claim much credit for this would always remain doubtful. Della Torre certainly had enemies in sufficient quantity that an addlepated don more or less could hardly have swayed the Venetian authorities. The silk merchants, glass-blowers, country priests, yeomen and sundry thugs who were perpetually eager to see a scholar sizzle probably found Matteo's denunciations of a fellow physician titillating, but by the time Matteo had married della Torre off to the infidel's granddaughter, exposed his cloven hoof, made him nephew to Louis Douze and the Pope's son, depicted his necrophilia,

murders, rapaciousness, and generally attributed to him
so many black arts and powers that only an idiot would
have tried to arrest him, by then pretty nearly everyone—
both those who wanted to bake the anatomist for the fun
of it and the more rational city officials who merely
needed a victim to divert attention momentarily from the
two thousand local sons they'd marched out a month
before against not quite three times that many superbly
armed French chevaliers who'd promptly fertilized the
earth with them—by then nearly everybody knew
Matteo for a crackpot. The Signoria's accusations against
della Torre would, of course, be lies, but the distinction
between decorous lies and outlandish lies seemed
important. It was one thing to look vicious, another to
look silly. The council muzzled Matteo, invoked high
principles, debated gobbledy-gook, wrote something
Latinate and commissioned the constabulary to arrest
the traitor.

And then the affair took a curious turn. While the
city fathers were busy conscripting a dozen yokels from
among the outlying peasantry—every Paduan youth
being either under fifteen, dead, or a proven coward—
fitting them with pikes, harquebusses, beavers, gorgets,
and trying to teach them to look like the nonexistent
constabulary the city fathers were counting on, Matteo
da Rimini paid a visit to della Torre's apartment. Exactly
why would never be clear to anyone, certainly not to della
Torre, perhaps not even to Matteo himself. By now,
annihilating the Antichrist, snatching a soul from
perdition, reproving an aberrant colleague, saving
Venetia and protecting his deceased friend's son had all
so run together in Matteo's mind that his every act was as
multilayered as Dante's inferno. Perhaps it was Matteo's
own yearning for the knowledge he meant to destroy, his
ache to thrust his hand just once through the veil of
words, or his fallen soul's recollection of the apple's
tangy meat; perhaps it was just bestial curiosity or even

24

an old man's boredom that finally drew him—now that his adversary's destruction was assured—into the circle of corruption. All Matteo would ever know is that while perusing Avicenna's medical poem on the balcony that evening he'd had a vision. Holy armies had suddenly appeared in the purple sky just above a neighboring palazzo, great clouds of roiling dust rising from the legs of frenzied stallions as black as the apostate's heart, swords, lances, cannons, rams, all galloping forth to do battle with what could only be described as an immense horizon of blinding light. Matteo shook his head, momentarily saw a sunset, distant hills, a pigeon perched on a roofing tile, and then lost himself again in the apocalypse. On which side virtue lay it seemed impossible to know, but Matteo sensed that after God's warriors encountered radiance a great peace would descend and, still more surely, that the site of this Armaggedon was Marcantonio della Torre's rooms. It was a call. Matteo would answer. He donned his cap and mantle, stuck a copy of Mundinus beneath one arm and, striding down the Via San Francesco, walked right into the anatomist's foyer.

Marcantonio, who was at the moment wrist-deep in the organs of an infant's cadaver he'd purchased that afternoon, no-questions-asked, from a local slime-bucket named Il Fortunato—a figure notorious on the streets for having only one nostril and half a lip as a result of getting overly intimate with a wheel-trueing device in his father's smithy as a child--and who was therefore committing a crime legally punishable by those very torments about to be meted out to him for political acts he'd never even dreamed of, when he heard the door crash open, could think of nothing but, Here are the extra pair of hands I need to hold this liver. Rushing downstairs he chose not to marvel that the hands were attached to his father's former crony, the principal nuisance of his daily undertakings, and not his arch-nemesis only by virtue of being too goofy. He merely grabbed the tassel of Matteo's robe, bolted the door so as not to be interrupted twice, and dragged the older man back to the table saying, Here, fool, hold this. Which for no reason I could ever convince you of, Matteo did.

Thus began the strangest of all anatomies the history of Renaissance science would ever know, an ordeal that continued through that night and on into the next morning when, pausing to drink goat's milk and chew honeyed toast on the veranda, the two physicians allowed their eyelids to droop for the shortest of instants as the sun boiled the streets, then were up again and working through the afternoon heat, gadflies, wasps, infernal midges, until blessed darkness returned and with it an autumn breeze that blew the stink away. During the entire time, they quarreled, shaking chisels, saws, kidneys in each other's face, and never had they despised their rival's pigheadedness so much as now. It was nothing less than human wisdom they contested, peeling back the tiny heart's wall and flushing its cavities with salty water, nothing less than light's path through blackness, how spirit dwells in the flesh, what can't be said and whether a mishandled truth is mortal. They hunted the three ventricles of Aristotle, the two and a half of Avicenna, the porous septum of Galen and Mundinus' honeycombed interstice. They found them all, they found nothing, they didn't know what they found. They pointed, poked, sliced, piddled, watched those shapes that when animate seemed so firm collapse now into puddles of purplish goo, saw eyes melt into the spongy forebrain, muscle tissues turn limp or hard, organs wither, lobes flop and nowhere an edge or outline or border to show that this thingamajig ends here. Again and again Matteo insisted that they'd never find what they longed to know by taking it apart, and each time della Torre countered, But look and see! Look and see! They snipped the vena cava, rubbed its surface with their

26

fingertips, sniffed its leathery edge, listened to the sound it made when whacked on the table, bit, licked, chewed it, compared its flavor with the triceps and concluded the heart wasn't a muscle. Twice peering down the esophagus their foreheads struck, once Marcantonio cut Matteo's thumb with the chisel, they hissed, swore. Both knew it was devil's work, but gazing into the same terrific ignorance, acknowledging that they had no idea—not just of what they were looking at, but even of what they were looking for—each man felt himself a stranger, someone lost in a country he'd mistaken for home, and in this shared misery and silence, they blundered on.

They didn't hear the pounding until the third time, but once they finally did hear it, they both knew they'd been listening for it their whole lives. They were bent over the infant's skull, fragile as a toy boat, with the saw halfway through the cerebrum and Marcantonio's fingers wiggling around in the eye, and as the sound rippled through the walls and floorboards, up their shins, spines, and finally merged with the beating of their hearts, they each looked up into the other's face and understood exactly how they'd arrived here and where it would all lead. At that instant della Torre acknowledged, perhaps for the first time, what a flimsy concoction the facts are, only slightly more reliable than nothing, and he saw that his confidence had never been much more than a refusal to look around him. He hadn't expected being correct to protect him. He'd just been too bored with the surface of things to worry about how his life appeared. As a result, he'd been transformed into all the specters flapping around in the darkness behind those very eyes staring at him now from across the table, and his only argument to the contrary was his absolute certainty that he'd been misunderstood. Precisely what every thief and murderer feels. Perhaps he wasn't innocent but he didn't feel especially inclined to be fairminded about it.

He supposed that he could endure having his knees crushed and his tongue cut out, but he would have preferred to watch Matteo chopped into tiny pieces and boiled in lard. He wondered if the iceberg forming in his pelvis was what ordinary people called terror. The air ceased to pulsate, the floorboards grew still. For a long moment the two men continued to look at one another, della Torre's fingers dribbling optic humors, Matteo holding the saw upright in the pink bone. Then Matteo shrugged: Well, they're here.

Della Torre frowned. I deserve better than this.

There's not much knowledge without virtue, Matteo said, but there can be really gruesome virtues with almost no knowledge at all. You've acted as if you didn't believe this. You've tried to destroy the benevolence you expected to protect you. Don't act like you're surprised.

Adder sputum! Vinegar piss!

Many things are more important than new ideas.

You knew?

Matteo smiled. I've felt a great longing to see you afraid.The pounding came again, grown fatter, bulging up into the beams where sticky spiders slouched, beating the air hot, filling each man's skull until it shook like a rattle. Della Torre's eyes throbbed. From somewhere came the sound of shattering glass. Della Torre decided to wake up from this nightmare. Then he decided to wake up again.

Stupid! Stupid! Stupid! he hissed. I've cut the veil away, flayed error, held nature in my palm. Here on this table, underneath your own fingers, can't you see?

You talk like a child, Matteo said. What do you have to show for your devil's meddling? Here on this table I see chaos, sacrilege. Wordless matter is a plunge into nothing. You're as benighted as I am.

Dotard!

Reprobate!

Della Torre glared back at him, then spoke slowly: I am the future. You're as commonplace as cobblestones. It is for you to make way. I am more important than you are.

They held one another's eyes long enough to purge the sin of pride as the pounding drew sweat from their pores, drove their teeth out the tops of their heads, rose up through the roof and became the hooves of a thousand stallions rushing across the plain of Armageddon, riders leaning forward on their weapons, cannons bouncing wildly behind, as God's army suddenly vanished without a sound into the immense kingdom of light. Then Matteo replied: I know.

When the band of armor-clanking yokels at the front door finally figured out that no one was going to answer, they fell to quarreling, and word had to be sent to one Arturo Gerli, a townsman of no great distinction but someone's cousin, to learn if he thought the Signoria preferred the house burned down, stormed with ladders, laid siege to, cordoned off, ignored, or just what. The neighbors were by this time awake and, leaning from their windows, offered suggestions of their own, exchanging news and insults, complaining of the racket, mimicking the soldiers' pronunciation, and generally enjoying the show. Beggars, mastiffs, and prostitutes worked the edges of the crowd, and one orange-haired bedlamite shrieked, Pickle the doctor! and flung himself repeatedly against a wall. The decision at last arrived from someone claiming to be in a position to make it that the door should be beaten down, and the ad hoc militia began applying its halberds, pikes, and axes to that end in what was surely the messiest forced entry in Paduan memory. The bolt wouldn't give; the hinges wouldn't flinch; the walnut planks were as thick as a forearm. Someone came up with the bright idea of firing a harquebus at it. The ball ricocheted off and struck a teenager from the banks of the Brenta between the cuisse and poleyn, badly denting the armor and dispensing with his knee. He had to be carried away sobbing, and the remaining constables eventually bashed a hole big enough to cram a skinny mule-tender through, running his hose on the splinters and nearly undressing him in the process. All of which left them feeling intensely shy and awkward once in the foyer, having not one of them ever set foot on carpet before, or seen a painting. They took their time working up courage to bellow the half-dozen authoritative expressions they'd memorized, still longer to venture up the stairs. They hoped nobody was home. They were disappointed.

The signoria had prepared them for what they might encounter in the anatomist's rooms, so the tiny shit-smeared torso with its duodenum curling down the table leg and a sawblade wedged in its nose didn't send anyone leaping off the balcony. Having grown up committing upon live pigs and calves atrocities that city-dwellers would've been loathe to commit on potted plants, the rustics weren't deeply troubled by the sight of gore, though one tender-hearted swain—called mockingly Lavender Giovio—had to lean against the wall till his head stopped reeling. What did surprise and baffle the soldiers, however, was the appearance of the traitor they'd been sent to subdue. Various councilors had explained that though an experienced Satanist, deeply initiated in bookish secrets, a Mason, hideously rich, probably in the French employ if not of Gallic parentage, and certainly a violator of custom, truth, virtue, nature, doctrine and ecclesiastical law, the damned physician Marcantonio della Torre was hardly older than the yokels themselves. But the debauched practitioner standing before them now was wizened and stooped with a weary sag to his eyes, and though he wore the black robes of a scholar, he could easily have been taken for an humble mendicant or someone's grandsire. He seemed unperturbed by their noisy entrance, continuing to gaze down at the large, pale cadaver on the table before him and whispering unintelligible incantations. The puzzled guards murmured that perhaps the sorcerer had compacted with his father Satan to take on this guise of maturity, but then the demon spoke—in perfect Italian!—claiming that the French betrayer they sought had been transmuted by Lucifer into gaseous sulphur in order to float out the window upon an icy breeze arisen from his frozen heart. They could see for themselves where his garments lay crumpled upon the floor, his body having melted with a hiss and the odor of boiling sassafras. The old man spoke without once lifting his face from the livid neck beneath his hands, and though his voice was calm, almost soothing, there seemed to be something furious in the way he glared at the naked corpse. He held a large cleaver pressed against the cadaver's throat, seemed on the point of ramming it into the tissue and bone, and it was this spectacle, far more than the ubiquitous carnage in the room, that very nearly unnerved the peasant youths. Human blood and organs might be indistinguishable from goose innards, but the thought of this human body, as healthy and whole as if it had walked the earth but moments before, the thought of these Christian remains staggering about mute and headless on resurrection day—now *that* was disgusting!

Then the old man begged for mercy, reminding the constables how much he too had suffered from the hellish betrayer, having—he feared—bartered his own soul for a taste of astonishing evils, and as the befuddled youths whispered among themselves, first, that the pitiful wretch was plainly not the man they sought and should be abandoned to his damnation, and, next, that this might be Beelzebub's voice spinning their minds around, and, last, that the impious pervert probably deserved stomping to death anyway, the man added that in gratitude for any modicum of leniency they might see fit to extend he was prepared to reveal a spectacle rarely enjoyed by mortals, a miracle to amaze townsmen and family, that is, the secret of life itself. And opening a large tome and plopping it down on the cadaver's naked pubis, he explained that, though the body of man was known to be a universe, it wasn't a harmony of constellations and moons as commonly believed, but rather a great principality at war. Conceive it as a city, he continued, brawls and swindling everywhere, walls tumbling, alleys twisting, a populace of tyrants, thieves, rebels, rogues. No one could know its purposes, for endless striving was its very nature. Bellies usurped reason, humors vied for dominion, the eye overthrew the sense of smell, and the heart would rule all. The ancients had mistaken life for equanimity and governance, just as he had once done himself, for their only study had been of death. But to glimpse the body's secret, to snatch a truth not yet decayed, one had to enter the fray, leap upon the enemy where he lay guileless and unsuspecting beneath your very hands. And here he paused, seemed to tense, then added: Nothing is less certain than the future. And raising the cleaver into the air he whispered in a voice grown luxurious and warm, For all knowledge is ambush, for triumph belongs to the wily, for everything living moves. And spinning on his heel, he flung himself on Fat Sacchi the goat-lover's son.

Sacchi squealed and vomited his dinner. The cleaver lodged in his gorget, somehow piercing an artery that promptly showered the room. Big Lothario grabbed the madman's knees, Little Lothario wrapped around his head. More or less everyone rolled on the floor in half-digested pasta while a fellow known to the others only as Him Yonder got his halberd tangled in a linen hamper and someone's matchlock exploded, raining down stucco, bits of rafter, and bewildered spiders. There was some cursing, the dead infant's pancreas got involved. At a crucial juncture the yokels figured out that whatever didn't have armor on it was fair game, and the demoniac's brains, kidneys, spleen and privates received a proper kicking. Exactly whose blood it all was no one could be sure, but eventually the assailant stopped twitching, so they dragged him by the whiskers down the stairs and were all delighted to be done with the place, its smell of sin and pesky flies. All but Lavender Giovio, who lingered momentarily over the two cadavers, poked a finger in a bulbous whazzit, twiddled squishy doo-bobs, flipped through the pages on the unmarred body's lap, then called out to the others that this one's soul had just entered hell. There was silence, a cough, some eye-rolling, then somebody said, All right then, how can you tell that one's soul has just etc., etc.? Lavender Giovio smiled, placed his palm on the forehead and pinched the nostrils closed. Still warm, he said, but no breathing.

Leonardo listened to della Torre's imitation of the swain's voice break into a snicker as the light on the men's faces flashed uncertainly and somewhere a shutter banged free. A storm was blowing up from the Ticino, and as the night began to come alive around the dark room Leonardo wondered how many deaths a man's bones could absorb before breaking through the skin and simply walking out from under him. Della Torre was repeating some portion of his tale, his back bent slightly and his head held almost at the angle of someone looking you in the eye, and for the first time Leonardo imagined that he might be bored. An odd thought. To strike the devil's bargain, plunge your fist into a heart, and bring it out again with nothing that amazed you—Leonardo would guess that this would be what boredom felt like and that the rage it sparked would become a conflagration, blackening your eyes, burying you in ash, slime. Yes, there'd been a betrayal, and della Torre would never understand whose or why. Watching the young man devour his life, Leonardo knew that one day he,

Leonardo, would say to Salai or Melzi or some besotted lens-grinder what he ought to be saying to della Torre right now and that the dazzled silence then would leave Leonardo wondering if he'd ever in sixty-odd years spoken an intelligible sentence and why, since understanding was going to come to you anyway, it never arrived while it could still do you some good. The room seemed darker now. Over della Torre's shoulder a shadow slid along the wall.

Suddenly Marcantonio shouted, "The candle!"

Leonardo lunged to the tall taper plunging toward the carrion basket as a gust ripped through the curtains, blew out the flame, and set the tapestry flapping wildly against a chair.

"Get the shut—"

"No, here!"

Kicking once at the window with his far leg, Leonardo leaned shoulder to shoulder with the anatomist, and together they wrapped their hands in a tight ring around the last light, a dirty taper in a teacup. The wind whistled past their ears, bringing distant barking and a wet smell like freshly bathed hair. A roof tile crashed on the paving stones outside. Leonardo watched a dung-fly shiver on the table's edge then blow away. The roar of air filled the room.

"Now!" della Torre yelled.

The two men grabbed the shutters, threw the latch, slammed the windows, pulled the drapes, just as raindrops splattered on the roof and the first thunder struck. Leonardo felt it rumble through the soles of his slippers and wondered what makeshift force of law had arrived to fetch them to a reckoning. He took a deep breath. With the windows closed the air would begin to gag him soon, though the flies had momentarily been chased into the rafters and the heat was gone. The room was dim now.

"Good fortune," della Torre said, holding up the

dirty taper as he relit the candles. "Our gratitude to the saints, Matteo da Rimini, Lord Vesta, and that apostle of resentment—Guido da Forli."

"Many hands to protect a small source of light."

"Claptrap," della Torre said. "The only protection I ever needed was from teachers."

"You are confusing yourself with what you study," Leonardo replied.

"Mock me, but where has there ever been a mortal I could learn from? After Galen only folly and the enigma here." Della Torre gestured down at the cadaver and then, recollecting the work, added, "Get the syringe."

Leonardo rummaged through a cabinet, pulled out a glass pipe with a greasy leather bag at one end. "Perhaps Matteo da Rimini was your kinsman," he continued. "There's much in his enmity that's curious. Not every cocksure youth drove him mad."

"Whatever bogey he worshipped it wasn't me."

"But still, what he saw in you seemed worth being afraid of. He possessed exceptional discernment, you said as much. Listen to your own tale."

"You needn't make riddles of commonplace things," della Torre said. "Nature may have blessed Matteo, but his education served him badly. The man's mind teemed with specters."

". . . such as the specter of a better mind."

"Claptrap. Give me your hands." Standing the head on its chin, della Torre worked the drill through the bone into the pulpy cortex as lightning flared at the curtains' edge and the floorboards shook. "Start confusing mistakes with miracles," he said, "and you'll end up baying at the moon. Matteo da Rimini was a rodent fawning on his shadow in the dark. The age of martyrs is passed."

"Nature must be an orderly realm," Leonardo began, "but I've watched fire streak down the clouds and never seen it twice the same. I find this and many other commonplace things remarkable. Tell me, what could the man have done to deserve your admiration?"

Della Torre didn't look up. "He could have driven the cleaver directly into my . . ."

With a terrific crash and gust of wet air, the darkness blew the windows back open and snuffed out all the lights.

Stacey Levine

My Horse

The horse was small and his name was Robin. The horse's skin was loose and slid freely about his body as he moved. He lived with me; he was my pet, given to me to be a pet, and whined incessantly at the back door or lay for hours on the hood of my car in the driveway. The horse was perhaps the size of a dog and his liver-colored, flaccid skin hung in sagging folds around his neck, legs, and chest; his mouth, open slightly, revealing his teeth, was always wet. Drool spilled from his mouth and he seemed always to be begging for something, though one could not always know what. He often wanted in the worst way to be let either in or out of the house.

I let him in or out accordingly, though he would only wander across the space of my living room or yard, whimpering and lying down when he did not know, at last, what to do. His neck was quite long and it was spotted, as was the rest of his body, with dried rings and sores, and a type of dark freckles that were tiny and almost black. The horse was my pet, meant to live at my house, meant to be fed by me; he moved incessantly; one noticed immediately his tremulous, skittish motions; he moved in and out of the house, whining, fearful, coughing, sighing windily in a kind of staccato that would break in his throat and cause a viscous mucus to blow from his nostrils.

Then he would go to lie on the hood of the car, half sleeping, eyes slitted, sighing further. As he slept his back would contract, perhaps in a kind of nervous exhaustion; the spasms were short, uncontrolled, full of the blind helpless strength in muscle which intrigues me; I watched the muscles move beneath the skin; I watched him carefully from my chair on the porch.

Clearly he had not lived in any one place for very long. He was always afraid; everything was ceaselessly horrifying to him, and he jumped in fear and whined in pain at simply every noise I made. He never even acknowledged that I placed the cup of food on the gravel driveway for him each night, that I was the one; without even looking up at me as I stood on the porch, he would trip blindly toward the cup and eat quickly, with great slobbering noises, often in less than a minute. When he was finished he would run away, often behind the car. He simply did not understand our relation and he made no effort in our relation; he rarely even looked at me, though when he did, his expression was always a shivering, guilty one. Otherwise, he spent his days straggling about my house and property endlessly, breathing heavily through his nostrils and whimpering to himself. It was hard to believe he had ever belonged to a family, or even to a mother.

He was quite ugly for a horse and very tiny and light on his feet; he did not walk firmly but rather picked his way across the gravel of my driveway or across my wooden porch and floors; it was as if he had no hooves, but only the soft heels that humans have. Indeed, when probed, his heels proved to be undersized and tender, full of bleeding scratches, not like hooves at all.

He often begged to be let out of the house and would then run immediately to the porch, carefully and nervously sniffing the wooden railing. He turned in awful circles and left the porch by means of the steps; he tripped to the gravel, stamping and scuffling there until he was exhausted and finally went to lie on the hood of the car.

He had been given to me to be my pet; he was my pet. He walked strangely; it seemed his heels hurt him quite a bit, for he would whine and sputter with each tentative step he took in picking his way across the patch of gravel and back. As for the rest of his body, I noticed immediately that the skin of his neck was tender and loose, though rough; the skin was pleasant to the touch, I noticed, though at first it seemed loose in a way that was strange and distasteful. His skin was queer and dense, I noticed; it locked around my fingers as I rubbed him though it also yielded to my touch; it was supple skin, smooth as velour; no one would have been able to guess he possessed such softness; I touched him often, and though at the very first his skin had seemed indeed strange and distasteful in its looseness, it was not a looseness that I would really allow to disturb me, I finally decided; so I knew, in the end, that I could touch him whenever I pleased.

I rubbed him very hard regularly, though he was covered with dried rings and sores as well as dark freckles, some of which were raised. I touched him, pulling at the looser parts of his skin as he would try to dart past my chair on the porch; I held his strange texture between my hands as he whined and whimpered, bewildered, looking only to the ground. He would often flatten his large, trembling ears, looking alarmed; I rubbed him when I wanted; his skin was very warm, after all, and because of the dried rings and sores, a bristly, rough effect was in fact achieved, an effect that countered his loose softness which, after all, was distasteful; I would hold him, lift him onto my lap upside down; his warm limbs churned slowly as if under water; I would knead him then; he never struggled, though he certainly could have, and once, because I held him for so long, he began to howl.

Since I did not know where my horse had come from I began to wonder if he was unclean, for this was a possibility. The scabby rings and sores on his skin could have been repositories of bacteria, and certainly his mucus, which often dropped onto my porch, might have indeed carried any number of diseases. And if he had been living in the wilds at any time prior to the time he had arrived at my house, that, too, would have increased his risk for picking up something from another animal, or even an insect.

I decided to wash him carefully. However, I could not find a suitable soap when I looked in my shed, though I did find a box of sterile latex gloves, and it occured to me that I could wear these while handling my horse. Yet if I did so, I realized, I would not have been able to feel his skin directly. Finally, after some deliberation, I decided not to use the gloves, for I would not undergo, to be sure, too much risk in touching my horse, though there might have been, in fact, some slender risk; yet that risk would not be significant in the scheme of things; and in the handling of any pet there is risk; in recognizing this, I decided I could touch my horse whenever I liked.

Still, I was uncertain as to whether or not he was free of disease; he quite truthfully could have been thick with germs. He could have been unclean, and still I was touching him whenever I wanted; I quickly decided that he should receive innoculations, and that I would make arrangements for this soon, though these innoculations could not take place reasonably soon, as it was summer now, and no one at all remained in the town.

One day, after I had placed his cup of food on the driveway, I noted with interest that my horse's belly had ballooned inordinately. It did not return to its usual size during the next four hours as he digested his food, nor when I fed him later. Instead, the belly ballooned even more hideously, swaying and juddering halfway down the length of his legs. Even more disturbing was that he did not appear to notice this change directly. Instead of truly noticing, he ran in and out of the house in even more of a panic than ever, sometimes spinning in circles for no clear reason; his screeching did not stop then, not for a minute; I slammed the door; he had not noticed this change in his body and had not even looked at himself; he only kicked about the yard hysterically now, wheezing and crying in his ridiculous manner.

I retreated further into the house and realized that now the sound of him was always in my ears; I had not noticed this before but the sound filled my house and yard; when he stepped on a sharp piece of gravel I would hear his high screech puncture the air and I would grow fatigued; I would even grow angry.

His belly had ballooned hideously and would not return to its normal size; it was obviously swollen due not only to the food within but also to an accumulation of fluid just beneath the surface of the skin, and soon, I made the decision to lance his belly, for this condition clearly needed to be relieved in some way. I knew that, sooner or later, I would need to take some action; otherwise, an emergency could arise.

I decided to prepare him for the lancing: I fed him a large meal. He slathered and whined piteously over the food, and when he was done, with his belly now incredibly distended, he went to lie on the hood of the car, whimpering still, and finally settling into a light sleep.

Then, in a few smooth motions, I strode toward him, rolled him over and pinned his thin legs to the metal; this last was not necessary, though, for even as I was lancing him he lay still as a baby. I lanced him thoroughly and in a fashion that allowed for quick and complete drainage, and incredibly he did nothing more than whimper once, quietly, and turn his head away. When I was done, I told him so and then let him go, noting that he only continued to lie there as if confused, with a pathetic look of weakness about him.

After washing myself thoroughly and then returning to the hood of the car, preparing to clean the fluid away with a hose, I told him clearly that he was entirely too weak, and that I would never feed him again. For it was true. I saw quite clearly that it would do him good to forage for himself, and since his belly now had been lanced and the fluid was gone, that he would be lighter, more agile, and therefore more able to forage out of doors for his food, and that I should have required him to do so from the very beginning.

I began, then, to leave the porch door unlatched so he could push his way in and out of the house whenever he wanted; it was mid-summer at this time. Because it was summer the streets, full of petals that fell from the trees and piled against the tires of parked cars, were empty; everyone had gone somewhere else. Because it was summer, the petals, smelling so sweet, fell everywhere and filled the always-silent yards and street; because he now was a foraging horse, my pet would hobble away from my property, onto the lots of the empty neighboring houses, foraging, his loose-skinned snout to the ground. He foraged well, though he continued to whine incessantly and often tripped over the stones in the gardens; I saw that he was, despite his whining, quite naturally good at collecting the blades of grass he needed, spreading his lips to extend his wet tongue, and collecting, in addition to grass, all manner of dirt and gravel.

After foraging, my horse would run to lie on the hood of my car, to loll his head there, and to close his eyes and whimper excessively, even though he knew that I sat nearby on the porch, watching and holding my drinking glass in the afternoons which were insulated and heavy with the stillness of a million petals. Incredibly, he made no direct protest about having to forage for his food; after all, I could not construe his constant blubbering as any kind of protest.

It was not long after this that he discovered the petals and began to eat them in front of me. He enjoyed their taste, evidently; he would go into the street, under the trees, to eat them, and even ate them with gusto; to see the way he enjoyed the petals disturbed me only because his pleasure made him more ridiculous; he drooled excessively and would lift his head suddenly while eating to bolt through the petals in excitement, audibly gulping air, too much air, and expelling it in spasms through his mouth like an infant. The sparse gray hair around his ears lifted in the breeze.

It seemed he was having some kind of happiness.

And since all the streets, the gutters, and the lawns in the neighborhood now overflowed with the sweet petals, for it was the season, I saw that his eating could not really be construed as foraging but merely as grazing: he would never learn anything, not strength, not cunning, nor survival, by simply strolling to the edge of my lawn and effortlessly satisfying his hunger there.

He was beginning, also, to grow a bit fatter on the petals which he scooped up in big mouthfuls from the street; there was a thickening around his small belly, though his skin remained loose, and he still made all manner of noise, bucking excitedly around the empty yards now; after thinking and watching him very carefully, I decided he might need something like a clamp. I went into my shed to look, and after finding there an actual clamp with two screws by which pressure could be increased or decreased, I decided to use it; I felt sure he needed something like a clamp, and that a clamp would help him. So I clamped the loose skin at his right side, just over his ribs; the clamp's metal edges were covered with a hard rubber that would prevent his skin from being pierced, and I told him so.

After the clamp was attached to his side, and, hanging there, beat against his flank with his gait until a few blisters appeared, I noticed with surprise that he did not try to reach for it, and did not attempt to yank it from his body. In any case, that would have broken the skin, and he sensed this, I was certain; still, he accepted the clamp completely, and had lain so still as I had attached it, with no struggling of any kind. And now, though he could have reached the clamp easily with his mouth, he made no attempt to tug at it, or even to test it; I knew this for a fact, because I watched my horse at all times now.

Perhaps, I thought briefly, I should now apply another clamp to his mouth. Yet despite the fact that this would have reminded him that he had a mouth with which to protest if he chose, it would also have kept him from eating entirely, and he might have died.

So I discarded that idea. Soon after, though, I quickly noted that his wailing and whining had stopped after I had applied the clamp; that he had grown silent. It was as if his attention had moved away from himself and somewhere into the distance. My house and property were quiet now, as was the entire neighborhood, which no longer echoed with his shrill voice.

He lost interest in the petals now, and returned to forage for grass, as he knew he was meant to. He foraged now along the patch of gravel for the few blades that grew there; he would not venture further than this, as he once had, and he now kept his head lowered constantly, even when he was not foraging but only standing, though one evening as he stood near the porch in the gravel, I caught him raising his head for a moment to glimpse at me.

He was now subsisting on this halfhearted foraging, as he had done before the clamp, yet now, I noticed, though he seemed to forage, he was not really foraging for food, but only for appearance's sake. The truth was that he simply had little hunger now; even to begin with, I recalled, his hunger had not been so great. This lack of will was sad, I perceived; it was self-destructive, and even shocking.

It was shocking how, as time began to pass away and the summer to wear on, his body grew smaller and smaller. The size of his body simply shrank and his skin grew even looser, sagging around his legs and chest.

Somehow he just did not enjoy the fact that he was a foraging horse and could not conceive of anything else to do with the time in which he was not making a show of foraging or lying on the hood of the car. In these few weeks he had grown quite a bit smaller, and his head began to look even more ridiculous, much too large for his small neck and body.

He was simply no longer hungry and I could tell he was no longer hungry; he took small lethargic bites of the grass he found; he had difficulty in swallowing and this was all because of the disturbance of the clamp, I knew. Yet, incredibly, he had done nothing in all this time to combat the painful presence of the clamp; he simply hobbled along as usual, making a show of foraging, severely disappointing, and even infuriating me.

His moist eyes would blink toward the railing of the hot porch; holding my drinking glass, I would sit watching; his eyes would dart to the ground, quietly fearful; I watched how his flesh shrank and shrank every day, how his legs grew more reedy. I sat on the porch, out of the summer sun, thinking how it had been so very easy for me to clamp him on the side where his skin was loose, so easy that I almost had not done it at all. He allowed me everything, my pet; I had not even needed to inform him, as I had been about to lance him, "I am a doctor," because he had lain so still and trusting.

I wondered why on earth my horse had even wanted to stay here with me this summer, during which all surrounding neighbors had gone away and left their silent parked cars to be covered with petals from the trees. I wondered where on earth he had come from, whimpering, ceaselessly taking such stuttering steps and crying out for so long until he was finally quiet. As the days grew even longer and more hot and the town ever more silent, it seemed the ground surrounding my house became flatter, wider; I could see for miles; I decided that I might someday remove the clamp, though I was not sure exactly when I would do so; still, I would soon decide. If he were in less discomfort, it occurred to me, perhaps he would be able to leave me: why not? Perhaps that would be the best thing for him; but also, having observed him all this time, I was able to see clearly that he would never change, never; he would always be like this, piteous and hopeless, with any owner.

Jeff Duncan

Spade Work

So long as the structural integrity of an organism is intact, it is alive; when that structural integrity is violated, the organism is dead.

John Crowe
Dry Biological Systems

Day 1: "Darkness lay over the abyss"

The trouble with that Indian Mound began early on a July morning in 1941, the beginning of what was to be known in those parts as the week of the "perplexin' rain." It was squat in the middle of the County of Fulton, Illinois' least extraordinary fifty square miles. When the clouds combusted on that midsummer dawn, it was not the variety of storm we normally see accompanied by sixty-thousand-foot-high cumulonimbus clouds, those anvil-shaped ogres that batter Amazon rain forests each autumn. Nor was it that index of sprinkle that comes in spits and hawks. This curious precipitation was more a maddened mist, a volatile vapor than a out-and-out downpour. It was a fog of moisture so pernicious that water came through the glass of windows. Granite rocks were like sponges and doubled in size. The skin of fingers shriveled and could no longer anchor their nails which dropped to the floor in piles of five and ten.

Had Don F. Dickson been a kid of the seventies, the reanimated bodies spawned by that dastardly drizzle would probably have reminded him of an advertisement for Sea Monkeys. You remember, the little amoebocyte prizes whose artist's rendering you would see on the back of Rice Krispies boxes and who you could have delivered to your doorstep and "bring to life" for fifty cents plus thirty proof-of-purchase seals. Those hybrid bits of multicolored grit that when dropped into a fish bowl or a glass of water for that matter were supposed to animate into entire cultures. They had the bodies of minute extraterrestrials and the faces of the young married couple next door, the corner pharmacist and other folks around town.

The tragedy of it was that when your Sea Monkeys finally came in the mail and you actually situated them in the bathtub, one by one with tweezers, with expectations of a veritable population explosion, they transformed rather pathetically into jumbo, faceless paramecia. Seven days later, there would be no more to show for your investment than a pile of lifeless worm-nothings—maybe fifteen in all—at the bottom of the bucket that your mother had made you transfer them into.

But Farmer Dickson had no such later-twentieth-century point of reference with which he might have better apprehended the Burial Mound's skeletons and the ramifications of their abrupt return to life. He was just a poor Illinois sod-buster looking to eke out a living for himself and his tuckered-out wife Grace. Don F. Dickson was born in "nineteen-aught-one" and knew nothing of the icy science of cryonics, or the discovery of fully preserved wooly mammoths in glaciers, and not a speck about modern-day tardigrade theory, which would be the life-blood not only of the Sea Monkey wonder-fad but of the bony residents of his own fleshly fields.

The "rain" of that wicked week had a nitrogen reek to it that you might expect to be troubled by in New Guinea but not in the relative predictability of Illinois' temperate Fulton County. Yet that is not to say that Fulton County was without its eccentricities. Its modest terrain boasted unexplored caves, insect-eating plants, and a prehistory that to this day conjures goose flesh on unseasoned archaeologists. As long as there had been settlers along the intersection of the Illinois and Spoon Rivers, there had been rumination about the contents of that Burial Mound. Most everyone believed it to be the mass grave of some ancient Indian tribe.

When he was not slugging it out with Grace, Don F. Dickson, himself, would fish around on that demon bed for squints at the past. He had been finding relics on and around that hump since he was a kid. His tool shed was "fit to bust" with ancient scrapers, projectile points, awls, bone pipes, ear ornaments and bean pots, while his own tools oxidized out in the yard.

Don F. Dickson was never without his lucky fossilized barley bean. He had found it on the Mound during the harvest of twenty-six. Indians had used their own blood to paint sacred beasts on these little pods. Farmer Dickson's barley bean sported the likeness of a prairie chicken, a powerful symbol of eros. He carried it in his front bib overall pocket. Driven by the spell of amateur archaeology, he would touch that bean during the course of the day and speculate that the Mound was simply chock full of dead savages. And more than once Grace Dickson had caught him worrying over that bean in the middle of the night.

"Why don't you just plant the God damn thing," she would say, catching him by the ear. "Least then we'd have a crop to harvest come fall."

Three or four times a day, Don F. Dickson would limp up atop the Mound and poke around with an arthritic foot, hoping that a hand would jut up sudden-like from the earth and grab him around the ankle. So he was not especially surprised on the first day of the "perplexin' rain" to find that the seasons had finally exposed a full torso, the Indian Maiden.

"It's a skeleton," Don F. Dickson whispered. "Bet it's been dead a long while, cuz there ain't no skin on it."

Though most of her bones were buried in an orderly manner, rodents and time had rearranged many. And so by nightfall, when Don F. Dickson had her reassembled and all laid out beside the Mound, like the hapless Humpty Dumpty, that Indian Maiden, Drink-Brook she had been known to her tribe, could not be put back together again without some pieces askew. There was a small pile of extras arranged beside her, a phalange here, a rib there. This calcified surplus wriggled and glistened in the mud like a bucket of worms.

It was not until that pregnant precipitate had seeped into the innermost fissures of her bones and she began to grow back patches of skin and sprout tufts of body hair that Farmer Dickson's lack of physiological expertise came to light. Though, in general, she looked human, her elbow was where her jaw should have been, and, what is worse, her pelvis had been left out entirely, lost to the rape of time. Still, to Don F. Dickson, who had gazed on Grace Dickson's squat, ever-corroding features, it seemed the Indian Maiden was an object of genuine beauty.

"Why, you're as purty as a tulip flower," Farmer Dickson told the reanimate, as she moved into his arms.

But when he tightened his hold, his hands found no skin on her back side to match the smooth, satin-like covering of her front. Instead, his fingers fumbled through a tepid chowder of exposed kidney, pancreas and sinewy liver.

Drink-Brook felt Farmer Dickson give a shudder at his unholy fistful, but he quickly recovered and said, "Ah, shucks, I still think yer as purty as a tulip flower."

Day 2: "Let there be a vault between the waters"

There was something aside from Sea Monkeys that Don F. Dickson missed out on by not being a kid of the seventies. He had been cheated of the moralizing virus of television. Grace and Farmer Dickson had their General Electric radio, but you can hardly compare the paltry audio contagion of *Fibber McGee and Molly* with the cathode ray germ of *The Courtship of Eddie's Father*, *The Partridge Family* and *The Brady Bunch*.

You might remember, for instance, the episode in which the whole Brady clan drove out west in their Oldsmobile Custom Cruiser station wagon—it was a two-parter—and little Bobby and Cindy Brady, the youngest of the bunch, lost their way at the bottom of the Grand Canyon. You never saw Mr. or Mrs. Brady launch into an accusatory tirade. Instead, they simply rented burros for themselves and their four remaining children and scouted around awhile. They even managed a chuckle as Alice, their wacky live-in housekeeper, ignited and fell into the mighty crevice like a comet, when she tried to light a signal fire on the Coleman stove. And, before you knew it, Bobby and Cindy showed up no worse for the wear. A ram's tendon necklace with a barley bean strung on it hung around each of their necks.

"Honest, this spooky Indian gave us these nifty charms," cried little Bobby.

"Yeah," little Cindy said, "and the Indian was real gross too. He was shaped like a big ol'. . ."

"Shush, you," little Bobby cut in, "or we'll be in trouble for sure."

Something happened to those two youngsters, alone at the belly of that great national wonder. But it was left to each of us viewers to decide just what tomfoolery they had been up to. All we knew was, that innocence we fans had subscribed to so faithfully each week was gone.

But television took its time setting root in rural Illinois. Rather than the Bradys as a model of appropriate domestic life, the Dicksons could only aspire to the cantankerous goings-on of the annual Fulton County Fair "Punch and Judy" puppeteer performance. Amos and Andy were good for a chuckle, but radio for all its noble stabs at verisimilitude would forever drift in one side and out the other of the Dickson's Midwestern ears.

Punch and Judy, though, with the "here-and-now" quality of their corporeal antics, were just as real as the Bradys were destined to be to seventies kids. It was through this well-pummeled duo that a workable balance of battering was struck in the Dickson home. A rural thrust and parry.

"Here's a stick in the eye," Grace would chortle, with quick, ruthless jabs.

"And here's one up the hole," Farmer Dickson would growl back, with a kick.

Though she could not explain how, Grace understood that a horrible portent accompanied Don F. Dickson's sudden almost distracted sighs at breakfast on that second day of the rain.

"How's about you helpin' me lift this here dress up over my big self" she finally offered, hoping to jolt him back to normal.

"No, no, thank ya kindly jus the same. That rain's got me a chill, and I think I'll jus sit here a spell," was Farmer Dickson's glum reply.

The remainder of the day he merely swayed in his rocker, gazing through the window in the direction of the Mound, his petrified barley bean rolled between his thumb and index finger. He fell asleep in that chair. Every hour or two, he startled Grace by releasing a crazed "Whoop, Whoop, Whoopie!" in mid-dream.

At four in the morning, Grace heard Don F. Dickson

fumble about in his dresser. And through a squinted eye had watched as he put on his "Sunday-go-to-meetin's."

"Got to check them crops, woman," he whispered in the dark.

She had followed him, still wearing her bathrobe, leaping behind trees, bushes, and nearby sheep or cows as he went into the barn, fetched a wheelbarrow, and moved off in the drizzle toward the Mound.

The Indian Maiden, Drink-Brook, had been rolling to and fro ever since her startling return to life. With no pelvis, she could only flop about like a carp in the bottom of a dinghy. Her nakedness was concealed beneath a layer of mud, a stringy film, wet and drippy on her front side, but baked on her horrid back side by the heat of exposed organs into a protective adobe flesh.

"Ya can't jus lay here in the mud, can ya?" Don F. Dickson asked, as he knelt down beside Drink-Brook.

Rendered mute by the elbow joint he had supplied her in lieu of a jaw, she could offer no reply.

"Course ya can't. Come on now with me, purty little fairy princess of the moist earth," he said.

Farmer Dickson positioned the wheelbarrow as best he could beneath Drink-Brook and secured her with a belt he had removed from his ruined suit trousers. Slowly, he worked his way to the tool shed.

Day 3: "The earth brought forth verdure"

What made that "perplexin' rain" all the more "perplexin'" for Fulton County was that it came out of nowhere, smack dab in the middle of the worst drought of the century. It was a dry spell even more blister-raising than the one we had had in the summer of nineteen seventy-two. You probably recall the strange lengths folks went to then to try and stir up a thunderstorm. The sky was seeded with phosphorus red dye, in the hope that indignant clouds would try and shed themselves of the gaudy coloring. Positive thinkers wore raincoats and boots under a humorless sun. "Nixon Now More Than Ever" buttons were pinned to chests all across the Midwest, in the hope that the slogan itself might, somehow, evoke a merciful drip.

Once when the omnipotent incumbent rode through Lewistown, the Fulton County seat, on the C & O railroad, a dark squall line rolled across the prairie sky, but it brought little more than a fetid thunderclap. The drought worsened as election day got closer. The rain never came. And when the votes were finally tallied, the becrumbled crops had long since made for a vile harvest, a parched horn-o-plenty.

Like the powder keg that was puppet-Judy, Grace would fester, mulling things over as best she could before surrendering to the violence which was her only recourse. Come sundown of the third day of the rain— "Medusa's own spit, it was"—Farmer Dickson came staggering from the tool shed, that barley bean glowing green in his bib overall pocket.

"What sort of tricks're ya playin'," Grace said, when he came inside the house.

"'Tricks'?"

"Where've ya been all night 'n day?"

"Checkin' crops, I told ya."

"Yer an ol' hound dog. Look at yerself, stickin' out like an ol' tree branch."

Farmer Dickson examined himself and was gratified to see that, sure enough, midway down, his bibs were not only sticking out but bobbing like a divining rod, following drips of rain water leaking from ceiling to floor.

"The big ol' thang's been there all day," he said, with a blush. "Now let me be afore I ferget myself."

Don F. Dickson waved off supper. He made himself comfortable in his rocker and began fiddling with his barley bean, just as he had done the day before.

Grace knew that with her uneven teeth and fully audible digestive ailments she could hold no candle to the likes of the Indian Maiden. Just the same, she figured she could serve up a message to her man every bit as painful as the blow he had dealt her heart. Come bedtime, she slipped out of the kitchen and made her way over to the form of slumbering Farmer Dickson and waited for him to let loose one of the joy shrieks that had assaulted her the previous day.

"I'll teach ya," she hissed in his ear, and smacked her sleeping husband on the head with a butter churn pestle.

"Woman, I'll teach ya to try'n teach me," Don F. Dickson responded, making a grab at Grace.

They launched into a regular knock-down-drag-out of a knuckle-buster.

"There now," she said, finally, patting a welt on her forehead. "Least ways I got some sign of life from ya."

It would be his last day in the farmhouse for some time to come.

Day 4: "The lesser light together with the stars to rule night"

In forty-one, Don F. Dickson and his contemporaries employed their share of rural remedies for drought. Yet nothing would shake a drop from the sky. Even the Hopis that were shipped by rail from Arizona to do a heathen rain fandango conjured little more than a vapid dust devil. Strangely enough, it was precisely when the parched Fulton Countians had given up that the sinister shower paid its visit. No meteorologist had foreseen that monstrous wetness. Nothing it moistened was immune to its effect. And, as wise as they were in the ways of the land, few of those folks surmised that even when wells are dry, a rain that brings back to life what is better off left dead is more curse than miracle.

In the Dickson farmhouse, water seeped through shingles, slipped down drapes and onto the furniture like honey. When the rooster finally cackled, Grace had been awake for hours. She plodded through the house, hurling china, kicking through doors, and tossing curses out of the bedroom window down toward the tool shed some fifty yards away, where she had sent Farmer Dickson.

"Ya can rot in there with the rest a yer relics, " she had told him.

That part of her that was sister-spirit to puppet-Judy advised she rid herself for good of the letch. But having reasoned this to be just what Farmer Dickson would have desired she do, she clung, instead, to her second impulse—a territorial nostalgia which was simply to get her man away from Satan's squaw and back into the farmhouse where he belonged.

With her head jutted out the porch door, she screamed into the yard, "What's good for the gander, is, by God, good for this ol' goose."

While Grace tossed Don F. Dickson's clothes into the fireplace, the perplexin' rain had continued to work its spell on that Mound. By dawn, a second full Indian torso was rinsed clean and into the air. The malicious moisture had lent no skin to this Indian ruffian, though, nor did it generate organ growth. Its brittle frame housed no heart or lungs. Where his eyes should have been were empty sockets. Only his costume had found new life. At the back of his skull, fastened with a ram's tendon bandana, was a single feather, plucked from the belly of a prairie chicken, a hypergenerative fowl so laden with testosterone that it could barely fly. Around his waist was a protective wrapping of phosphorus gauze.

Farmer Dickson caught a glimpse of it, as this bony undead brought itself to its feet and began to scrape toward the farmhouse.

"What're ya up about there?" Farmer Dickson had shouted.

But the reanimated Indian only moved down the lane which had been transformed into a river of earthy ganglia.

"Hey, feller. I sed, what're ya doin' there?" Farmer Dickson shouted even louder.

Grace opened the porch door to see what the fuss was all about. She saw right off that it was another of those Burial Mound skeletons come to life.

"It's about time ya got here. Come on in, deary, 'fore this perplexin' rain gives ya yer death," Grace instructed the skeleton.

"I'll be go to hell," Don F. Dickson muttered under his breath.

It was not just any homewrecker who had rattled into the Dickson home. That Woodland playboy had been the Indian Maiden's promised one, called by his people, Dude.

"My heart bursts inside my chest when you are near, brutal red man" the Indian Maiden had told Dude, hundreds of years before, "yet I want to harm you. I do not know why."

"And I love but despise, honor but mistrust, cherish but shun you as well, red-skinned flower of the prairie," Dude had assured her, day after day, when their tribe had thrived.

Thus was their fate sealed.

While Farmer Dickson peered through a window at her and her skeletal guest, Grace led Dude over to her husband's rocker.

"How's 'bout a lil' kiss deary," she offered.

"So sorry, but I haven't any lips," Dude replied with a disturbing click, "but I wonder if I might trouble you for a tumbler of rain water."

Grace, with the crude know-how of her puppet mentor, reached out and untied the phosphorous bandage which hid the come-to-life's manhood. The gauze dropped to the floor. But instead of the juicy tomahawk she had desired Grace saw only her husband's rocker through the barren cavity of Dude's hollow hip.

"I'll not give you squat," she replied.

Day 5: "Fill the waters of the sea"

Had he lived long enough, Don F. Dickson could have seen busloads of grade school children scramble pell-mell over his acreage, in the mid-seventies. By then his farm buildings had been torn down and replaced by Dickson Mounds Archaeological Museum, a massive, modern, sleekly contoured structure. It housed a Woodland village mock-up, complete with life-sized Indian figurines, their bulbous brow ridges wax-locked in brute thought. One wing protected the partially excavated skeletons themselves, some with toothy grins on their faces, others in confused tangles of three or more and another with a shagbark hickory grown up through its rib cage. The most notorious of them all, though, and the one that engendered ghastly phobias in classrooms of Midwest field trippers, was that of the "Phallus," as it was known to the kids.

The perplexin' rain continued to wet the Mound, rinsing away what the topsoil had helped shelter in a death-like cryptobiosis. It was a long, thick, beating pattern of powder, the remnant veins and elastic tissues of *It* which had been the embodiment of generative power. In the midst of this pixie dust slavering was a petrified barley bean, no bigger than your thumbnail. That bean was of the same germ as the pod Farmer Dickson stowed in his bib-overall pocket, only this wormseed boasted no blood-inked prairie chicken on its slippery hull. It bore no sacred tattoo at all, yet it was Nature's freak, malformed in the likeness of a wretched penis. Threaded through it was a cord fashioned from the tendon of a ram. It was a potent little kernel and, like Sampson's bountiful locks, that barley bean had been the well-spring of the Phallus's libidinal prowess.

With each thunder clap, endogenic clumps of Satan's sputum dripped from the clouds which hung over the Dixon homestead. And with this devilish rain, the Phallus grew back skin, joints, ligaments, all that had made up the stuff of its life. As it moved away from the Mound in the direction of the tool shed and farmhouse, its grotesque Member began to swell and inflate. Its feet, legs, arms, body and head fell away, and rejoined the inky humus of the grave. The wind lifted what was left, a penile club and pouch, big as a dream.

In their heyday, the Woodland Indians were much more hospitable than other tribes of this continent. Strictly speaking, though, they were not a tribe at all. These North American originals were something of an autonomous, quasi-nomadic commune, with a kindly politic little resembling the classist aquatics of your Sea Monkeys. Still, it takes only one ornery brave to bring down on his people the vile stigma of "unfriendlies."

Outside the tool shed and Dickson home, the Phallus hovered like a zeppelin, its solitary eye-mouth foaming. The barley bean dangled from its tip and dragged along the ground as anchor. Etched with war-paint on its bloated, lighter-than-air scrotum was the likeness of a prairie chicken.

"Come Dicksons," it sang. "Come into the courtyard. Hear what for you has been chosen."

Compelled by the Phallus's siren-like song, the Dicksons could do only what it bade. Farmer Dickson came out of the tool shed, as Grace left the farmhouse. They met before the well and stood facing the Phallus like zombies.

"My two fellow tribespeople, whom you have so graciously entertained during the storm, they are star-crossed lovers. When they were alive, they were as you. They were cohabitants of a violent affection. Among my functional people, such . . ."

"Hey, feller," Farmer Dickson cut in, "alls I know is that all a sudden I got my manhood back. This great tree trunk o' mine ya see stretched out afore me, for thirty odd years, up 'til this rain, it's been hanging useless as a rooster's wattle. Now that it's come back to life, alls I got to use it on is a Injun gal whose even worse icy than my wife here. Sure enough she's a purty one, but she ain't got herself no reservoir for me to bury this ol' feller in."

"Same fer me," broke in Grace. "The young Injun in the house yonder, he's polite as a preacher. He ain't once took a swat at me. But what's the use of me whorin' if the damn fool skeleton ain't no lips or nuthin'."

The Phallus nodded in understanding.

"Oh, but try to understand, gentle Dicksons," the Phallus sang on, "Drink-Brook and Dude, you see, killed one another, so great was their love and so deep their hate. And so may you. Already you have evidenced stinging snakes' tongues. When will you let fly your venom?"

Grace and Farmer Dickson eyed each other with suspicion.

"It is through those ill-fated lovers," the Phallus sang on, "that you may be released from your earthly roles. I propose a swap."

The wise Phallus manipulated his thousands of pubic hairs to lift and remove the malformed barley bean necklace from his Head. He offered it to Grace.

"Why're ya givin' me this here bean fer," asked Grace.

"This charm will help you," the Phallus responded, draping the potent seed over Grace's head. "Only through the power of your beans can you, Don F. Dickson, and you, Grace Dickson, mesh with the brother and sister of the Mound."

Grace held the ram's tendon cord which threaded the little bean while Don F. Dickson removed his own from its bib overall nest. They twisted them around, comparing them.

"Tell ya the truth," Farmer Dickson said, " I've had me my fun and jus wanna come on home."

"Sure enough," Grace put in, "I'm tired o' teasin' after that bony critter in the house. So you an yer Injun friends go on back now from whence ya came."

"Nonsense. Now sleep," the Phallus instructed, "sleep, Dicksons, sleep, sleep as if you dwelled in the soil."

Day Six: "Let us make them in our own likeness"

You probably recall that in the seventies, as they drove over the belly of the country, families like the Brady Bunch gaped at great mountains of discarded tires along the highway. Occasionally, a pneumatic castaway would dislodge from its pile of abandoned brothers and roll down the highway in pursuit of a Chrysler or Ford.

61

"Stop. Take me along," it seemed to call, "I've got a few miles left in me. Honest!"

It was a municipal nightmare. Aside from burning it and stitching the air with black toxic threads, there was no getting rid of a spent radial. And if you bothered to bury a blow-out, it repealed its decay. Sooner or later, like a sliver under your skin, it would work its way back to the surface.

The Dicksons awoke to the sound of tom-toms. They were still in the yard. Their clothing had been removed. On their skin had been painted the images of a thousand prairie chickens. Around them danced the disjointed fragments of the Woodland nation. Skeletal feet danced alone. A gleaming stack of teeth chattered in rhythm to the beat of the drums. Detached fingers snapped and twisted. Skulls spun like tops or rolled in figure eights.

"It looks bad fer us, woman," Farmer Dickson managed to say as the Phallus itself floated down some ten yards in front of them.

Using its hairs, it lifted a nearby jagged femur and with a mighty sweep slit into the maw of its own potent duffel. It burst like a pinata. Indian limbs, tissues, and bones of all shapes and sizes spilled forth, along with spears, bows and arrows, feathers, charms, teepees, sticks, and a buffalo hide. These spare parts were quickly gathered by the tribespeople, who helped one another reassemble. Soon they looked as they had in life. All that remained of the Phallus' secret hord was a single pelvis, a gummy jaw, and a thin pair of lips. These were placed on platters fashioned of tree bark and delivered to Drink-Brook and Dude, who were seated in two chairs that had been removed from the Dickson home.

Don F. Dickson looked at Grace. Grace looked at Farmer Dickson. Against his will, his bib overalls bulged out like the big top at the county fair.

"I have my lips on now, lady," Dude called to Grace. "I'm ready for you at last."

"And I you, Don F. Dickson," said Drink-Brook, exercising that speech newly engendered by the jaw. "My birthing bone is restored," she went on.

The love struck Indians joined hands and began marching toward the Dicksons. The animals were hushed. The rest of the tribe threw themselves on the ground and hid their eyes.

"No, I just couldn't bear it," Grace screamed.

"Come on, woman," Farmer Dickson said and grabbed her by the hand. They broke free from the circle and hobbled hurriedly to the side of the well.

"It's these here barley beans been gummin' up the works," Farmer Dickson said.

He ripped the sacred necklace from his neck and hurled it into the well.

"Come on, woman, toss yers in there, quick now, fore it's too late."

Grace hesitated, turned to look back at Dude with a tear in her eye. She tugged at her own ram cord necklace, dislodging the horribly fashioned barley seed from its spongy burrow. She gave it a stroke or two before she dropped it into the pit.

At breakfast in the seventies, if you looked closely, you probably saw that the artist's rendering on the back of your Rice Krispie box affixed crowns on what must have been the king and queen of the Sea Monkeys. These royal ornaments paraded a hierarchy that stood in ruthless contrast with the egalitarian family rule of T.V. Time's benign matriarch and patriarch, Mr. and Mrs. Brady.

As the Dicksons heard the splash of their two barley beans at the bottom of the well, the earth began to shake.

A gruesome groan, like two mountains grinding in metamorphic passion, came echoing up from its depths. The well burped and coughed up warm streams and veiny clots in a sizzling geyser of life.

Farmer Dickson hefted Grace onto his shoulder and scrambled atop the shed. The Woodlands managed to gain the higher ground of the Mound.

Five, maybe six, molten eruptions and it was over. Yet the fiery silt spawned from the blast sported a hyper-fertile energy that made that week's already astounding fecundity impotent in comparison.

The primordial gravy covering the farm began to steam and churn. Fragile bubbles raised and exploded, out of which flew sparrows, wrens, and a moist pterodactyl. They flapped furiously, rising a few feet before falling back into the ooze only to lift again as dogs, horses, cows, deer, raccoons, or opossum. Out from the barn thudded a parade of mastodons, iguanodons, and a lone parasaurolophus. Rabbits, turkeys, passenger pigeons, bobwhites, turtles, beaver, and muskrats clung to the bellies of these horrid, oversized lizards feeding on trilobites which fed on still weaker arthropods which, in turn, fed on fragrant sumac, elderberry, dogwood, sassafras and hog-peanut which sprouted, grew, flowered, wilted, turned black, decayed and grew again.

"Look over yonder, woman," Don F. Dickson yelled, nudging his wife.

Drink-Brook and Dude had dived from the Mound and were swimming toward the shed.

"I jus can't bear no more o' this," Grace cried, throwing her arms around Farmer Dixon. "I don't want that Injun man no more. I jus want you."

The rain came down harder still. The two Woodland Indians were nearly to the shed, when they got caught up in a strong eddy. The lake began to move, slowly at first, but quickly became a cytoplasmic whirlpool, with the well as its center. Stuck like tar babies, one by one the creatures were sucked down into the well. Without sound, the animals and plants and all that had been reborn were gone. Drink-Brook and Dude fought with fury, but they too were drawn into the relentless black hole.

"Lookee here," nudged Farmer Dickson.

That unspeakable peak in his bib overalls was subsiding, eroding, little by little, until it was no more than a humble butte. But Grace was unconscious, her mind unable to sustain the horror.

On the Mound, the Woodland Indians shuffled single-file into the infinity of the Phallus's testicular mass. When the last had entered, its nimble hairs resutured itself, and it went flaccid and melted into the quiet of the grave.

Day Seven: "Thus was the universe and its array all finished"

Thirty Rice Krispies box tops plus fifty cents seemed a lot of cash for a kid to lay out for a handful of grit that would be dead in a week. But, as your parents pointed out, at least your Sea Monkeys, those social protozoa, could generate no more trouble than what little disasters might occur in a fishbowl.

Before the week of the perplexin' rain, the sole experience Farmer Dickson had had with corpses was following the demise of his ma and her brother, his Uncle Seth. Theirs were not unusual deaths. His uncle died from plain old age and his ma followed him three months later, from sheer loneliness. But neither of them came back to life. Death took hold of those two and stuck. So this whole business of dying for Don F. Dickson had mostly been a permanent sort of thing, though even for him there was something deceitful and undeniably transient about it all. Up in the family cemetery plot, for instance, between the graves of his mother and Uncle Seth, was a marker for his pa. The thing of it was, though, that his pa had high-tailed it when little Donny was new born. Don's pa's was a decoy grave in which Don's ma had buried all of the runaway's "lily-livered" belongings—in that sense, his grave truly did contain his remains.

Not all the Woodlands could have been brought back to life. Many had been unearthed and rinsed down the Illinois River and on into the Gulf of Mexico in the centuries before the "perplexin' rain." Others simply lacked the karmic momentum to allow the vile wetness to boost them back to life. But, though it had been reduced to no more than a chalky residue, the Phallus could have reanimated, with or without the sinister saline that fell from the sky that week, through its residual erotic energy alone. Still, it seems the Woodland Indians of Dickson Mounds and the Sea Monkeys shared little more than a tragic anatomical fragility.

Your Sea Monkeys were another breed entirely. As quickly as they were born of that grainy mail-order seed, they would skid back again, past hibernation, careening madly into death. Perhaps it was the sheer momentum of their watery leap from dust to culture which sped these curious pets through their life-cycle in just seven short days. What brakes could they possibly have applied to slow their penchant for sterile citizenship? Imagine the terror of such a brief, well-ordered existence. Still, to a humble amoebocyte, the Nothingness of death may be less grisly than the Foreverness of homeostatic pause. Maybe, that is, the suspended grip of dehydration is so fierce a concept that any horror death carries for Sea Monkeys pales by comparison. And there must have been, after all, some consolation in the immortality carried in the artwork of a cereal-box advertisement.

The Dicksons could take a beating, as it happened, with as much resiliency as Punch and Judy. On the final day of the perplexin' rain, Farmer Dickson and Grace worked side by side, clearing away debris, rounding up the farm animals, repairing what they could. Grace chortled with glee when Don F. Dickson transported his artifacts from the tool shed and piled them in the yard. Together, they poured bacon grease and corn oil on what had been his treasures, so that the foul rain would not extinguish them once lit.

"Go on now, woman, " Farmer Dickson said. "Light up the damn lot of 'em fore I think better on it."

By the time his arrowheads, awls, bone pipes and bean pots were no more than charred and shattered remnants, the rain had stopped entirely.

"It's sure enough good to be home, woman," Farmer Dickson told his wife.

Yet whenever it rained just so, Grace would find Farmer Dickson's rocker abandoned. And had she bothered to look out the kitchen window she could have spied him peering down into that well, fishing around with a rake or a hoe.

Edward Kleinschmidt

Face Value

I picture Wittgenstein as a boy playing with a Quaker gun. No simple bang-bang, just simpler silence. What was he to do with this object carved of wood, like a piano, or like his clarinet, but no sound and, beyond that, no purpose? I picture him sitting on a rock in a park, thinking about this.

Now I picture a man in a barn milking a cow. I can not picture the vice-versa of this situation and do not want to and nobody, nobody even in this room, can make me.

The carton of milk in the refrigerator has a date stamped at the top, and I can't tell you how many times, how many, many times, I have thought about that date. Where was I on June 21st, the last date this particular carton of milk can be sold in the grocery store before it is yanked off by the milk-delivery person and made into cottage cheese back at the processing plant (and it will then reappear with a new date)? Ah, November 10th, do not buy after November 10th—are we talking about this year? And here is my father's birthday, here the date I graduated from high school, here Christmas, here Labor Day. And on this date, July 25th, ten years ago, I am telling the three people at Safeway who have gathered around the dairy department—on this date ten years ago I fell truly in love.

I know that five days after the date of sale, the milk will turn. It had been squeezed out of some cow, it had been squeezed into this carton, the carton had been squeezed into my refrigerator. All this time, the milk's biological clock is ticking. There are so many biological clocks in the refrigerator—on the butter, the cheese, the mayonnaise, all stamped with "best when purchased before" and the date—that I hate to open the door, the sound is so loud. It keeps the cat up. I know that one day I will look in the refrigerator and find everything in it spoiled, the dates glaring at me with I-told-you-so's. If the dairy industry could only embed in the cartons a tiny digital clock that would count down the time each product has left, with a set alarm, then I would sleep better.

Now I am picturing the face. Not the face of a clock, for a clock hasn't any more of a face than it has hands, and what would hands be doing stuck in the middle of a face, right where the nose should be? And a clock hasn't hands, arms with no hands perhaps, but even then, where are its elbows, its wrists, its biceps.

I am picturing the human face, known as that area from the top of the forehead to the chin and from ear to ear. No need now to become self-conscious and make a face: the face has been made.

And now I am picturing a book, but I can only guess at its title because I can't yet see it clearly. It lies open on a beach towel. The wind has blown the bookmark into the plate of potato salad. Someone has been reading but is now swimming.

There is another book. This one on a table in the living room. It is large and jam-packed with words.

When I fall asleep reading a book, the words slide off the page onto the white comforter. The book falls from my hands, the long drop to the floor, and the cat under the bed stretches and yawns. So be it for books.

As a child I had a picture book, its corners chewed by the dog who lived in the house. It had only as many words as the plastic flowers in the pot on the window sill had petals. The number never changed, even when I skipped over words I didn't feel like saying on a particular day. I've since used all the words in that book. I've rewritten the book without knowing I have every year. I probably say cat every day. But where has garden gone? I would prefer to say well more, the kind of well that is dug in the backyard, with a bucket I could lower on thick rope, and could pull up well water, could water the real flowers that still bloom when the book is opened.

Can you picture this: This sentence is a picture. That is, I think of Joan Dingfelder in seventh grade reading aloud to the class as she was told to do and saying pitcher for the word picture. I thought of a picture of a pitcher, a picture of pitch, a picture of a pitcher with flowers in it. That day, there was only one word I stumbled on, Cairo. I had been absent the previous day when we began Egypt, our first country in the African unit. And here was Cairo; when the teacher told me how it was pronounced, I thought of my mother pouring syrup on her pancakes that morning, thick and clear, pooling on the sides of the plate.

Now I have pictured Joan Dingfelder (who knew a little German) and Ludwig Wittgenstein (who died in

71

1951, the year Joan was born) on the same morning, in nearly the same breath, something Joan never would have believed if I had told her in seventh grade, "Joan, someday I will mention your name in nearly the same breath as the name of Ludwig Wittgenstein." Who had, I should add, but I couldn't to Joan, in seventh grade, a picture theory about language, which, if Joan were reading this sentence, she would call a pitcher theory about language, something Ludwig would have thought about and thought about.

Constance Pierce

In the Garden of the Sunbelt Arts Preserve

1.

With great propriety the woman seems to drive her dog, a lhasa apso. The leash is pulled so tight that it looks like a goad pestering the animal's neck, an impression encouraged by the woman's vague scowl and the dog's single-minded advance. They are moving rapidly down the green that separates "Common flowers of the Region" from "Tea Roses." It's a testament to the woman's handling of her posture that she can seem to be in command, for it is of course the dog who is determining their pace and direction.

Whether because she's focusing so intently on her immediate situation or for some other reason, the woman doesn't acknowledge us: three women drinking coffee and sunning our legs on a terrace just to the side of her course. Though the sun is beginning to warm from the outside what the caffeine has constricted within (the veins of our extremities are cool as snakes with the drug's effects), the rest of us—head, shoulders, and trunk—is warm enough in the shade beneath the umbrella of our table.

The table itself is patterned with coffee rings, errant pens and pencils, a barrette shaped like a pair of kissing swans, legal pads and note pads well-doodled, an address book on whose shiny blue surface a pink flamingo stands on one long leg and curls the other in reference to its curled neck, which is the shape of a question mark. Our paperback novels are spotted with suntan oil, and if a person were to squint from my vantage, at least three nipples are visible through the gauzy fabric of my companions' brief clothing, a fourth implied behind the camouflage of a silk-screened rose. My clothes are brief and loose too, but not transparent.

The woman clipping along is wearing golf togs. Suddenly I wonder, as this part of the world always makes you wonder, if the woman, who is perfectly groomed and the picture of propriety, is consciously ignoring us because we have transgressed . . . in our clothing. If this is so, I know that we'll hear about it soon enough, that justice will be swift, stupid, inconsequential in the larger scheme of things, but that it will put us in our places. I know this in spite of the other thing I know from eavesdropping on her conversation yesterday in Cheese 'n' Things, when I dipped in for a pack of weeds (to smoke outside, of course). I could hear that she is from elsewhere, a snowbird. But something in her demeanor and her bearing make it clear how well she's adjusted. It occurs to me that she has assumed something like the place that might have been reserved for me (no matter that she is clearly one of the "smart women" of my mother's generation), if I'd been born into receptivity to a certain kind of polishing and a more calculating instruction, a different kind of class anxiety.

No, she does not acknowledge us, does not appear to note us on the terrace, loaned for the occasion: for taking possession of her and her dog, the robust birds, the flowers and trees, anything in range (unless, of course, we wish to ignore all that and look forward or inward or backward instead). Everything is open to us. Except certain rooms, maddening behind their

74

burnished doors. The patrons are secure nothing will come of our being here, no tattle or bad taste. Our kind comes and goes without incident, grateful for the mornings that prickle with pine, mint and boxwood. Here, arts are preserved, sweet and pungent as English sachet.

"I could use some more of this," Heather says, having sat up and wedged small cotton logs in between her toes. She is holding up an almost empty bottle of nail polish and watching its sluggish progress down the side of the bottle. "It's a good shade, Tea Rose."

"We could go to town," Rosemary says, not opening her eyes.

They are pretty women, with hair in floral shades and husbands in the Professions. They say they're poets, and I believe it. There are always more poets than anybody else here, I've heard. Heather says she's writing a villanelle on the varieties of mint in the Garden; Rosemary intends to perform a meditation on the pines. Upstairs, our fellow Fellows are still asleep: a painter, who seems to sleep a lot, and a person I haven't met yet, but I've heard the tortured cello in the night.

The woman clipping along is perfectly groomed and tanned almost violet. Her head is tufted beige, something like the ornamental grasses that grow out by "The Natural Pond." I see now that she is swinging a plastic bag of something—probably fresh mint—in one fist, as if to balance the other, managing its enormous clump of her animal's rein. With a quick economy, she surveys the sunny roses, some nameless wildflowers contained in the shade, the monumental house buttressed by her deductible donation, the tiny gift shoppe where she volunteers her hours. Her efficient eyes are everywhere, and still she does not notice: the trio of scribbling women taking an endless break, barely covered by halter scraps, beneath the table's big umbrella, which is brash as a sunflower.

Are we too much in the flesh?

Or has she made the proper gesture already, and "Good morning" would be an extravagance?

Perhaps she thinks that she and the others who sustain the Foundation have done their share in maintaining the house, the stables and grounds . . . and all that comes with them: the cryptic practices that must be taken on faith to be good for civilization and order, humanity and the uncommon weal.

"I always go in the mornings," I heard her tell the fellow refugee yesterday over *bisque des crevettes* at Cheese 'n'Things. "To walk Aida . . . you know, smell the blooms, listen to bird-song, check on the help. See what's *disappeared* in the night."

She spooned her soup away from herself, in keeping with instructions absorbed somewhere along the way. Fascinated with the parsimony of her clean sips from the large European-style spoon, not a drop lost to its source in the European-style soup plate, I missed something her companion said. Suddenly, the spoon was back in the plate, the fuchsia linen pressed to pristine lips.

"Oh, Sugar, no," she said, instructing her companion in the droll markers of the region, draining all sweetness from the word. "Never in the Public Hours. Some *chèvre?*"

"No, the *bisque* is quite adequate," her companion said, over-exaggerating the French.

"Hours—," the woman went on, emphatically cutting off a large ring of the cheese and scraping it quickly onto a ring of baguette, "—*much* too generous, by my lights. . . ."

At the gift shoppe she miraculously uncurls a set of keys from the tangle of leash in her hand, then pushes into the quaint outbuilding, yanking the dog in behind her, and shuts its rustic door.

In moments, the resonating strains of a concerto for violin coalesce and begin to wend like a lush serpent toward the terrace.

2.

My companions have gone to the Village, leaving me with the demons of excess caffeine and the too-bright sun. Vertiginous birds dip through the last reek of moss and dew as the Garden dries out and the boxwood and myrtle release their smells, which have never been described very well. They are neither floral nor medicinal. Like almost nothing left in the natural world, they are "incomparable." Anything else to be said about them must be left to the poets.

Though recent inhabitants prefer "Village," the town is more a crossroads of rural exchange transmogrified. The new ferny restaurant retains the signs of the old feedstore. The surprised faces of the country people and displaced entreprenuers of modest aspirations now meet at the Convenience Mart on the edge of town or at the service entrances to the golf clubs. Ancient black men who remember mixing toddies and unseasonal juleps for the Gentlemen who came in winter by private railroad car, now grouse along the sandy paths connecting the old estates, muttering an aphasic language that tells much more than it says. A skink with a bright orange head skims the terrace slate like he's on fire. There is resin in the air, resin in my head, suddenly distilled from the loblolly pines edging the Garden, and beyond: longleaf, the last virgin stand in the South. I've been gone for fifteen years, and even this relocation— brief and only approximate, since I am not from this Village/town, but only from a swampy place near it, lacking its pastoral name—is dislocating. In part, I'm reeling from the reel of smells, the sweet and the incomparable; but most of all from the overwhelming pines. To calm myself, I go through the names you might use to name a town, or a motel or campground, or a trailer park or golf course. Tall Pines. Two Pines. Three Pines.

Whispering Pines (of course). Lonesome Pines, Fallen Pines, Burnt Pines. Pineland, Pine Glen, Pine Hill, Pine Creek. Lost Pines (?). Green Pines, White Pines, Black Pines. Piney Pines. About these pines, my long-dead host wrote much, perhaps from this very terrace. He was a writer of regional reputation, host of last resort to the brilliant novas of his boozy generation. So often broke and sick to boot, they crisscrossed the nation from host to host, by trains that always arrived in the dead of night. They were men who were delirious to find this gracious house with its door unlocked, a fire lit, brandy on the mantle. They wrote of dissolving life in exile, in the great capitols of Europe, or in its picturesque towns, or along its jewel-like Sea. He wrote of things closer to home, like the declining market for naval stores—pitch, tar, and resin—the remote sources of his largesse. His early forte was historical fiction, encoding advice on how to handle Negroes for northerners new to the South, words of caution on Yankee parsimony when retained at the expense of play. Later, in poetry, he took on the Revolution and the Civil War, writing (as he said of one of his characters) a verse that was born old, full of couplets and strophic dazzle. He was to the manner born, as they say now, in their punning way, so let me say it too. (My sinuses are killing me!) But in the end, he lived up to his times, in his fashion. He wrote of children bombed in London, Jews in the hands of ruffians, all the pillage and wasted promise of that vast backwater, Europe. Perhaps he'd had its number all along. He wrote, finally, some poignant remarks on factory work, a social issue of the region; he wrote of Negroes with empty pockets in the mill towns. He reviled the KKK.

He meant well. And he was generous in all the ways he could afford to be. He loved riding to the hounds on Sunday morning, spreading a lavish hunt breakfast around a well-cured country ham, inviting all his neighbors. *Loving* his neighbors, turning his other cheek for their grazing kisses as they entered his door, as if he had never had politics on his mind, or anything questionable or in bad taste. No one person could save the world, anyway.

The soft and fragrant lips of the women moved easily from his cheek to the rims of the glasses black Virgil had filled, the instant they walked in the room, with an icy liquor clear as turpentine.

The fire crackled. The morning sun caught the gold tones of the carpets, where the heels of the women's shoes, wrapped in the skins of reptiles whose cellular structure seemed displayed there, were sinking into the wool of yaks and goats. Cigarette smoke was rising like incense. A local spinster in her best dress was playing Cole Porter and George Gershwin, out of sight behind an arras decorated with the images of knights on horseback in gold leaf. Voices rose in indeterminate talk, classed together by their happy tones and regular laughter. The sugar glazing the huge animal part had begun to give up the ghost and collect in dark splendor on the Sèvres platter. The honey jar was waiting for the hot biscuits Sukie would be bringing in any moment, suspended just this side of disintegrating into buttery crumbs. The plates of sausage and fried apples, the grits flecked with pepper, the bowls of fruit out of season, the candied ginger and orange peel and clementines his guests had brought as gifts and set on the sideboard, the silver lined up on the Madeira cloth—these were pleasures too rare to forego, whatever one's convictions. It couldn't be done, and why should it be done? He didn't see how or why. He loved his neighbors, wherever they came from. But he loved his famous writer-friends the best. He loved to see them ranging his terrace in late afternoon, drinking his liquor, squandering his luminous garden, the rare roses and tamed deer. He cherished their books with their witty dedications to him by name.

He loved writers, loved writing, a noble enterprise. He loved the simple dichotomies—Man Against Nature,

Man Against Machine, Man Against Himself. He wrestled humility from his inflated circumstances, but never failed to thank his lucky stars that the messy business of extracting viscids from those lonesome pines was two generations behind him. America, for all its faults, gave one hope, nearing the end. If poetry made nothing happen, as one who had never partaken of his hospitality had proclaimed; if all couldn't be construed—some things could still be taken on faith. If a person had tried to be a good host, and tried to do right, and write right, accepting the critical responsibility of a good citizen, things would work out. Sure as natural law. One would be allowed to make a dent in the nature of things.

He died in a plush room full of books, stores of words sticking to his tongue in the end, dark as pitch, gummy as resin. He left it all—the signatures, his own books, the grounds, the elaborate house that privately even his friends had found slightly monstrous in its antebellum detail—bestowed it all on the State, to bestow on writers. Now there could be a perpetual unlocked door, a fire in the grate, food and drink and virgin pines whispering to soothe their sleep. But the State let it dwindle near decay, an outrage to art, architecture and gestures of the public spirit, so incensing their champions that the Foundation sprang into furious being and saved the day. A melange of retired golfers, scandalized members of the Historical Society, a young specialist in Corporate Giving, and several PR men from the Mill, who insisted on the Public Hours.

Everyone lent a hand, and a check, volunteered to trim the grass, prune the roses, mind the gift shoppe, check to be sure the artists had a regional connection, didn't write smut or pilfer the library and garden, and kept to their designated quarters.

The deer that had thrived during the era of neglect

were donated to the zoo. And after a scrupulous consultation of the conditions of the Trust, it was concluded that surely more than writers might avail themselves of the benefactor's generous legacy. Oh, many, many more. It was concluded further that the private quarter-horses of the most serious donors might be sheltered in the stables, that the ballroom could accomodate a weekly chamber group, occasional *lieder*, and that now and then a symphony might be feted in the pines.

3.

It's close to noon. The tabula is rasa, except for a fetching nuthatch sketched—for want of a shrike! What kind of ingrate takes this bountiful sun and scent, feeds on brie-ends and pinenuts, the scraps of a brunch in the ballroom, left discreetly on a serving tray by some friendly Friend of the Foundation . . . and then bites the hand that feeds, fouling a comfortable nest?

The caffeine and sugar have worn off, the sinuses cleared by a spray that, interestingly, seems itself to be made of pine.

A BC powder has dulled a bad headache. But still groggy with useless malice, I'm receptive to the retired surgeon from Dayton who is trimming the boxwood in his shorts and running shoes. He talks about his children, who majored in political science and English lit, then graduated and went out West to work in computers. He says he can't figure it out and shakes his head.

"Youth is mysterious," I say. He laughs.

"That's right," he says, shaking his head again, as if to clear it, then laughing again. "That's right." He looks at me a little more sharply. "What is it you do?" he asks.

"Video," I lie. I must seem young to him.

He suspends his great shears. "You mean, that MTV stuff?"

"Without the music," I say.

He lowers his shears and trims a little. "I just can't figure it out," he says. "I thought the boy would go to Washington. I thought maybe she'd move down here, close to us, get married."

He stops trimming with each new thought. He tells me he thought his daughter would give him grandchildren, living right down the street from him, that the kids would ride in the Loblolly Chase and study the Suzuki violin.

It doesn't matter that he dawdles. The Foundation is flourishing now, and there is a full-time groundsman, black, as energetic as the New South. I see him piling pinestraw around Don't Pick signs in the background.

"Youth is mysterious," the surgeon says, more to himself than to me. I like him, in spite of certain reservations . . .

. . . Borne out by his driven friend, the piston engineer from Cleveland. The friend disapproves of us. He is furiously working the iris beds as though they're his own, spading, and driving the classifying labels into the ground with relish, in spite of his pique.

Both men are elaborately ignored by a silver-haired Professor Emeritus of the Classics, out by the roses, muffled stubbornly in an ascot in spite of the heat. Retired on patrimony and the sale of his oriental rugs, he speaks to me sometimes when the northern Friends are gone, his genteel tongue lolling about his mouth like a netted fish, garbling his Old Tidewater speech. Now he frees the roses of aphids, plucking them from the leaves and crushing them in his handkerchief. He eyes the process, and his hand in it, with a voyeur's fascination.

The strains of "Water Music" click off in mid-note. My eye explodes like a roman candle from a sudden dip in blood sugar, and I grab the coffee creamer and drink it down. The woman is coming out of the gift shoppe and locking it carefully, a walking stick tucked under her arm like a riding crop. She tests the lock, hesitates, then tests it again, before turning her attention to the matter at hand: taking possession of herself, assuming the proprietary posture that will obscure her willful dog pulling her by the leash. She achieves the effect she's after. The two take off, steady as dividends.

The men from Ohio say they'd better cash it in and head over to the lake. They are the color of steaks, sweating, neatly tying things off. The surgeon hesitates.

"Would you like to join us," he asks, gallant as a native, of a certain kind.

"I think she'd need to be a Member," his friend volunteers quickly.

"Oh . . .," the surgeon says, looking uncertainly between us.

"Another time," I say. The noon sky is full of stars and rockets.

"Well," the surgeon says. "I enjoyed talking to you. I'll look for you on MTV."

"I'm best known for 'The People, Yes,'" I say, giving him my friendliest smile.

"It almost sounds like something I've heard of already," he says.

"Let's get going," his friend says, peeling off his work gloves, encrusted with dirt, exposing his paler hands. "Before it gets too hot to take."

They leave, each carrying a Baggie stuffed with mint. Suddenly burning, I move out to the shade for relief—before I die! Go to be a Member of that great writers' colony in the sky. . . .

The signs staked in the vegetation (in the cool dapple, in the truncated vision of basal distress) almost seem put here to serve the new poets, so singularly obsessed with the quaint names of plants. There are twenty kinds of mint, and twenty country-sounding

labels.   Also "Rue," "Red Bee Balm," "Tansy,"
"Lovage"—a whole chapbook's worth.   The irises are
refreshing, with their as-yet-unbeaten names: Lime fizz,
Loud Mouth, Whoop Em Up. They sound like the names
of race horses, and then, given my state, I can't help but
think that's because both were named out of the same
kind of leisure. I'm in no shape to indulge this thought.
I seek out the herbs and daffodils bubbling up on each
other nearby: Libation, Swizzle, Cheers, Angel Baby.
Wow. Beau. Voilà! Forty Winks, Stony Eyed. Men Only.

In my struggle to ignore the horsey names of even
these modest plants, I fall into a slough after all. It is as
if a train of dead writers has suddenly arrived, a
generation so conspicuously lost that others may never
find themselves. Names give up the ghost of things,
narrate a frantic cycle of jazzy nights and working days.

It is a tale so Modern and magical that flowers, even
fed on leafmeal of "Bloodroot" and "Heart's Ease," bleed
further away. Word capitulates to story, becoming twice
the host—Boo, Betsy Boo, Laced Lemonade.   The
fabulous couple whoops in, in the dead of night, Zelda's
pathetic trajectory curving in the background: Dixie
Pixie, Spreckled Sprite. Baby Toes, April Ballet, Mini
Plie. Already. Men Only.

"I hate their goddam putting greens," the old
professor says, clear as a Bronze Bell, gathering aphid-
remains into a ball of handkerchief, freeing a corner to
sop at his brow. "They've got two hundred already, and
six man-made lakes. When will they get enough?"

He begins to garble again, something about the
Moneybelt, a subject he discursed on earlier in the week;
something else in Latin. Then his eye is caught by the
wealth of mints at our feet and he begins to file sprigs in
his different pockets. The others are on the terrace, back
from the Village with beer and (I feel sure) their new felt-
tip pens. Heather and Rosemary are greasing themselves
against the sun, down to their strong pointed toes. A

young oriental man is standing off to the side, watching them, wearing long pants and a long-sleeved shirt. He must be the cellist. I want to hear about his regional connection this afternoon. He probably goes to Duke.

"What do they do?" the professor asks. He has slipped up behind me and is watching them over my shoulder, a piece of mint leaf held like a short pencil. I think about Heather and Rosemary. I haven't seen them do much of anything but what they're doing right now, but then I haven't done much of anything myself but stew and "read" everything around me like an untended sensor. I know they've studied with the Masters. They talk a lot about "poetic mistakes," and they are intimidating with their secret lore on the line. They talk a lot about dishonest writers and believe that writing coolly from the heart will necessarily yield the universal truth. One's refrain is No Ideas, the other's Make It New.

"What you see them doing," I say to the professor. "And they say they're poets too. I believe them."

The cellist is still standing in the same place. He looks hot. Heather and Rosemary have collapsed on the chaise longues and have begun to play a new cassette very loud. They know that the Friends are gone for the day, that the professor is odd man out, not a friend at all.

Again, clear as the lyric of an old song, the professor speaks: "Nobody's minding the store."

4.

By late afternoon, the light is washing everything the color of jaundice. The pines are slanting across the garden, the terrace, a big piece of lawn, making a tarn of shade. I have bathed in the cold water barely trickling from the old pipes, washed my hair and put on a clean shirt too much like a golf tog. (At least I've written all this, easing my conscience.) But meanwhile the others have gone, Heather and Rosemary, the Japanese cellist (who does go to Duke), even the painter, still rubbing sleep from her eyes as they all squeezed into the cellist's tiny Honda. The house is spooky as a forest near evening. Time to seek out the library. It is ringed with mullioned windows, bringing the garden inside. Exposing anything anybody might do.

This has become a habit, the library in late afternoon on the days I don't go with the others to whoop at the Pub. In the library, on its one wall that isn't glass, there's a portrait of my host in pastels. His wife is blooming beside him. They are wearing pink riding habits and one of them, I can't tell which, is carrying a crop. On the same wall, there are many photographs of horses decked with wreathes and roses, and there are lots of loving cups in a built-in cabinet with a glass door. There are books too, locked behind glass in another cabinet. And there are several free-standing display cases in which books are opened to the famous signatures and scrawled, unreadable messages.

The Foundation pumps arias and sonatas through the rooms like water all morning, accompanying the Volunteers. But this silence calls for something from a dusty collection, uncatalogued on a dark bottom shelf— blues, jazz, country, and several sub-genres that layer one people over another, something like the woman's saying Sugar, her tongue salty with goat cheese.

I stack them on: a history of something. I listen to white women moanin' low. Black men named Count, Duke, and Earl make sophisticated rhythms; others in white tuxedoed orchestras play a white Beguine. Fiddles speed up the rhythms of Renaissance kings to tell a lonesome tale. And a cryptic discord out of a black North city, a triumphant Idea, pure and private as the Longleaf Country Club, releases a thin serpentine sound that winds and undulates briefly, disappears, returns and returns.

I have been reading my host's forgotten stories, novels, and poems as though it were a debt. Reading the Foundation's offical bio, I've learned that in the Argonne Forest, he sustained a minor wound to the chest. I wonder why he never wrote of that. Naturally, what writers write away from tells its own story.

I have been reading away from a Poe-ish tale, full of lurid moonbeams, magnolias, palmettos scraping in the wind—the host's most fascinating remains, read several days ago and nagging. I give in, begin it again. It is a story set in a coastal backwater, with ripples of necrophilia. There is the treacherous undertow of class, the only American subject.

The narrator is a Cavalier, that curious Southern affectation. He is well-meaning and, of course, well-born—a wit, with a Moral Sense, a faithful black retainer named Scipio. The servant is a wizard with rum and mint. He has been well- trained to rise, even in the dead of night, to mix his Master's a masterful julep from a special Jamaican reserve. It is a kind of leitmotif, this cliche, this mint julep, infusing the story with its liquid content. The Cavalier's aristocratic chum, the Doctor, experiments on "darkies" from the swampland with impunity. He is a kind of Doctor Blood or Mabuse, a caution to his gentler friend. That the Doctor has a radical notion of noblesse oblige, the Cavalier seems to understand. But his protest is the essence of discretion and gallantry, even in the most serious verbal tussles. The Doctor's use of the darkies is a moral scandal; both author and narrating Cavalier make that clear beyond a doubt. But oddly, the greater transgression (pandered in whispers and puzzling perhaps even to my host) seems to be that the Doctor has married a pale-faced country girl, barely in shoes.

Who of course must die.

One night, when the moon hangs in the sky like a

Stilton cheese, the brooding Cavalier leaves his house, determined to get to the bottom of an uneasy feeling he hasn't been able to shake, not since the wife's funeral. (The pall had been so easy to bear.) His brain curdling with theories and juleps, he reels through the ghostly moonlight to dig like a ghoul, unearth the empty coffin and some whiff of the worst he'd suspected. Not without shame, he creeps to his friend's house and spies through a louvre. And then, in that latter-century convention— the telling, shocking tableau: the Doctor-aristocrat holds his vigil near the corpse of his country wife, his great folly, and they are shown to be joined in a way the bride could never have imagined, their two arms linked by a telltale tube.

I put the story down, marvel at it, the quaintness of its House-of-Usher-Rappaccini-Dr. Heidegger aspect, overlaid with celluloid, and all the story hints about my host and his conflicts. Was the Cavalier politely horrified that his friend shifted the subject of his research, or that he'd married her to do it? It's hard to tell. Was it Frankenstein or Dracula my host was after? Mad Promethean science run amok, or a shameless aristocracy seeking to refresh itself at a stream of peasant blood? Is the story, for 1945, an anachronistic mistake? Or did history make it new, absolutely to the point?

I ruminate on viscids and juleps, a stake in the chest of my host in the Argonne Forest; his postwar trauma that ranged, like some monster or vampire, from War to War; his late social conscience and philanthropy, his die-hard investment in the Cavalier (or was that an interrogation of the Cavalier?). Ruminating on the whole mysterious tangle, I am shocked by a face at the window. I jump and my host's book falls from my lap to the floor. It is the pale country face of a woman, with eyes the color of swamp water.

It is, of course, the Public Hours.

5.

The woman lowers her eyes, embarrassed to be caught out looking in on the lush interior of the house. She turns and heads toward the Garden, catching up with her little girl, who has the neutral coloring of our race, the dishwater hair and swamp eyes that I've learned to like in myself after all, in spite of the names. By now, I know absolutely why.

I leave the library, filch a beer with somebody else's name on it from the Artists' Refrigerator, disguise the liquid in a coffee cup and head outside, trailing the two of them.

It's close to dark. Time to check the windows upstairs, windows to the forbidden rooms. They make you half-expect to see a range of ghosts propped up to regard the property—my troubled host, his famous friends, ironic and melancholy. Besotted by words and signs, a condition of their Trust. Tubes tying them to a history of their own making. How to justify the private extravagance so publically displayed, the excessive texture and suggestive metaphors that only half-reveal? The voluptuous babble every time they wrote near the American subject? They were time-obsessed men, living in the dark night of denial, grazing things, and veering away politely, leaving the safer hint. Men whose public hours were full of craft—ingratiatingly poignant, clubby, a bit inchoate, working the magic "ineffable" like music on the brain. And it left us all in thrall: no clear exit. A blast from the "warm" radio station lets me know the others are back. Lights are going on in our designated quarters. It's dark in there. It's almost dark out here. But I can see by the extra bodies filing out onto the terrace, that the others have brought company. The radio goes off in favor of Heather and Rosemary's favorite cassette, the golden oldies that were used to score a hit movie several years ago. Already, Heather and Rosemary are nostalgic for the movie and have bought their own copy. All week long, after a certain point in the evening, they have put it into the painter's VCR, poured more wine, and danced and sung along. The movie itself is nostalgic: a troubled "ensemble" nearing middle-age reassembles after many years for the funeral of a friend. They pack into the bountiful home of their rich and successful host (entrepreneur extraordinaire), dance to the oldies, long for their lost selves, for the happy days at their expensive university, where they had been happily committed to the important causes. They drink wine, confess, dance some more. In the end, everyone is happier and wiser. Most of their problems have been addressed wisely by their genial host, whose hospitality is boundless, whose wisdom is smug and unreflective, but nobody seems to notice. They love their host! He and his wife become Pater and Mater, save the day. Everyone leaves happier and wiser themselves, Pater and Mater smiling beatifically from the yard of their expensive house by the sea. The movie was a big hit with everyone, all across the nation. I can't see it. The self-congratulation alone is insufferable. The new entrepreneur as pater, patron, patron saint, and savior of the day is a suspicious idea. It gives me a chill.

Last night in the dining room, where we had sneaked the VCR—while the painter was dead to the world on a French settee and the cellist made himself known from above each time the movie quieted down for its earnest heartfelt moment; while Heather and Rosemary rocked and boogied and laughed every time they spilt wine on the carpet that was already hopelessly pitted by the reptilian heels and idly poked riding crops of long-ago guests; while I drank my beer and pondered why the politics of the movie were so palatable to so many, why conservative rhetoric is so invisible that it seems natural to most people, why the movie's self-satisfaction didn't seem to goad and pester—I suddenly saw exactly how the movie had cast its blinding spell. I saw it in one of the commercials that sponsored a TV show we were watching intermittently when Heather and Rosemary wanted to rest from their dance. The commercial was scored with solid gold, drawing Heather and Rosemary up out of their slump and back onto "the dance floor." They sang along and kept their eyes focused on the screen where an ugly black and silver car was careening through a lush suburb lined with palm trees. Heather and Rosemary were smiling and singing softly as if to encourage the car in its progress. Neither of them would have wanted that car on the last day of their lives. But watching them smiling and singing along, mesmerized by the image—held to it by the song—I felt that car might be in their futures, and suddenly I understood the movie's fatal attraction.

(I know what you're thinking: I should look to my own house. You're thinking about my own self-satisfaction. I see what you mean, and I'm working on it. I concede that the tone is sometimes insufferable, the relentless hackles a pain in the neck. Sometimes I'm too clever by half, as our anglophiliacs say, and let me say it too. But I don't exempt myself [Heather, you are more myself than I am]. And, Reader, don't misread me: I am not satisfied, not satisfied at all.)

Heather has just seen me and held up a clear bottle which must be gin; I can almost intuit its coat-of-arms label from the shape of the bottle, which she has begun to wave in the air, balanced by what must be a lime. I wave back, hold up a finger as a minute. Then I follow the woman and the child. They have sped up with the racket from the terrace. The woman is wearing the furtive look of a trespasser.

"Don't pick anything," she warns the child.

Then, maybe to compensate, she leans down and begins to read the signs to her in a falsely lilting voice.

"Bleeding Heart," she says. "Blue Bis . . . Bids-kew."

"What's a bids-kew," the child asks, ignoring the other name, the gory one that speaks of Dracula, my wounded host, and me, at once—a name, an image, and a flower pressed into service to repress the public spirit, to make a metaphor out of the impossible Democracy that drives a person crazy, ruins writing, maybe even affects metabolism. . . .

I fling caution to the bluster of something. It's starting up in that old boondoggle of The People, of people created unequal, their pain reduced to platitude and sentiment that never reaches the heart or brain. It gains force from the complicity of pirouetting on time 'n' things, which breeds research on poignance, that blissful hurt in "epiphany"; from appropriating the straightforward names of weeds, herbs, and flowers in telling indirection—

If poetry makes nothing happen, if it seeks no Ideas beyond Things that are more and more the same (stones, bones, snow and snowdrop), if all can't be construed, it isn't natural law!

I draw on my cup like a hookah, make a little *jeté* to miss a thorny pyracantha, follow my leaders into the blue anti-crime light that has just come on and thrown the door to the gift shoppe into cunning relief, as if there are Fates that concur with this sermonette, this tune in one key, this old-fangled flyting, urging me on.

(Well, what about it? Does it scan?)

My host, in his way, knew and spoke his bad conscience. Good for him! I like him more and more. And what's wrong with wanting to be a good guest, not a parasite or ghoul, a solo bump in the dead of night, angling in on the brandy?

"I don't know what it means," the mother whispers, and the child looks at me: The Perpetual Instructor, who must be giving off a scent, who is sugar-drunk again, and no special believer anyway in what things mean— though she always has a theory; though she detests like a serpent's bite the big-hit notion that things shouldn't mean but be. It gives her a big chill.

"I don't know what it means either," I say, refusing to instruct. "But there's a can of soup inside called Tomato Bids-kew." (Don't laugh: I mask no irony. I say the word as earnestly as they have, giving it their best shot. Some things are more important than instructing, perhaps many, many things. I congratulate myself a little on that. Why not? Such forgoings are as rare as common courtesy and common sense. They're not the nature of the beast, so give a little credit. Take a little note.)

We are standing so close by now that I know they can smell the beer. Maybe they can smell the ruse of my old half-forgotten backwater speech, too, trying too hard to make them at home where I'm just a parasite myself. It's a bind, this meaning well. It's forever turning you into some kind of patronizing host. (I seem to have just stepped in dog shit.)

"The Campbell Soup people have a house around here," the woman says as I scrape my shoe on a label-holder; then she begins to lead us back into the trees. "It's bigger'n this," she says over her shoulder, a little triumphantly.

At last you're almost off the hook. At last, we are down on our knees, the two of us, straining to read the signs in the almost-dark for the child.

"It was nice of them to label ever'thing," the woman says, breaking my bleeding heart.

Our swampy eyes strain, despair of seeing much. Some of the deadliest things look beautiful, like this deadly beauty blooming to my right. Even to the jaundiced and vigilant eye, most of the time.

"Hard to see," she says, looking into my eyes, which, like hers, are always surprised, never sure. It's almost our racial trait. Our eyes collect so much color from the sky they could almost become any color, given the chance.

The little girl fidgets, claims there are chiggers in the pinestraw. We scoot around to take advantage of the crime light. The woman begins to tick off the names of the common mints—"Ginger . . . Pepper . . . Lemon . . . Apple"— resolutely, like she wants to say them all and never have to come here again.

The rocking on the terrace has given away to a loud game of charades, lots of laughing.

"It's a movie," the painter says in her usual flat and resigned voice. Heather is nodding and flapping her arms.

"The Birds!" Rosemary squeals, but Heather is shaking her head. She continues to flap her arms.

"Well, is it a bird?" Rosemary asks indignantly.

"Superman," the cellist says.

Heather has stopped flapping her wings and is standing on one leg, curling the other up behind her knee, extending her neck in a funny undulant way.

"A snake!" Rosemary shouts. "Snake Pit!"

Heather stops undulating and begins to do something with her face, still standing on one leg. "Lips!" Rosemary shouts. "Mouth! Tongue! Yuck! . . . oh . . . Bad taste!"

Heather is still standing on one foot, nodding wildly, and flapping her arms.

"Pink Flamingos," the painter says in her defeated voice.

Heather is jumping up and down and clapping her hands.

"That's not fair," Rosemary says. "I got all the clues."

"That was a weird movie," one of the mystery guests says.

"It's camp," the painter says.

"Stone Mint, Horse Mint," I read, squinting, wishing I had the equilibrium to make a poem out of them.

"Creeping Thy-me," the woman says, lending a fricative of refreshing good sense, straightforward and reassuring. "Caraway Thy-me, Sweet Woodruff. . . ."

Thy-me and the River, I think, crocked on half a beer and lurching into another mode. Nick-Carraway Thy-me. I fumble for my cup on the ground, drink to the old whitehaired goatman poet, living still in the shadows. I drink again—why not? It seems silly not to—to all the dead men in the windows of my head and (molecules and imagery swirling under their own steam) to the professor, somewhere across town, who must be having his evening julep swimming with pocket lint: Thyme marches on. And on.

"Smell it!" I exhort the little girl, putting to her face a great clump of mint, torn up so carelessly I can feel its roots tendril against my wrist. She watches me in the blue light, all of us colored blue by now. The clamor from the terrace has receded behind a sudden jam session of crickets and the knee-deeping frogs that live out in our host's cracked swimming pool, "The Natural Pond," now covered with algae and lily pads.

"I didn't see one rose," the mother said. "They're supposed to be famous for the roses here."

"They're just hybrid tea roses," I said. "All the sweetness has been bred out of them. What do you smell?" I ask the child.

I can feel her breath on the inside of my wrist as she takes another whiff and looks at me. "Mint?" she asks.

"Just ordinary mint," I confirm. "Doesn't it smell good? Better than anything here?"

Tentatively, she sniffs again. Then she makes a leap of faith, gives me the benefit of the doubt. "Yes," she says. I can feel her strong little hand on my fingers, her warm breath, the closeness of her face, eyes, and hair, as she holds my heavy hand steady, for a long time.

Beverly Brown

Gardener

Having once worked for a gardener for several years.
A real brute when it came to plants.

How we hated the torment they underwent at his
hands. He, however, found great pleasure in brutalizing
them, and even greater pleasure in our agony over his
behavior, their pain. He wanted us forever working for
him. (Didn't he?) So beautifully did we complete his
dream: hearing expressed the pain he delivered. Always
before, he must rely on his distorted and inefficient
imagination to supply the idea that pain was really felt.

He even tormented the ground. But so much
ground was there, ground only laughed when assaulted,
knowing it could swallow this brute, and knowing he
knew it: one reason he despised it and gave it so much
trouble. So even more the plants. Thinking they were the
children of ground and that ground was far more
disturbed by their trials than by its own. Which must
have been the case. Ground began to act on its feelings
when we gave voice to the plants.

In the mornings we'd find the gardener savagely
ripping at a bed of sweet peas, ignoring entirely a fire he
had begun in the corn, an entire row of tomatoes
squashed.

All this in the name of parasite control.

He was mad with the idea of parasites. Often he
would scourge his own flesh with a knife heated in one

of his vegetable fires. Because he thought he spotted a louse. He was so filthy that lice were not impossible! He never bathed for fear of facilitating entry of perhaps invisible parasites through the fluid medium.

He left it up to us to plant and maintain the garden. Parasite control, in his eyes, the far greater task for the higher-level gardener.

And to nurse the plants after his treatments. Our saddest duty. Bathing their crippled stalks, clearing away the abundant, useless, rotting carnage.

Fallen, oozing, humiliated and defeated. Without having put up any kind of a fight. How could they? The idea unknown to them. However, ground did not take this business lightly.

One morning in our hut—on a tiny plot abutting the garden—we awoke to cries from the gardener.

His feet were stuck in the ground, as were his hoe and pick. He didn't need a pick! we kept saying. But for the worms, the pick's the thing, he'd say.

"Step out of your shoes."

He'd already stepped out of his shoes.

At once we recognized why his feet were stuck. Brought him a watering pail.

"Water something."

He watered the nearby cauliflower which he had hacked with a hatchet just the day before, thinking he had found evidence of a leaf miner.

Instantly his feet were released and he stepped out of the ground.

But learned nothing from this event.

If anything he was more than ever on the rampage, thinking the parasites had formed a coalition against him. Now whenever he went into the garden, he wore a belt loaded with anti-parasite ammunition, brandishing a lit acetylene torch, large knife in his teeth. He'd seen this in a Sunday afternoon movie. Wearing a safari hat. And war growls.

"You'll not get me you worms and mites. Grerrurir. I know you're hiding, waiting for me to turn my back." Turned his back: "Thought you'd pull one over on me." Ripped a cabbage out of the ground and stabbed it over and over.

We cooked produce he gathered from the garden. Took our meals with him. He demanded that all produce be cooked beyond any possibility of nurturance. All meat must be cooked until charred inside and out. Meat he got from his brother, the farmer: pork, beef, chicken and lamb. Meat frightened him even more than vegetables. Even when it was burnt, he didn't trust it, and after every meal, he took his temperature on the principle that infestation would at once raise body heat. If it were the slightest bit above normal, he gargled with kerosene and drank disinfectant which caused great retching fits and diahrrea and put him into bed for several days. But this was purgative, he thought, absolutely necessary.

He was certain we were infested. We were required to wear gloves while preparing his food, and we were not allowed to use his toilet.

Nor would he touch us, and after ever meal we must thoroughly disinfect the kitchen. We brought from our hut a separate set of dishes which we laid atop newspaper all at the far end of the rectangular kitchen table. He wore gauze over his nose while we were in the house.

We had a separate set of garden tools as well.

Curious that he allowed our employment at all, so much of a strain was our proximity.

But at times our comfort was necessary. When the ground caused him trouble, rendered him helpless, held his feet tight, then he cried for us. Allowed us to touch him, begged for our touch. We answered his pathetic pleas at once. Perhaps he would see that our touch did not infest.

Far from it. Ground episodes were followed by his greatest periods of hypochondriacal convalesence. Brief hospital stay. Surprisingly doctors seemed concerned with his opinion regarding infestation.

"My feet," he screamed, "the ground. Unbearable!"

Clerks typed out forms. Asked him about his insurance.

"My shoulders," he shuddered, "my help. Intolerable."

They'd wheel him off to parts unknown and we'd spend a few days alone with the plants. Tending them and healing them as best we could. Amazed that they still tended to grow. And, in fact, in his absence, they flourished. Ah, when he returns, we'd think, he will notice the change and finally recognize that it is the tender touch which yields the greatest and healthiest production.

On the contrary. Upon his return, with renewed vigor he'd set about hacking at them, burning them, molesting them in every manner conceivable. By the end of his first day, they'd be in worse shape than they were the day he left. Why didn't the ground swallow him altogether?

Ground was a curious body. It gave him all kinds of unlikely allowances. Perhaps it, like us, had the hope that he would one day see that if in fact plants were infested, destruction of plants did not follow as a cure. And that a mistreated plant was all the more prone to infestation.

He never saw it, and he never got more than a little swallowed.

One day while he was convalescing, an incident occurred which raised grave questions in regard to ground.

We were tending the sweet peas and basil which were in adjacent patches. Sweet pea tendrils stretched out to us as if yearning for our touch, acknowledgement

of our concern. We readily gave. (We had a special soft
spot for sweet peas; basil called us with its scent, opened
our heart to sweet peas.) While giving them a gentle
shower of water we'd carried all the way from the brook
in the downlands, we noticed our feet were up to the
ankles in the ground. Having no great horror of ground,
we calmly continued our sweet pea/basil nursing.
(Perhaps sweet peas were dear to us because Gardener
was more intensely ill-disposed towards them than
towards any other plant. Perhaps his attitude stemmed
from our great affection for them. Or perhaps it stemmed
from ground's apparent favoritism: sweet peas had the
greatest recovery rate in this garden—which may,
however, have been the result of our preponderance of
attention towards them.)

Surely ground had not confused us with Gardener.

Up to our knees.

Tendrils elongated and caressed our face, and their
fragrance overshadowed even that of basil. We could not
think of leaving them, even had it been possible.

Which it was not: up to our waist in ground.

Ho, Ground. Why are you so hungry for us?

Black, warm, heavy bed and a fast sinking
underneath the garden. A great sucking from all sides;
we feared we might be turned inside out and endeavored
to organize the evidence of our exclusive good will
towards garden. If we should find an opportunity to
present our case. In the ground. To the ground. Though
we couldn't even open our mouth. Had no idea of
mouth. Only dark and pressure. And an awareness of
the closeness of decomposed plants which had gone by
the way due to centuries of abuse. Even in this state, they
had not forgotten their lives above and we heard their
screams. That they were cheated out of life and someone
was to blame. They became aware of our presence. All
around us we saw dark hues in fossil patterns of all sorts
of garden flora. Their tints grew bolder and their voices

were directed towards us. A kind of proto-language which we comprehended immediately: a human was responsible for their multigenerational tragedy; we were human and the ground, their only consistent defense, had seen fit to swallow us. We felt ourself rapidly decomposing, dissolving. Ground acted as a ready medium and conductor for their long-delayed attack. Bit by bit we were no longer. In ignorant hopelessness we gave way to this dissolution and lost any consciousness of "we."

Apparently.

At least knew not of ourself.

Knew a thick pounding pain. But not in our body. A vast, unfathomable, blasting heat, like existing in the screams of a child dying in a fire.

Wasn't that a peculiar thing for ground to allow?

We thought so. Later when we were thinking as usual.

The out-of-there we do not remember.

The incident came to us as we were once again comforting the gardener whose little feet had been gobbled. Suddenly we thought, big deal. He knows he'll get them back, and they're only his feet.

After this realization we were never so kindly disposed towards plants or ground. And at times could not resist stomping an innocent blossom or slicing an unripe tomato and inserting into its young flesh a thriving worm.

Nor did this give us any great comfort. We ceased it altogether and took up even more peculiar habits of smashing our toes, slicing our arms and filling the wounds with maggots.

Oddly enough, this behavior yielded a kind of relief.

When comforting the gardener, we felt now a kind of real sympathy; perhaps at one time he had felt the same love for the plants, and had suffered a similar ground betrayal.

At night we heard it pounding, throbbing with the screams of its dead and gone inside, nagging it for compensation. When not terrified of its possible focus upon us, we felt sympathy even for it. How it never could escape these never-to-be-satisfieds. Suppressing the accumulation of all the centuries of suffering without any possibility of relief. For they could not sleep. And they could not be satisfied. And the ground could not help its hold in. And we could not help our despair at its despair.

Sometimes during these nights when the pounding was particularly intense and therefore unbearable, we would venture out into the garden and with a long knife cut deep slits of five or six feet in order to allow the dead captors some open vent so that ground might not have to contain the entire force of their horrible, unceasing expression.

No doubt, the idea for this course stemmed from the tilling periods during which we recognized a decided drop in the rate of gardener-toe-bite. Although the plant screams were worse, the ground throbs were less. (Plants knew they were to join their ancestors in a permanent mourn and scorn.)

Our interpretation, implied before: ground did not have to give so much pain if it did not receive so much. Air could take it. Better than we could.

But this theory, thus far explained, does not reveal the cause of the periods of screaming and throbbing and toe-bites and swallowing of us.

We found, however, a possible answer: these periods coincided with greatest incorporation into the earth of slaughtered plant offal.

What caused the range of slaughter, what prompted the gardener to slaughter a little or a lot?

Do we really have to go into all that? Can't you leave us alone for a while? You have no idea how tired we are and how we can hardly think straight. How could you?

... And continue your demands for our constant analysis of this living at various stages.

For all you know, we were never in a garden, nowhere near a plant our whole life through, nor in the future, nor never having read a word in regard to the subject. Merely a fancy. Or others told us about their experiences. We have in fact the barest minimum of response to the idea of botany. For us, say "botany," and we'll not even talk to you. Which is really saying something. Can you imagine? Not talking to you?

Or you knew we were in a garden.

It is we who do not know whether or not we were there. But if we were not, how is it we have such a great store of memories . . . ?

Gardener kept the barbwire fence ensconcing the garden in excellent shape, taut at all times, fence posts painted nicely white. He kept this fence well. He never trusted us to work on it, not in maintenance nor repair. He did, however, allow us tasks just outside the fence. Paint white halfway up the trunks of all trees for a radius of approximately one mile surrounding the garden. As a deterrent to parasites. What else? Then he got the idea that we should paint white halfway up the stalks of all plants in the garden. Even on the vine types. We spent almost an entire growing period painting these strips and this included many hours before sunup and after sundown.

Can't we move on from here? We don't want to be here any longer with this . . . .

In his house, a scratching or chewing, he heard it constantly, as did we. It drove him mad often enough. He tore at his furniture, threw us out on our ear, pulled at his ears, struck his head against the wall. For some purpose, presumably.

Then one day we were preparing a meal for him. We remember it very well. Our senses were unusually acute; we had not eaten for a week or more, having been temporarily exiled: he thought he spied a tick on our arm. Though we showed him it was only a mole. It was not the first time we had been banned and gone hungry because of this mole.

You might ask why didn't we gather food from the garden and prepare it ourself.

We wouldn't take a risk like that.

Why didn't we go into the forest and gather foods? On our paint-the-tree jaunts for instance?

You ask such troublesome questions.

First of all, we were absolutely forbidden to eat any foods except those secured by the gardener in town, from his brother, and from the garden. Secondly, we were not to eat anything except under supervision. This was deterrent to infestation. He did not trust our preparations, our discrimination.

What did it matter to him, you ask, since he thought we were infested already?

He wished at least to keep it to a minimum.

How can we ever get on with it if you keep interrupting?

Yes, that mole got us banned more than once.

Not that. It was the day we were preparing foods in his house and he wasn't watching.

Thirdly, we were deathly afraid of woods and never went there unless ordered.

Why didn't we harbor foods from the house and eat them on the sly during these periods of us-on-the-outs? Because we had done just that three times and the consequences were humiliating and devastating. We don't have to tell you; you are interrupting.

Ravenous, we were standing by the range watching the vegetables and meats cook for another hour according to his specifications. He had his back to us. In the next room, which was separated only by a waist-high counter, he was having trouble with his nose-mask strings, twisted and knotted. An impatient applier of nose masks.

Looked as if it would take some time, this unknotting and his muttering.

All the while the scratching, chewing.

So we helped ourself to a spoonful of stew. Which he spied. Flew into a wild fury. Dashed into the kitchen, towards us. We ran to the other side of the table. He threw the pot of violated stew. Missing us, it crashed through the wall and revealed millions of teaming, thriving termites, happily consuming his house.

His face went white and he sank to the floor, mouth open, eyes wide. In shock.

We carried him to the sofa. Filled the hole with paper bags and took to our hut.

And shall not tell you our punishment for that episode.

The least of it was a four-week fast.

The rest. At night. With fire and long, barbed instruments he must have welded himself, so unusual were they in shape and unique in function.

You don't really need this knowledge. It excites you. Why should we spend our time exciting you?

When we were on the verge of expiring from starvation, and properly purged by his tools and fire, we were again allowed entrance to the house. Immediately we collapsed onto the kitchen floor, so overpowering was the smell of the insecticide. Our task at that time: dispose of all the mounds of dead termites. At the very outer border of his land. Through the forest.

We had never sojourned to this area, nor were we overjoyed at the prospect. The trip could not be made in a day's time, but the gardener made no mention of foodstuffs we might bring along.

He could have been thinking of our health. That we should not break a long fast while in unfamiliar territory away from his eyes.

Possibly.

Dead silence in his house save the scrape of our shovel, termites into burlap sacks. Six huge bundles, as big as cotton bales. Fortunately termites are lightweight, although the bulk was quite cumbersome and one of the bags ripped as we attempted the doorway. He wouldn't supply us with another. We had to darn the slit and stuff the little bodies back into the sack.

And off. Despite the fact that by this time it was night, and we were outside, beyond the usual nocturnal terror in our hovel under our rags, safe and sound, more or less.

Nor did he offer a torch or flashlight or turn on the back porch light or smoke a cigarette or kiss my foot.

"Maybe we should wait until morning."

He opened the gate for us and locked it after we were on the other side, already without the slightest idea of direction. Presumably direction was of no consequence: we would come to the end of his property no matter what path we chose.

However, there were no paths. That we knew of. Whoever ventured in this wild inhospitable? The tree painting was the only occasion which had ever demanded our reluctant appearance. No paths were necessary at that time. It was daylight. We were something atremble admittedly, but we knew Gardener would come after us; we had his paint and brush, and he wished a second coat on the fence posts, and on the plants.

But now he had exhibited behavior which made us fear that he might wish to be shed of us altogether. Had he not starved us for a month?

Perhaps he thought his house infestation was in some way by our hand. That we had passed on the infestation we had ourself. Deliberately, maliciously, because we resented his position. Or that the disease had progressed to such a degree that we could not help but spread it into whatever we contacted.

Why then would he have spent so much time purging us? Did he not think we were well purged at the end?

Why do you make us explore these possibilities?
No wonder we're always exhausted.

No question but that you are responsible for this never ceasing, on and on . . .

He was right to send us away.

He must have known we would not return.

Did he?

Did we? Return.

We must go on and find out.

Here then, we can at least say that we left with our burden and an idea that if we found a more amicable ambience, we would take up with it. But we weren't in search of it. Because we would not have known where to look, or what it might look like, the earmarks of better.

Also we did not wish to have him know that we would break our allegiance to him. What a depression he would have fallen into. All alone with no one to pull his feet out of the ground. In absence of us, ground would swallow him. He would not know how to deal with the scream merge and so forth. By leaving him, we were condemning him.

All this we thought only to make ourself feel better about our having been thrown out. Though this directive was never clearly spoken.

Ground would stay clear of complete Gardener destruction.   Who would continue to plant if not Gardener? But how would plants survive without us?

And who's to say he was not on the phone in the same moment in which he sealed the gate. To the employment agency. Requesting another one of us. Poor fool who doesn't know the difference. Some ignorant lover of nature.

In which case we would look for any other environment which had any possibility of supporting us. We would not be able to stop in the thick of the forest and live for any length of time.

Already on the first night, our knees were folding from fear, without any more imaginative provocation than forest, night, no companion.

His forest. We could never stay here anyway. We would be shot for trespassing eventually.

David Wong Louie

Social Science

From the house's second story, Henry watches Mrs. Steiner climb from the backseat of a hired '67 El Dorado, and before its tailfins completely slip from view, a second car pulls up to take its place alongside the curb. A tall, bare-legged woman in white pops from out of the cherry-red Porsche and shakes Mrs. Steiner's hand. They turn as one and face the house. The old woman points at the date palm on the front lawn, diverting the other's attention away from the house and its flaking coats of paint. More than once he has overheard Mrs. Steiner rave about the exquisite sweetness of the palm's sad inedible fruit.

The women go through the first floor, discussing square footage, carpeting, plumbing, and interest rates. They open every door they pass. On the second floor it's more of the same. When they discover Henry lying shirtless in his hot study, Mrs. Steiner apologizes to her well-tanned companion: "Henry's my tenant. His wife used to live here with him, but she's gone. Henry doesn't need all this space now, so don't go feeling sorry for him."

After the Porsche drives off, Mrs. Steiner returns to Henry, still half-naked in his study, and says, "I wouldn't sell the holes in the wall to that one. Belongs to one of those cults, I bet. Got more things hanging from her ears than a Christmas tree has decorations." Mrs. Steiner shakes her head, and her blueish hair bobs and weaves.

She takes her leave and goes outside to wait for her cab. Henry eyes her tidying the patch of grass that surrounds the FOR SALE sign. She picks up broken palm fronds and plucks weeds, working with the fastidious devotion of one on a visit to the family plot. Henry feels a twinge in his stomach. This happens whenever the

FOR SALE
By Owner
No Appointment Necessary

sign crosses his line of vision. It's as if his body were trying to tell him something's wrong, the way a toothache calls attention to invisible decay. When Mrs. Steiner first put the house on the market, she and Henry struck a deal. In exchange for a reduction in rent, he has agreed to show the house to anyone who wishes to see it. But doing so leaves him feeling like a condemned man advising his executioner on the best way to do him in. He hates the thought of moving, hates equally living in a renter's limbo, never knowing, from day to day, if he'll have a home. At times, he wonders whether Mrs. Steiner is deliberately delaying the sale just to torment him. She has certainly fielded several credible bids, but in every instance she has invented excuses for prolonging the process. She turned away one guy because of his turquoise ostrich skin cowboy boots, another because he wanted to put a hot tub in the yard; there was the couple with the McGovern sticker on their car, and the black man she suspected was a professional athlete of some kind.

Henry relaxes a little the instant he hears Mrs. Steiner's cab pull away. He is lying on the maroon couch by his desk, where prior to the interruption he had just finished grading a composition by his favorite student,

Agnes. Trained in grad school to penetrate the surface of literary texts, Henry rereads the paper, analyzing the pellucid symbolism and the quivering tropes that riddle the paper she calls "How to Make Melon Balls." The subtext is obvious, her message to Henry clear—she has a crush on him—but the problem of making the proper response is, from a professional standpoint, a tricky one. He imagines combing the essay for grammatical flaws— this isn't as simple as it sounds since she's an exceptional writer—or, failing that, fabricating a few; next he might invite her to his office to discuss, let's say, dangling modifiers; the minutes fly by, and he awes her with his mastery of the rules of grammar, she's swooning as he fleshes out subordination; and just as this scene, playing in his head, swiftly moves to its inevitable and well-deserved climax, Henry hears a strange voice out in the hallway, putting an end to the private lesson. Someone knocks. The door swings open. "I'm Dave Brinkley," says the man stepping into the study. "Nice place you have here."

With his head pillowed comfortably on his arms, Henry tells the stranger that he's too busy to show the house. He can go look for himself. Henry closes his eyes, hoping to find Agnes there under his lids. But Dave Brinkley, awash in cologne, steps deeper into the study, apologizing for the intrusion. He explains how he had seen the sign and thought the place deserted. He's standing within an arm's reach of Henry and sees the stack of essays on the desk. He says that he too is an "educator," an assistant professor of psychology at the state college across town. Having established this professional bond between them, Dave Brinkley pulls the chair away from the desk and parks it at the end of the couch where Henry's resting his head. He sits down and they engage in faculty lounge chitchat, covering comparative salaries, course loads, and the quality of the student body at their respective schools. Dave Brinkley then starts to describe his impression of what Henry's mental state must be at that precise moment. "You see me coming between you and this house. To you, I am an interloper, a sexual rival of sorts. If I bought this house, you would probably feel emasculated, and we might not be friends anymore. That is why we need to talk."

When Dave Brinkley finally leaves, the sun in the smog is the color of iodine. By then Henry has long forgotten Agnes and split infinitives. Dave Brinkley occupies his thoughts. He had come to California to find his estranged wife when he heard she was "doing time in Hollywood." He wanted to buy the house and try to salvage their marriage. "I can see why she loves the West Coast. The sun, the surf; and the air is not all that bad when it is the right color. This is her world. I can never hope to take her away from paradise." He unscrewed the wedding band from his finger, and said, as he handed it to Henry, "I was a fool to think I could keep a girl like her in Ohio." When Henry had some difficulty deciphering the engraved name, Dave Brinkley started to spell it, enunciating each letter with the phoney suspense of an emcee reading the winning digits of a lottery number. "C-H-R-I-S-T—"

"Wait, you're married—to the model?"

"Good, you are familiar with her work then. Don't you just love how healthy she looks?"

A few days later Mrs. Steiner phones. "I like that Dave Brinkley fellow. So educated and forthright." After she hangs up he calls the psych department at the state college. The secretary corroborates Dave Brinkley's story but adds a significant twist. His name wasn't Brinkley when he applied for the position. It had been changed only after his arrival in California.

Henry drives to the university library and descends into the stacks. He locates back issues of *People, Glamour,*

Mademoiselle. He sees the model in swimsuits, in evening gowns, in every imaginable shade of lipstick. Such teeth, he thinks. Photo after photo she smiles as though she does it for free. Then, in *Self,* in an article entitled, "Blondes Are Back and Bare as Ever!" Henry uncovers the vital statistics he has been seeking. In boldface type the caption under the bikini-clad model reads: "One of the most eligible bachelorettes in America, Christie's looking for a man to complement her busy life-style."

In class that day Henry stares suspiciously at the rows of faces before him and tries to reconcile the names on the registrar's roster with the students who claim them as theirs. To his own dismay he realizes he even doubts the authenticity of his prized Agnes. When her thin, braceleted arm lolls weak-wristed in the air, waiting to be acknowledged, Henry can only nod in her direction, forsaking the name that once had given him such pleasure to say.

Weeks pass and the FOR SALE sign remains firmly in place. It probably will withstand the earthquake. Mrs. Steiner keeps showing prospective buyers the house but can't decide who truly "deserves" it.

Dave Brinkley drops by often. He comes armed with questions about the wiring, the roof, the septic tank, and then hangs around for conversation. At first these visits annoyed Henry, but gradually Dave Brinkley's persistence won out and he started talking to the psychologist about Marybeth, their marriage, and their subsequent divorce in the same quasi-professional way people came to Henry for help with their cover letters.

One night Dave Brinkley knocks at the front door. They shake hands as usual, the psychologist smiling, his facial muscles tensed to the twitching point. "I just want to take some measurements," he says with a giggle, pulling a tape rule from his pocket.

"Not tonight, Dave," Henry says. "It's late and I have papers to grade."

"Me, I have exams at home. But I am too excited. I think the house is mine."

Henry offers his congratulations. He pumps Dave Brinkley's hand once, then abruptly extricates himself from the grip. He excuses himself and goes upstairs and mans his desk. He searches for Agnes' essay, in hopes the sensual loops of her script might relieve, at least temporarily, the uncomfortable pressure building beneath his scalp. But before her penmanship can work its analgesic magic Dave Brinkley bursts into the study. He says, "I have a date with her Friday night."

Henry turns in his seat. "With her?"

"Yes, yes, with Marybeth."

Henry jumps up from his chair. "Marybeth who?"

The psychologist sits on the couch and crosses his legs and drapes his arm across the backrest. "Marybeth," he says, "your wife, your ex-wife." His eyes fix upon Henry as if he were watching a stranger undress. "You are angry, of course," Dave Brinkley observes. "You are burning up inside, and that is only appropriate. Marybeth has betrayed you, and to a lesser degree so have I." He tweaks the tip of his nose. "Relax your fists, Henry, forget the macho stuff, it doesn't suit you. Let us talk. Let your unfiltered feelings out. Express yourself to me." He opens up his arms in an all-embracing gesture of peace.

Henry stalks to the door of the study. He looks across the hallway at the bedroom, or more precisely, at the spot in front of the mirror where Marybeth lifted her dumbbells in the morning and brushed her hair a hundred times at night. He remembers watching the hem of her nightshirt rise to mid-thigh with each upward sweep of her arm. He tries to visualize her there in front of the mirror but his imagination is weak. At best she is an erasure, barely perceptible, lacking definition. "How'd you find her?" he says to the hallway.

"I did nothing more devious than dial 4-1-1."

"And like that, " Henry snaps his fingers, "she agreed to go out with you. You must have the wrong girl."

The psychologist chuckles, "Remember what I taught you? By calling her 'girl,' you reveal to the world your basic hostility toward her. Have I not established that as the root of your marital problems?"

"You're not going out with my Marybeth," Henry says, shaking his finger in a threatening way.

"Now that's better. Let your anger out."

Henry waves his hand in disgust.

"Look, I am not leaving until we talk." Dave Brinkley gets up from the couch and looks around the room. "I just called her and said you and I were good friends. We are good friends." He goes to the center of the floor and addresses the light fixture in the ceiling: "I am new in town. You tell me about this nice girl. What am I supposed to do?" He peeks in the closet. He sits on the edge of the desk, folding his tweedy arms over his chest. "Back in my apartment I already played this scene out. When I took your part, you said some hateful things about me. But now that I am here, you are all but silent. We must be adult and work on this." He claps his hands together. "You be me, and I will be you." He tweaks his nose again. The sight of the gold band on Dave Brinkley's left hand revives Henry. Like Popeye after spinach, he can feel his inner resources galvanize. In the murky pools of his memory, a school of Christie Brinkleys, toothy and blow-dried, swim to his rescue. While the psychologist—as Henry—twists his face and prepares to deliver a diatribe against himself, the real Henry launches a preemptive strike: "What's become of your model-wife?"

"Good effort. I can hear that nastiness coming through." Henry repeats the question, and after a few seconds, like the lag between a flash of lightning and clap of thunder, the question finds its mark. Dave Brinkley

117

stops talking and lowers his gaze, sweeping the floor with it. For the next few seconds, he seems only to be exhaling. He fidgets clumsily with the things on Henry's desk. The psychologist is sputtering, he's winged, and Henry knows it. But he lets him get away: When Dave Brinkley—he does this innocently, biding his time, trying to catch his breath—picks up the top essay from the stack on the blotter, Henry says, "Put her down."

"What pretty handwriting," the psychologist says, as a grin brightens his face. "Do you want to tell me about Agnes? Come Henry, out with it. How can we be friends otherwise?"

Henry can see her shaking her head like a robin tearing a worm from the ground. She's holding the phone on her hip, collecting her thoughts. The song "Psycho Killer" is playing on the old phono she bought years ago at a yardsale so she could listen to music while she worked, stuffing envelopes in the garage. Through the telephone lines, the singer sounds like poultry. "You promised you'd leave town," she finally says into the mouthpiece.

"How do you know I haven't left?"

"Your friend told me."

"What friend?"

"Forget it. I didn't say anything."

"Turn off the record. I can hardly hear you."

"Good."

"What?"

"I said I hope he buys that house. Maybe then you'll leave." Her voice is lean and aggressive. He can picture her: raking her hand through her long hair, sniffing her fingertips, shifting her weight, cradling the phone between cheek and shoulder. This was how she ran her direct mail service out of the garage; stuffing envelopes, licking stamps, while talking to printers and clients over the phone.

Because the house is on her mailing list, he still receives mail from her almost every week.

"Why'd you think I agreed to meet this Brinkley character? Because he's a chum of yours? Not in a million. I'm gonna see to it he buys that house. If he needs cash I'll sell part of the business and I'll give him a loan, cheap. Then maybe you'll leave."

They hang up without the conversational equivalent of a concluding paragraph that marks a resolution of conflict. Henry turns to his students' papers for solace. He reads one by a Vietnam vet who, writing about his experience as a POW, tells how he was unable to remember during captivity a single detail of his wife's face.

Mrs. Steiner is standing by the FOR SALE sign. She looks as squat and round as its red letters. A man in madras slacks and green sports coat joins her on the lawn. He is carrying a briefcase. Together they admire the sign.

They enter the house where Henry is sipping coffee in the kitchen. Mrs. Steiner says, "This is Mr. Escrow."

"No, ma'am," the man says with a chuckle. "I work for the escrow company. My name's Mooney."

"How silly of me."

"Happens all the time, ma'am," The escrow man then reaches his hand out to Henry and says, "And you must be Mr. Brinkley."

"Oh my, no," Mrs. Steiner says, giggling. "Aren't we a pair! This is Henry, my tenant. I would never have imagined anyone confusing Henry with good Mr. Brinkley."

The escrow man sets his briefcase on the table and removes a manila envelope which he hands to Mrs. Steiner who turns it over to Henry. She says, "You must perform this duty faithfully or not do it at all. Henry, I want you to give this to Mr. Brinkley when he comes on Sunday."

Henry looks at the escrow man who shrugs his shoulders and says, "Mr. Brinkley's intrigue, I assure you. This is highly irregular practice for a firm such as ours."

Using a roll of packing tape she pulled from her purse, Mrs. Steiner tapes the envelopes to the refrigerator. "So you don't forget," she says. "And so you don't peek and spoil Mr. Brinkley's surprise."

Thursday after class Henry drives to the state college. He arrives too early for Dave Brinkley's office hours. As he waits he reads the psych professor's door, covered not only by the kinds of cartoons and new clippings academics find amusing but a 200-question true/false personality test with such items as #47) I sleep with my clothes off and the lights on. #89) I am as healthy as a blonde. #152) Fashion models adore the touch of tweed.

Henry tires of this excess and tries the door. It isn't locked. The place smells like a bottling plant for cologne. Henry is stunned by its overall neatness. Papers are in folders and meticulously stacked at the corner of the desk; pens are capped; pencils sharpened; the typewriter wears its dust cover. There's an impressive wall of books, clothbound and alphabetized, with stately brown spines. Henry peruses the titles until he uncovers, wedged between Boggs' *Sexual Deviation in the Tropics* and Blumbergs' *Blondes: A Subject for Scientific Analysis*, an unusual tome with an oaken spine. It's a framed collage of dozens of Christie Brinkleys in tennis togs. Spurred by this discovery Henry searches the desk drawer and finds, beneath a pile of soiled running clothes, an 8x10 glossy of the model's broad lunar face, one rouged cheek adorned one rouged cheek adorned with a dedication executed in a loose, flamboyant script: Dear Dave, Hey, are we related? Thanx for the letters. Luv, Christie.

Henry's looking through a folder labeled "At the Beach with Christie B.," filled with scissored Christies in swimwear, when the phone rings. After some consideration, Henry decides to answer. A student in Dave Brinkley's Psych 101 course is on the line pleading for an extension on her paper assignment. Henry grants it.

Once he cradles the phone he suddenly feels uncomfortable with his body, as if he were clothed, from head to toe, in a new pair of Levis. His hand trembles slightly as he turns the pages of the desk calendar. On each leaf CHRISTIE? has been scrawled in the time slots set aside for his office hours. Then the phone rings again. He picks up the receiver but doesn't say anything. "Hello?" a familiar voice says. "Hello? Is this David Brinkley's line?" At first, Henry thinks it's the same student calling again. But as he slowly depresses the clear plastic nib on the cradle, he realizes the person on the other end had been Marybeth. With his finger still on the nib, he stares at the phone's black mantle, trying to see her: hip out, fingers raking her scalp, peeved Henry's friend has slipped her a wrong number. As he expected the phone rings again, and this time he's prepared. Holding his nose, he pretends he's Dave Brinkley's answering machine: "Hi. I am not in the office at the moment—"

"I hate these stupid machines," says Marybeth. She speaks rapidly trying to fit her message within the allotted time.

"Listen, something's come up. Seven's out of the question. See you at the Dolphin around seven-thirty. And don't bring your machine." She slams the phone down, and it pops like a pistol shot in Henry's ear.

That same afternoon a short, bearded man in a white

linen suit comes to the house. "I'd like to make you an offer for this property," he says. "I guarantee you won't get a penny more from anyone else."

Henry steps back from the door so the man can enter. "I'll have a look at the interior when we sit down to sign the contract," he says. "I'm well-acquainted with this vintage." He hands Henry his business card. "I already own similar units in the neighborhood."

The Golden Dolphin is one of those seafood stops along Route 1 specializing in redwood decks, seagulls, Cinzano umbrellas, and food served on mango halves. Marybeth was particularly fond of it when she and Henry first came to town. The place is packed with the usual Friday night crowd of faculty members, students, tourists, and third-rank Hollywood types. Seven o'clock. Henry's sitting at the end of the restaurant bar, near the hostess's station, waiting for Dave Brinkley. He orders beer and nibbles goldfish crackers. Ten-after-seven. As he had been for his office hours, Dave Brinkley is late again. Perhaps he won't even show up. The mere thought of Marybeth being stood up by the likes of Dave Brinkley upsets him almost as much as the thought of the two of them actually meeting. Perhaps she got her message through to him after all. Perhaps they suspect Henry and have changed their plans accordingly.

Henry goes to see the hostess, a pretty coed he believes he has seen on campus. "Don't you go to the university?"

"Biz Admin," she says, smiling big. Her hair is a shade lighter than her teeth. "You go there too?"

"I . . . I work at Student Services," he says. "I counsel kids on academic probation."

"Guess I'll see you there someday," she says with professional good cheer. "Will you be dining with us tonight?"

"I have a reservation for two."

"Name?" she scans the date book on the hostess stand.

"Brinkley. At seven."

"The Brinkley party. Wow, lucky you showed up. We almost gave your table away. She picks up two menus. "We all here?"

"Not yet, but I'll wait at the table."

She tosses her hair and leads Henry out to the deck.

"Voila, just as you requested, one of our most romantic tables." She hands Henry a menu. "Mr. Brinkley, everything's special tonight."

The cocktail waitress, a starlet in an oversized T-shirt with dolphins riding silk-screened waves over her breasts, takes his order. After his beer arrives he sees the hostess winding her way through the crowded dining room, followed closely by Dave Brinkley, who's gesticulating wildly and saying such things at her that diners turn around in their seats to stare. When they finally arrive at tableside, Henry springs to his feet and reaches for the other's hand. "Dave, old pal!" The psychologist's hand is puffy and extremely warm.

"Wow, so you two do know each other," the hostess says, relieved. "Gawd, I thought I really blew this one. I mean, you both said Brinkley: okay? So I figured, hey, brothers; okay? But he," she nods at Dave Brinkley, "he said he's expecting a lady friend, so I thought, wow, Lisa, you've made a major screw up." She drops her hands to both men's shoulders and exhales dramatically.

"That will be all, miss." The psychologist tries to shoo her away with a flick of his wrist.

"But are you or aren't you expecting a third?" she asks.

The men answer simultaneously. One yes, the other no.

"Now that's really . . . wow," she exclaims.

"Incredible. Like twins." She stares at the two as if they're talking fish.

"By my watch you're twenty-two minutes late," Henry says, the instant the hostess leaves.

"Your watch doesn't count here." Dave Brinkley is ready to leap at Henry. A plumb line dropped from his chin would strike the center of the table. The surf tumbles behind him. Smog or clouds obscure the moon. A storm candle casts a rare light that reduces Dave Brinkley's face to a series of simple planes; he has the look of a crude portrait executed with a knife.

"Marybeth can't make it," Henry says. "She called me and said something's come up. Those were her exact words."

"This is delusional fantasy. Why didn't she call me?"

"You're the expert, you figure it out." He peeks at his watch. Seven-thirty. Soon Marybeth will make her appearance. "Dave," he says, "let's go somewhere and talk."

His face buried in his ringless hands, the psychologist appears deep in thought. Perhaps he is paging through the textbooks in his mind for advice in resolving the present conflict. When the waitress comes to the table, he abruptly drops his hands from his face and fixes Henry with a strange look. "I see no reason to go hunt for another restaurant. We are here. And we have our table."

Henry says, "I know a better place for seafood." He glances at the waitress, then down at his watch. He scans the interior dining room for Marybeth. "We used to eat here a lot. The food's mediocre. She probably chose this place for sentimental reasons."

The waitress leaves them to make their decision. As she recedes into the dining room, framed in the crook of her arm and the curve of her waist, he thinks he spots Marybeth; he's almost certain it's her.

"No, this was my idea. Their Louies are simply—"

"Dave," Henry interrupts, "did I ever show you a picture of Marybeth?"

"No. Nor do I recall hearing you describe her. Which is odd," he says, reverting to his clinical voice, "because most people start with a physical description of their ex."

Marybeth wades through the busy dining room, squeezing past chairs, ducking trays, avoiding busboys darting in her lane.

"Excuse me," Henry says. "Back in a sec. I see a former student who owes me work on an incomplete from last quarter. I've been trying to get hold of her."

"Ask the young lady to join us," the psychologist calls, as Henry enters the dining room.

He intercepts her before she can set foot on the deck. She looks different than she does in his memory; her metamorphosis is utterly disconcerting. Not only has she picked up several well-placed pounds, she's tinted her hair a silvery blond and wears it short so her facial bones are more prominent, attenuating the shape of her face. And her eyes, could she have had them tinted too? And her skin, is she tanned or is this Mediterranean complexion hers? "I'm late," she says, her equaminity incompatible with the surprise of Henry's presence. "Let me pass, Hank." Had she always called him Hank? She steps away in her simple black dress, cinched at the waist with a red patent leather belt, and a pair of ankle boots. Then she stops, turns, and says, "What're you doing here?"

"Brinkley can't make it. He tried to reach you but you weren't home. So he called me."

"And like a pup you came running." She sweeps her fingers through her new short curls. "Hank, don't be an ass. What're you after?"

"Seafood," he says. "I know a new place not far from here. Come on, the bum stiffed you. Aren't I at least second best?"

"Drop it. The girl said Brinkley's back on the deck. In fact, she said two Brinkleys are out there." She goes out into the salt air. Once there, she appears lost; she must be looking for a table occupied by two men.

The instant Henry catches up to her, Dave Brinkley stands and waves and grins and mouths "Hi." She moves toward him. Although Henry can't see it, he can feel the heat of her smile. "So you are a former student of Henry's," Dave Brinkley says, holding out his hand to Marybeth.

As acid burns the whorls from fingertips, last night's dose of Marybeth has erased that part of Henry's brain that controls forgetting. All Saturday morning she has been unforgiving. She haunts the house, going through her old routines. He sees her in the tub, inflated pillow under her neck, her stockinged legs crossed, her feet covered with the same frumpish ankle boots. In the kitchen she licks the lid of an open can of soup. In the bedroom she lifts her weights in front of the mirror, her eyes, fierce and anthracitean, concentrating on the slip-slide of the dozens of bracelets on her arms. How easily those same eyes found Dave Brinkley's last night and softened. Instant friends they were, linked by a common annoyance. "Dave," she said, loud enough for Henry to hear, "I know a quiet place where we won't be disturbed."

Mrs. Steiner phones. She reminds Henry to stay near the house tomorrow when Mr. Brinkley comes for the envelope. "Maybe you can put on a suit and look nice for him. I bet you haven't done that since your wedding day."

Henry climbs the stairs, his legs heavy, as if chimpanzees were clinging to them. In his study he shuffles a stack of essays, and miraculously Agnes's rises like cream to the top. Divine providence! He picks up the phone and dials the campus switchboard. The operator rings Agnes's extension number in the dorm. Without any pretext he'll ask her to lunch. They'll go to a place where people in ankle boots aren't served. But after too many unanswered rings his enthusiasm for the adventure dies, and for a fleeting instant he thinks Dave Brinkley has waylaid Agnes too.

Upstairs, he reads her essay, a paean to a boy named Buzz. No camouflaged emotions here. Not a single cryptic trope. Just unadulterated, unfiltered, irrational goo from the heart. No matter what methodology he employs in his reading of the text one sentiment prevails, "Buzz is best." Henry puts down his pencil and takes up the red ballpoint reserved for his other students. Soon her essay resembles the latticework of arteries and veins on an anatomical chart. He populates the margins and the tight spaces between lines with convoluted bloodworms. He maims every sentence, bad or good. Finally Henry awards a grade: D+. Then he reconsiders and whites-out the vertical component of the plus sign. He has seen it happen so many times before—as love grows writing skills decline.

"I've come to sweeten the pot," the man in the white linen suit says. "My original bid was very generous but it seems you need more inducement." He plucks a checkbook from his breast-pocket. "What'll it take to close the deal? $500?" He steps past Henry into the house. They sit down in the kitchen. "As I had said, I'll bump my bid by three G's, and you get this $500 as soon as we shake hands."

"This sounds like a bribe."

"It's a bribe only if you don't take it. Otherwise, it's called sound business practice." He sets the check down at the middle of the table. Henry studies the check, made out to no one, and he smiles, and then the man smiles.

"I'll take it in cash," Henry says, letting the check fall from his hands.

The man frowns, massages his beard, then whips out his billfold. "Let's see. I only have $285 on hand. I'll give you a check for the rest. My signature is as good as a gun in a bank."

Henry nods. "Looks like you just bought a house."

"I did? Are you sure?"

Henry shrugs and goes outside. Inside a minute he returns with the FOR SALE sign. "She's yours if you want her."

The man laughs and pumps Henry's hand. "I like you. You're an odd one." He sits down to write a check. "You just sold me your house and I don't even know your name. Who do I make it out to?"

"Brinkley. Dave Brinkley. But don't give it to me now. Send it to my box in the psych office at the state college."

The man laughs again. "Didn't I say you were odd?" He slips the checkbook away. He picks the cash off the table, neatens it into a pile, and presses it into Henry's open palm. They shake hands. The man says his lawyers would contact Henry Monday to work out the details.

The man drives off in his silver Seville coupe.

Henry's sitting on the front steps, replaying the events that have left him $285 richer, when the red sportscar, top down, pulls up. The same bare-legged woman, now sporting a big sun bonnet and wrap-around shades, strolls up the front walk toward Henry, but then abruptly cuts across the lawn to where the FOR SALE SIGN once stood. She stares at the hole. "Excuse me," she calls to Henry, "does this mean it's sold?"

He goes over to her at the hole. Her lips are the same red as her car. "I was just driving by and thought I'd take another look. But I guess I'm too late."

"Hasn't Mrs. Steiner contacted you?"

"No, why?"

"Isn't your name . . . what did she say again?"

"I'm Dorrine. Dorinne Weiss."

"That's the one. Dorinne. And you haven't spoken to Mrs. Steiner? The house is yours. Honest. She told me, 'Henry, take down that sign. I want that lovely Dorinne lady to live here.'"

"I can't believe it. This is a joke, right? I better call Mrs. Steiner."

"No," Henry says. "She's out of town. Went to see her mother."

"Mother? She must be very old."

"That's why she went to see her." He invites Dorinne into the house. For the next forty minutes she examines the rooms, inch by inch.

The house immediately takes on her particular smell. She says, "Henry, come help me celebrate."

They go to her car. He opens and shuts the driver-side door for her. He watches her settle behind the wheel, knock off her shoes, adjust her sunglasses in the rearview mirror. Henry wonders how long it'll be before she feels comfortable enough to let him drive. She looks at Henry and pats the passenger seat.

"One second," he says.

In the kitchen he rips the envelope off the refrigerator door.

The Porsche's engine revs noisily. Henry jumps into the sun drenched bucket seat. Dorinne smiles. Her teeth are magnificently white and even. Her shades hide half her face. "What sounds good, Henry?"

"Hank," he says. "Call me Hank. That sounds good." He suggests they try the Golden Dolphin. "I've heard good things about it. Champagne on the deck. Ocean breeze. My treat."

The little car lurches into gear. Its engine buzzes. The rushing wind pulls his hair by the roots. His eyes water. The faster they go, the noisier the engine, the more thunderous the wind. She slips a tape into the cassette player and drives and sings and dances and talks. Occasionally she taps his leg to get his attention but then speaks in her normal voice, as if she were unaware of the noise. Nonetheless Henry nods, she talks, they're wrapped in speed and sound.

He opens the envelope. Inside he finds important looking documents which he believes are the title and deed to the property. He understands Dave Brinkley's plan: he literally wanted Henry to hand over the house to him.

Dorinne points to the papers and rolls her palm up to the sky: "What's that?"

Henry stuffs the documents back into the envelope. He weighs his possible answer. He wants his words to be generous and expansive.

"One's my marriage license," he says, "and the other proves that I'm divorced." But Dorinne doesn't hear. He tries again, now louder, but she remains in profile, eyes locked on the road, the scarf holding her hat in place, twirling in the wind, parallel to the ground. She's smiling broadly. Those teeth! White as the sky is blue at the shore where they're headed, where the sea breeze has already chased the smog into the valley. Wrapped inside all this speed and sound, Henry has found a pocket of silence. He leans back in his seat and tells his story into the wind, which carries it back to the house where it will live on forever. In this way they drive off, the road straight and obvious.

Jacques Servin

Still Life with Disaster (U.S.)

THE CAT-WOMAN CLAWS, RED-CAPED AND SENSUOUS, CLAWS CLAWS CLAWS AT THE SKYSCRAPER. SLOWLY HER LIPS BARE ELLIPTICAL MOON OF TEETH, THE MOON ARCS LEFT TO RIGHT, RIGHT TO LEFT, SLOWER, RESTS IN CENTER, HER HEAD TURNS, SHE FACES US. THERE IS NOTHING, HER FACE SEEMS SUPERIMPOSED ON A TATTERED LAMPSHADE, WE CAN ONLY IMAGINE WHAT IS LEFT SILENT IN THE DEPTH OF HER FOLDS. HER HEAD TURNS BACK SLOWLY, SLOWLY, BACK TO THE SKYSCRAPER, HER LIMBS ARE MOVING ALMOST IMPERCEPTIBLY, THEN SHE SHIFTS AND CLAWS AGAIN, CLAWS CLAWS CLAWS, SLOWLY, SHE IS THE CAT-WOMAN.

Mary swivels by the coffee machine her arms a galleon of tuck-and-wave proofs, and stops. She tilts a lazy head and stops. Suddenly she stops in her tracks and her head sticks out, she is listening.

"Oh gum," she says to Chip as she stops, "this is spooky, Chip. There's a clawing coming from this wall. I swear."

Chip stops and comes over. He hears the clawing as he stops. "Damn. This is a nice place, a really nice place, but then this clawing, it's like a nightmare but you can't wake up even when you stop breathing, I'm barely breathing (because I hate it so much when something hideous like this happens, I mean what could that be, it could be anything), what is it? What do you think it might be, Mary? What do you judge?"

"God, I don't know. It could be anything, Chip. Hey, Mr. Hubert! There's a clawing coming from this wall, Chip heard it too. It could be anything. What do you think it is?"

Jon stops, rotund. "I don't know," he bellows, "I haven't heard it." He starts to walk on.

"Please stop," Chip says. "We're kind of freaked out, this kind of thing doesn't happen in regular life, couldn't you just stop here for a minute like we have and listen, please?"

Jon stops and tilts his head. In the relative silence he hears a clawing. A gasp escapes his throat. He lifts an arm and waves it frantically behind his back. "Mr. Brass! Mr. Brass! There's a thing here, there's a weird thing going on. Mr. Brass?" Jon stops and turns around just in time to catch a view of Huck Brass coming out of his office.

Mary announces the discovery. "We've found a clawing, Huck! There's a lot of clawing going on."

Huck arrives and tilts his head, holding up an arm to dim the hubbub. "My God, you're right, Ms. Seminal, you're right indeed. There is a veritable clawing going on here."

Bunko and Killer and Swine pass by and stop. "Well then there now. What's this here going on here?" No one notices them and they tilt their heads.

Randy calls out from the hallway, "Is someone hurt? Should I get something on my way out?"

"It's clawing!" He stops but everyone is suddenly gabbing.

"Quiet?" Someone hears him and nudges the rest to silence. He listens. "Okay," he says, "Mary, Mr. Norse,

Brass, Jon-Jon, Messrs. Grunnheck, we've got a weird situation on our hands here, friends, we're swooping in the mad endeavor now, we're swivelling on righteousness over monkey-tunes, let's not screw, let's not do boners, we're heavy on this one, ladies and gentlemen, we've got to be a little bit heavy with this, let's see, let's see, let's see."

Huck steps up then and puts an arm on Randy's shoulder. "Randy, I think we just need to stay calm, is all. I think if we just weather this like we've weathered the other disturbances in our office, I think if we just do that it's going to be just fine. I don't think there's anything to worry about. I think we've got angels in our desks and that's all we need." (Mock-conspiratorial wink to Chip.) "Now nobody panic, okay? Okay okay?"

Jon steps to the fore and takes off his jacket. "I've got the say on this, Mr. Brass. This is the simple outcome: We are going to lay low and find a television. I have a feeling this is something serious. Everyone stay put."

"Well yes," Mary says, "but we don't have a television. Why don't we just all have coffee?" Everyone agrees provisionally and the discussion goes on for four more minutes and thirty-six more seconds.

THE CAT-WOMAN TIRES AND SAGS. SHE TURNS ON A TELEVISION AND WATCHES SOME CEREMONIES. SUDDENLY A MAN IS KILLED, IT IS A CAT-WOMAN IN SEOUL WHO HAS TIRED AND EXPLODED A GYMNASIUM, THESE THINGS ARE HAPPENING SAYS THE ANNOUNCER, BEWARE, THE CAT-WOMAN PULLS OUT SOME EXPLOSIVES AND TIES THEM TO THE SKYSCRAPER. SHE TURNS AND LOOKS AT THE STREET, HER EYES LOST IN THE IDIOTIC PLAINS OF HER FACE, HER LIPS SAGGING TOO MUCH NOW, THE TEETH TOO PROMINENT. . .

HER CARRIAGE SAGS MORE AS SHE WATCHES THE
PEOPLE STUMBLING ABOUT AND SHE HAS TO
ACTUALLY PULL HERSELF AROUND TOWARDS
THE SKYSCRAPER . . . IT RAINS. THE CAT-WOMAN
SHIFTS HER EYES TO THE EXPLOSIVES AND EVERY
MUSCLE IN HER BODY TENSES IN RAW
ANTICIPATION.

Gerald Vizenor

Bad Breath

Mildred Fairchild was convinced that bad breath caused cancer. Surrounded by bad breath she measured the seasons on a calendar of private theories and moved west to teach at the government school on the White Earth Reservation in Minnesota.

"Inhale the sunrise," she told her sisters. "Pure breath is the path to a clean mind and body." Her buttons were too tight but she never raved in the dark. Mildred inhaled the sunrise and hummed near water. Twice a week she trimmed her nails on the back porch; she was clean and worried about her appearance but she never searched her smile in a mirror until she moved to the reservation.

Mildred was fifteen when her mother died, the sudden victim of bad breath. She hummed at the river. Later, over the grave, she promised to serve the survivors: her father, a miserable politician who practiced admiralty law with a morbid fear of the sea; twin sisters who turned to a secret language; and an elder brother who mourned for six months and then he disappeared. Mildred cooked, washed, gardened, attended to her sisters, searched for her brother, and studied to be a teacher, in that order from sunrise to the back porch at dusk. She was clean.

Three years later she smelled cancer on the breath of her chosen professor, the poet with psoriasis. Late that summer she bought a rail ticket west to the wilds of the reservation.

"Christians must not solicit praise for their simple missions," she told her father and sisters at the depot. "Hence, my promise to serve tribal children, while a proper sacrifice, must be held a secret."

"Dred, come back when you must, no one will know where you were," one sister said in a loud voice. "We know how to keep secrets."

"Catholic priests are not to be trusted," warned her father in a cloud of cigar smoke. "You know how we feel about them . . ."

"Father, no need for that now."

"Beware of the savages," he complained.

"Indians, father, not savages," said Mildred. She was eager for the train to depart. "Take care of your feet and remember not to eat too much pork."

"No Catholics."

"Yes, father."

"Dred, promise me," he insisted.

"Yes, father."

"No savages."

"No, father."

"Dred, you could still teach here at the country school," said her other sister as the train lurched backward and then forward a few feet. "Remember me, send us picture postcards with the wilderness."

"No Catholics, promise me that."

"Yes, father."

"Dred, do you hear me?"

"Yes, father."

Mildred waved from the open window as the train started and stopped several times at the station. No one could turn back at the right moment; last waves were repeated, hesitant, lost gestures.

Back in the spring of 1886 there sure was plenty of good excitement out here when them Beaulieus published the first newspaper on the reservation. White Earth never has been the same. Theodore, he had a cousin with the same name, and August, they tried all kinds of things from selling sewing machines to newspapers. Sewing was not a serious problem, but words, little words with white around them, attracted the evils of the government. Reservation Indians weren't supposed to know anything about words, so it was the mixedbloods that caused all the trouble the way the agents saw it. Government agents could cheat the fullbloods with words but not the mixedbloods, and who were these mongrels who started a newspaper without permission? Printed words attracted the broken crows and not far behind them was the old Indian agent Tipi Milcho. His real name was T. J. Sheehan, but we called him Tipi for the shape of his head and Milcho, well, I'm not really sure where we got that name but we know what it means. Someone evil, I think, someone who gave an Irish saint some trouble and a good name.

The Beaulieus called their little paper The Progress, dedicated, they wrote, to a "higher civilization." Now, can you imagine that bit of idealism in the middle of a federal trust reservation with an Indian agent strutting around like some sort of colonial monarch? Well, the Beaulieus took after old Tipi with a vengeance. This was one headline on the front page: "Is it an Indian Bureau? About some of the freaks in the employ of the Indian Service whose actions are a disgrace to the nation and a curse to the cause of justice. Putrescent through the spoils system." You must understand that the Beaulieus weren't writing for us on the reservation, we knew that and more, they were throwing those words like "putrescent" around for God-fearing people living back east, back where Tipi comes from, some say. Anyway, the agent choked on those words so we knew what they meant.

Tipi Milcho was at the door and he said those were fighting words. More than that, he put the newspaper out of business. He took the printing press in the name of the government, made a few drunks into deputies, and then he ordered the Beaulieus out of town, even before sundown. We sat on the porch of the Hindquarters Hotel and laughed at the deputies trying to move an old printing press. They gave up, ink on their hands and clothes, marked by the government forever.

Listen, if you knew the Beaulieus as well as we did at the Hindquarters Hotel that day, you would know that no one tells that family to leave the reservation, no one. Not even the government. They weren't mean, or anything like that, but they were part of a big and important mixedblood family, the first to settle on the reservation, and they were Catholics.

Tipi arrived at high noon at the big white Beaulieu house near the Mission Pond with half a dozen deputies hanging behind in the trees. Dummy Funday and his cousin Birch were up front with the agent, they both wore giant silver stars on their vests, the kind we saw in cartoons. The stars didn't change them much though, they still stumbled and stammered, always wanting to be in charge of something or another. Birch was white, he married a skin, they were both pretty good boys, but they sure do hate Catholics, especially halfbreed Catholics. Tipi put together a pack of Catholic-hating deputies to run the Beaulieus out, but not one of them, not even the agent, had the courage in the end. They came up the dirt path and stood for a long time below the porch stairs. The longer they waited the more people gathered on the road waiting for the action. Catholics were the real enemies but nothing happened.

Tipi started up the stairs of the Beaulieu place when someone in the crowd yelled, "Hey, watch out for the fifth step." So he stopped and looked around. He did look stupid with his pointed head and sixgun at his side playing the western hero, but he was really the loser, not a twig of humor in his bones. "The board is loose." We all laughed. Tipi thought the whole thing was a joke, and we knew he would, so he threw both feet on the fifth step and fell on his ass down the stairs. He caught a sliver on his right thumb, drew some blood. We laughed again because it was his shooting hand and we called out to him, "Tipi, watch out, those Catholics learn how to fast draw at confessions."

Colonel Clement Hudon dit Beaulieu, the elder of the mixedblood families, was at the door to meet the agent. He was no stranger, but even so, Tipi yelled his orders out: "You Beaulieus leave this reservation by order of the United States and the honorable Secretary of the Interior." He had the government behind him and he was still scared. His voice wagged like a mongrel at a picnic. We never did hear what Colonel Clement said back to him through the screen door. The old man wore a black morning coat, sometimes visitors took him for the priest. He had a real quiet voice, he was educated, and so were his boys. They all went to private schools out east somewhere. He was in the fur trade for a time, before the reservation was created. That's when the governor of the state made him a Colonel, but soon the fur was gone and the Indians were removed. He and his boys did the best they could as educated mixedbloods on the reservation, they went into business, what else, and now they started a newspaper. The old man still tells a good story, he even plays a good poker hand, and he has a way with bears and horses. He drinks with the priests.

Tipi kicked his heels at the door, looked down and around to see who was watching. We were sitting on the porch of the Hindquarters so once more he ordered the Beaulieus to leave. Birch said later that Colonel Clement invited him over to the church and that scared him more than a shotgun aimed at his head. That's just what the Beaulieus did, they went over to the church and Father Corner, that weird old man with a hatchet face, held a special service. The next thing you know, there was a United States Senate Subcommittee hearing about corruption at White Earth.

Listen, that was a long time ago, back in the good old days when words still had some power and people sat around and laughed over a good story. We laughed over that story many an afternoon, sitting on the porch of the Hindquarters Hotel. Father Corner talked about the devil and Colonel Clement went all the way to Washington to testify. Tipi Milcho never came back once the word was out. No one was surprised because he never should of been here in the first place. Tipi never laughed, everything was too serious to him, he even reported the doctor for dancing in the hospital and said that all the jerking around would weaken the foundation of the building. Dancing, now there's a way to destroy government property. Tipi never came back from the hearing and the Beaulieus went back to publishing their newspaper, maintaining, as they said, our "higher civilization" on the reservation. Like I said, Colonel Clement had a way with bears, and horses, and priests.

Father Laurence watched the sun crawl over the mount named for Saint Columban and then he plunged his narrow head deep into cool water and thumped his fingers on the rim of the wooden rain barrel. There, in that manner each morning, he balanced his otherwise uncertain spiritual worlds under water. He confessed that the resound, like the distant thunder in tribal creation stories, stopped sacramental time; he descended into a pacific sea.

Sister James, a conservative throwback to the old school of pure and simple sacrifices, complained to

Father Corner, whose flesh was corrupt enough to retain a thin beam of humor, that Father Laurence was possessed, that he had been touched by savages and evil shamans. She reported that the young priest, new to the reservation, his first appointment to "clear his unsettled mind," chanted on the mount at night, talked to insects, and inhaled rain water from a barrel at first light.

"Father Corner, the wicked ones like him too much, they ask him several times a day, 'How was your plunge this morning, Father?' and he says back, 'Just fine, thank you for asking.' And he even smokes bark with those pagans at the hotel." She confessed to her superior and then she explained that she had passed these rumors to others, and she even told unkind stories about the new priest to the sisters at the mission school. Sister James had enormous feet, long and narrow, so narrow that she ordered her shoes from a custom cobbler who supplied circus clowns. She looked down at her shoes in the confessional and noticed a thin crack in the leather. She tapped the toes together.

"Sister, this is your confession, not his," said Father Corner. He was harsh at confessionals. He pinched his eyes closed and pictured the young priest on the loose. "Please, please continue the stories." She never failed to please the old priest with her wild and paranoid imagination; his curiosity and absolution each week was implicit.

"Father Laurence calls me Big Jim."

"So what, you confessed that last week," said Father Corner.

"He ridicules me."

Father Laurence was not certain how to answer the letter from Mildred Fairchild. She explained her situation: the Bureau of Indian Affairs had hired her to

141

teach at the White Earth government school but no one in the main office could provide her with information about tribal children or the reservation. He wrote a note, "Big Jim, please answer."

"No," she wrote back. "You be the expert."

"Dear Sister James," he addressed a second note. "Please, would you kindly answer the attached letter from Mildred Fairchild."

"No," she answered a second time. "Must we point out that Miss Fairchild is a federal teacher and we are a mission school?"

"Thanks again, Big Jim."

"Praying mantis have four thin legs," Father Laurence told Little Baron, son of Dummy Funday, and his little friend with no name. The two had been lurking all week in the woods behind his small house behind the mission school. The tribal boys sought the attention of the new priest as an excuse to avoid their classroom teachers in the government school. Now, during the summer, Little Baron and his friend waited to time the priest in the rain barrel. The gamblers in the village started a secret cash raffle on how long the priest could keep his head under water. Colonel Clement Beaulieu loaned the boys his gold watch, the best one on the reservation, to keep the average time for seven plunges in the barrel. The fifth plunge was short, but the first four ran between three and four minutes. Colonel Clement believed that the new priest possessed unusual spiritual energies so he bought each third second between three and four minutes. Imar Funday, and his son Dummy, bought the other marks on the clock but for different reasons. Imar, who hates Catholics, was convinced that beneath the black robe of the priest there beat the black heart of an evil shaman. Others in the village, with much less cash on hand to risk, measured what the priest could do as a mortal white man. "Not much," said a wood cutter. He lost.

"Now, watch the neck, see there, see how it moves over the shoulder," said the priest as he touched the green back with a twig. The boys leaned on their elbows, close to the earth, to hear the lecture. The priest turned his head with the mantis, his face was round and tender, a hint of green from the trees. A scar creased his right cheek at the same level as his mouth. When he was twelve he chased a fawn across a field and caught his cheek on a barbed wire fence. "Mantis eat insects, and sometimes the female eats the male for dinner, what do you make of that?"

"I like dogs better," said the little boy.

"How long can you hold your head under water?" asked Little Baron, a mixedblood with pale green eyes. He leaped to his feet, excited, and waited for an answer. A grey mongrel barked.

"Why do you ask?"

"We saw you in the barrel," said the little boy.

"Never thought about the time."

"We got a watch," said Little Baron.

"Where did you get that?" asked the priest.

"Colonel Clement gave it to us."

"Really?"

"We didn't steal it, we didn't," pleaded Little Baron.

"Well, I suppose you better time me with it then," said the priest. He brushed his black hair behind his ears and leaned close to the water. The boys waved their arms to mark the time and the priest plunged his head into the rain barrel. One, two, three, four. . . . One minute, thirty-eight seconds for the sixth plunge beneath the water.

"You did better the last time."

"Never thought about it until now."

"Can we time you tomorrow?"

"Don't tell me about it," said the priest and then he

plunged his head into the barrel once more. The water was cool, he could hear animals at a distance, and then he pictured the new teacher at the window of the train.

"No, we won't," said Little Baron.

Dear Miss Fairchild, the priest thought to write with his head deep in the rain barrel. Please forgive this tardy reply to your letter. . . . Where should we begin to introduce you to the unusual people of this reservation?

At the beginning, but then where is the beginning of this tribal place?

"In 1863 the Indian Office submitted a plan to unite the scattered tribes," he continued to write at his desk. Through three narrow windows he watched the poplar and the oak leaves shiver in the warm breeze on the mount at Saint Columban. "White Earth was established by treaty in 1867, and one June 14, 1868 the first Indians, most of them were mixedbloods, began to arrive at White Earth from Mille Lacs, Pillager. The Beaulieus and the Morrisons, two prominent fur trade families from Old Crow Wing, were the first to be removed to the new reservation.

"White Earth was a beautiful forest then, quiet and clean beneath the tall red and white pines. It was a good place for the first settlers. The Indian knew himself better in those days than he does today, and he had the pride of being on his own good land, until the enactment of the Dawes Allotment Act of 1886 which led to the illusion of individual ownership of the land. The trees were cut to build cities and a few men became wealthy and in their guilt built monuments in their name at a great distance from the stumps they left behind on the reservation. Now we measure who we are from what we have done to them.

"White Earth village, which is where you will teach,

was subdivided into small blocks and homesites. Some roads were paved, a water tower was erected, and there were even plans for a sewer system which was never completed, but things are much different now. . . .

"This, of course, does not tell you much about the people who live here now. Well, let me tell you two stories, which is the way most Indians explain their time to a visitor.

"The first is about two Indian boys, they could be in your class next year, who came by to see me this afternoon. Rather, they were lurking in the trees behind the house. God knows why, but they have taken an interest in one of my peculiar practices: in the morning I rinse my face outside in a rain barrel. The water is so soft. Well, the boys are up to something because they have been timing how long I keep my head under water. Little Baron, the mixedblood grandson of the shaman Imar Funday, is quick and full of wit, and he reminds me of the tribal trickster we hear so much about here on the reservation. Naanabozho is his name, or her name, a sort of cultural hero who creates and contradicts classes, manners, and political authority. There are many tales of his growing and learning. His grandmother told him that when Indians first ate the meat of animals the trees and plants got together and decided to punish people with diseases. The plants and trees, however, decided that the Indians had not been unkind to them so they agreed to offer humans the secrets of herbal medicines to cure diseases given to them by animals. A rational balance, but the trickster upsets the balance, if for no other reason, to keep people alert to their own survival and powers to heal. The mixedbloods are the tricksters, they settle new worlds in their own blood.

"The second story is about Saint Columban, a sacred place on the earth which I can see at this moment through the window. We call it the mount, a meadow near the pond, and it is marked by four poles which have been carved down to stubs in the past few years. Tribal people come from all over the state to touch the earth at Saint Columban and to cut sacred slivers from one of the posts. The slivers, and the earth there, some believe, will cure cancer.

"Saint Columban, and most of this reservation, is unlike any place I have ever known or dreamed about before. It is truly a sacred place on the earth; it is a place where some are touched by visions and where religions begin, and some end. White Earth, on the other hand, cannot be introduced. This place must be a collection of every changing trickster story, and the longer I am here the more we seem to change each time a story is told.

"White Earth might be one of those transitional places on the earth where the past is never the same in the memories of the people who lived here. This reservation is a story."

Father Laurence imitated the water strider, he touched his hands and moved on the surface. He could feel the tension there, but he was not small enough to walk across the rain in the barrel. He leaned over and rolled the reflection of his face from side to side with his hands and then he plunged his head up to his naked shoulders. He listened to the distance in the cool rain water, his meditation at first light.

Little Baron, tucked behind a tree with the gold watch, timed the priest at three minutes, forty-two seconds. Imar Funday, his wicked grandfather, was the winner; but when others in the village learned that his grandson had been the official timekeeper they withdrew their money from the raffle.

Colonel Clement Beaulieu paid the mixedblood, made good on his bet as always and then he drove to meet the new schoolteacher. Perched high in the seat of his plain black motorcar, he confessed his basic needs to the priest.

"Basic needs?" asked Father Laurence.

"Education, women, priests, and red wine."

"No song?"

"I had no idea the new teacher could sing," he said and then burst into laughter. Colonel Clement looked around the fields; the slant of morning light raised the corn. He waited for the priest to ask the most obvious question.

"How many basic needs do you have?"

"Seventeen, at last count," he said.

"What might one or two be?" asked the priest.

"Not until you tell me how you can hold your breath for such a long time under water in that rain barrel," he said and leaned into a curve.

The broken road from White Earth curves near the Mission Pond, circles the mount, and then unfurls like a ribbon snake between the corn and alfalfa fields. Ogema is a white town on the border of the reservation; the nearest railroad depot, a place where the plains begin and alcohol is dispensed at a high price.

Mildred Fairchild stood beneath a pale blue parasol at the entrance to the Paradise Bank and Trust Company of Ogema. The church was hidden behind the public school, not obvious to a visitor. Mildred waited near the pillars of the bank, between her valise and a small trunk. She was tired, but she stood erect with her small feet close together on the broken concrete.

Her blond hair was bound in a loose bun low at the back of her neck. She watched the street, alert to the gestures of others. She did not know that there was more behind those mock pillars than a bank.

"Miss Fairchild, I presume," said Colonel Clement.

"Your name, sir?"

"Your chauffeur," he said and smiled.

"Your name, sir?"

"Colonel Clement Hudon dit Beaulieu, at your service."

"Do you live on the White Earth Reservation?" she asked and then folded her parasol. The blue cloth was faded and clean. She was nervous, insecure, and she avoided the priest.

"Indeed, since the night it was invented."

"What do you do there?"

"Twice retired," he said as he reached for the small trunk.

"Twice?"

"Fur trader one and farmer twice."

"My father is a lawyer," she said.

"So he is," said Colonel Clement as he walked to the car. "Perhaps you would not mind waiting here for a few minutes with Father Laurence while I conduct some business at the bank?"

"Not at all, Colonel. . . ." She settled in the middle of the back seat.

"Here is my response to your letter," said Father Laurence. He was standing outside the car and handed the unsealed envelope to her through the window in the back door.

"But I never wrote to you." Mildred hesitated and did not open the letter; she placed it beside her on the leather seat.

"Your letter was forwarded to me because the other teachers have left for the summer," he said through the window. She looked past him when he spoke. "Forgive me. . . ."

"For what?" she snapped.

"Forgive me for not writing to you sooner about what to expect here," he said in a slow and awkward speech. "When I finally took up my pen to answer, well, I noticed that you would be here before the letter could be delivered."

"Thank you."

"Did you notice the bank?"

"Well, of course."

"What I mean to say is, did you notice that the bank is more than what meets the eye?" The priest rested his bare arm on the window. The black metal was hot in the sun.

"Not really." She turned toward the entrance to the bank. Her face came too close to his arm on the window, too close to the thin black hair that spread down to his fingers. She pinched her lips and moved back from the window.

"The bank is in the front, as you can see, but behind that is a liquor bar," he explained in a louder voice, "and behind the bar is a land trust company."

"My father would call that a western."

"Western, indeed," said the priest. He pushed his head through the open window. "They bank on one end, grab land, Indian land and valuable timber, on the other end, and then drink and celebrate in the middle."

"What would they think of me," she said and leaned forward on the leather seat, "standing there at the door to the bar?"

"There stands the new school teacher," he said. "People seem to know just about everything around here, not much gained with a pose."

Katydids sounded in the trees. Mildred opened the back door and placed one foot on the running board. "Colonel Beaulieu, would he be a banker or a drinker?" she asked.

"Both, and he would agree."

"Father Laurence, would you show me the bank?"

"The bank?" He took her hand and watched her move from the car. He opened the door to the bank, stood behind her, and imagined that he saw her small bare feet move on the cool marble floor.

Mildred followed a path worn in the marble from

the vestibule to the bright white entrance and to the bar in the back. Two men watched from behind brass enclosures at the side of the bank.

"Where is the bar?" she shouted.

"Through the back door." The priest pointed to a steel door that had been the entrance to the vault. The door handle, a wide copper wheel, had turned green. "Not a comfortable place for a woman."

"What could be so bad about a bar?" she said. Her shoes ticked on the marble, a determined measure. She never would have entered a bar at home, but this was a western, on the border of civilization, and she was moved to experience deceptions. She towed the green wheel and walked into the bar ahead of the priest.

The room was dark and smelled of mold and liquor, cigar smoke, and perspiration. Mildred pinched her nose at the masculine emanations, but it was the smell of bad breath that forced her against the wall. She gasped and retreated to the back seat of the car.

Father Laurence, meanwhile, heard his name mentioned when he entered the bar. He approached Colonel Clement who stood at the end of the bar with several other men from town. The men talked about bankers and games, winners and lovers.

"Saint Laurence of the rain barrel," said one man.

"No saint could survive on this reservation."

"Much less around mixedbloods," said another man.

"Laurence has been touched . . ." Colonel Clement stopped in the middle of his sentence. "Laurence, I would like you to meet some of my friends . . ." When the mixedblood turned, the four men at the bar had disappeared. "Some people fear the best in a man."

"Mildred Fairchild. . . ."

"Father, forgive me, she was lost in the stories," he said and wrapped the opened bottle with several others in a small leather case. "She was under the stories."

"Colonel, would the game you mentioned to your friends at the bar be of interest to me?" The priest walked and talked to the bank entrance.

"Yes, it would indeed," said Colonel Clement. He covered his eyes from the bright light. "We bet on how long you could keep your head under water in that rain barrel."

"Little Baron borrowed your watch to time me then?"

"The average time for seven tries," he said and handed the leather case to the priest near the car. "Funday won, but the game died because the others would not trust the timer."

"But he is an honest boy."

"Fundays are honest to the seeds, but few trust them."

"People fear the dark," said Father Laurence.

"Miss Fairchild, forgive me, for we have sinned," said Colonel Clement. He started the engine, turned, smiled, and nodded toward the back seat.

"Priests and mixedbloods are ritualists," he construed with a flourish. "We are the creatures folded in stories, better told, better remembered than morals and manners."

"Such ritual banking could be bad for your health," she said in a serious voice but then she smiled and leaned back in the warm leather. She had removed her blue gloves.

"There you'll find a gentle argument," he said and started the engine. He slipped his hands into large gloves to handle the hot wooden wheel.

"Father Laurence?"

"Yes."

"Did you retrieve the letter you gave to me?"

"No, I thought you placed it on the seat."

"I am afraid the letter is missing," she said.

"Father, please see that her trunk is tied to the back."

Colonel Clement turned and stopped the car. "Some people borrow too much in this town."

"Trunk is here," said the priest. He looked in the back seat, and under the seats. "Miss Fairchild, I am afraid that someone has borrowed your valise."

Colonel Clement reported the missing valise to the local constable and then, as best he could, assured the new teacher that the letter and her personal properties, nightdress and underwear, would soon be returned.

Mildred listened to the wind and smelled the hot timothy, corn, and meadow flowers. For a few minutes she was alone, for the first time in years, at peace in the back seat. Redwing blackbirds cracked the air on both sides of the narrow road back to the White Earth Reservation.

Mildred moved into a small private room attached to the back of the Hindquarters Hotel. The outside wall was stained and the fleu-de-lis border paper had fallen near the corner. She pulled the lace curtains back and opened the windows on both sides; there was a trace of mold in the room.

She was tired, the breeze was warm and humid. She removed her shoes and stockings, loosened her dress, and leaned back on the hard bed. The linen was hard and clean, the pillow smelled fresh; she thought about her mother and burst into tears.

"Dred, come rest beside me now," her mother said in a dream. The linen was pure white and scented with clover. Mildred buried her head in the pillow and counted silhouettes until she was lost in sleep.

Mildred smelled bread fresh from the oven. She was home with her mother at last, but then she awakened; the linen was coarse, the wallpaper was stained and pared. She was alone on the reservation with savages late in the afternoon.

Two boys, one with cat-green eyes, stared at her from behind the window screen; one pressed his nose hard to the wire and crossed his fingers.

Mildred screamed; she pulled a blanket over her bodice, and then burst into tears a second time.

"There, there, nothing to fear now," said the hotel cook and baker who heard the screams. The stout brown woman lowered the blanket and soughed until the teacher turned a smile, however thin. "There, there, come with me now and we'll have some coffee and fresh bread."

"Thank you," Mildred said and then she dressed. Her movements were slow, deliberate, she was ashamed to be alone and dependent on strangers; afraid that she would forget her name. She studied her face in the mirror, the irregular glass rolled her nose and cheeks flat. She tried to smile but each gesture brought silent tears. She had never come so close to her face in a mirror; she had avoided such vanities at home.

"There, there, nothing to worry about now, you'll be up in the new house with the other teacher in a week or so, as soon as she returns and they put in the water," she said with her hands on her wide hips.

"The room is fine, really. . . ."

"There, there, never mind now," she said and held out her fat hand. "Mildred, is that what your mother called you at home?"

"Dred for short. . . ."

"Well, we'll just call you by your whole name," she said as they walked down the hall to the hotel kitchen. "My name is Gracie Bobolink, but my friends call me Greasie because I'm the head cook here."

"Greasie?"

"It's good to call me Greasie," she insisted with a wide smile. Two front teeth were broken. "Before that name they called me Beaucoup Bobolink."

"Bobolink?"

"Yes, my mother came down from Rat Portage with

153

no name, and in those days government agents gave us bird names." Greasie chirruped.

"Greasie, I'm pleased to know you," said Mildred.

"See there, you feel better now."

"Yes, I was dreaming about my mother, she died eight years ago, and when I woke up I saw these two boys at the window. One of them had strange green eyes."

"That would be Little Baron, no trouble," said Greasie.

"Little Baron?"

"Nicknames, tumble names . . . ." She started to explain tumble names and then looked out the kitchen window. "Some people wear out their names and get new ones from time to time."

"Dred never wore out . . . ."

"Little Baron, come here, boy." Greasie called through the window. When she moved, the flesh under her arms waved like wattle. She held the back door open for the green-eyed boy. "What you got there?"

"Letter from Father Laurence."

"Well, who did he write to now?" asked Greasie.

"Letter for the teacher," he answered and handed over the unsealed envelope. He turned his head, looked to the corners of the room, hid his eyes.

"Look up now." Greasie held her hand under his chin. "Look up, let's see those bright green eyes." She pinched his cheeks, "Where's the smile in those eyes?"

"Where did you get this letter?" asked Mildred.

"My grandfather, he told me to bring it here."

"Who is your grandfather?"

"Imar Funday, he's a big shaman," answered Greasie.

"I came to the window with the letter." Little Baron raised his head and looked at the teacher in the same way he watched her through the window screen earlier.

"Little Baron, will you be in my class at school?" Mildred leaned over a few inches, closer to his answer.

He nodded that he would, his green eyes flashed around the kitchen like a monger, stopped at the loaves of fresh bread. He touched his fingers to his mouth.

Greasie gave him two thick slices of warm bread covered with lard and sugar, one in each hand. Little Baron nodded and then he butted the door open with his head and ran out.

Mildred sat at the kitchen table and read the letter. She sipped coffee but stopped when several flies paraded on the rim of the cracked cup. She waved the flies from the table, from her hair, from the letter.

Greasie watched the white teacher read and wave, she swatted the flies around her with a folded newspaper. Mildred nodded her approval with each smack of the paper. When she finished the letter she smiled and counted seventeen dead flies on the bare table.

"Colonel Clement said someone would bring it back," Mildred told Greasie over supper. The valise was on the bed when she returned to her room that night.

"Funday returns things around here, whatever is lost or stolen," said Greasie with a mouthful of sweet peas. "He's the shaman and he knows where things get lost and what people think about, so watch what you think around him or he'll say your mind back."

"Shaman, is that a witch doctor?"

"You should ask the priest about that."

"My father told me to avoid Catholics." Mildred leaned on her elbows and waved her fork over the table, an unusual gesture. She heard an echo in her voice; she watched her gestures from the inside, the rituals from word to hand.

"The priests be good to me." Greasie made the sign of the cross and then she wiped her plate clean with a thick slice of white bread. Three fat black flies pursued her hand from plate to mouth and lost.

Thunderbirds overturned the prairie and late in her dreams that night the bed trembled and the room blazed with lightning. Pillars of hail crossed the Mission Pond and hammered a barrel at the back of the hotel. The rain smelled of meadow flowers and twittered on the narrow wooden window sills.

Lightning cracked at the tall white pine.

Thunder chattered at the panes.

Mildred lost her place in the world, the scenes beneath her hands burned. She told her mother to wait, whispered secret fears to her sisters, and then she called out her own name to be sure that she was there that night. Nothing returned, her voice was lost in the thunder.

The wild wind pulled at nests in the trees, turned signs around, tore shingles from the hotel. The ceiling in her room leaked over the bed and in three places near the windows. Drops of rain hit the brass headboard and splashed on her face, soft and cool.

Mildred imagined animals on the oil lanterns. There were bears at the windows and an owl screamed from the bars at the end of her bed. A snake uncoiled and hissed from a corner near the ceiling. Her wet flesh tingled; thunder trembled in her pillow.

Mildred called out for Greasie but her voice was lost. The room came alive and then died with the light, nothing could be darker. Images danced on her hands, on the walls, at the windowsills.

Shamans were at the windows.

Little Baron was a white cat in a flash of lightning, his green eyes blinked and splashed at the foot of her bed. She opened her mouth to scream but there was no sound.

Trees snapped on the hill behind the hotel.

Imar Funday appeared at the other window as a black bear with his front paws on the sill. Lightning flashed from his maw and sharp teeth, and his roar rattled the lanterns and shook the bed.

"There, there, never mind now, you are good," said Greasie. She touched her hot cheeks in the dark. "We get storms like this every few days in the late summer, thunderbirds from the mountains, the weather of the shamans."

"Greasie, they were here."

"Who was here?"

"Funday and Little Baron, at the windows."

"There, there, Funday is a shaman, he has the time of the night to go where he wants to, he was at my window once, he even moves in dreams," she said in a calm voice between the low rumbles of distant thunder. "Funday can scare the ears from a corn stalk, but he never hurt anybody, sounds to me like he might have taken a liking to you."

"No, no, not me," pleaded Mildred.

"There, there, you'll just have to learn how to talk to a shaman at night and then you won't be scared." Greasie rubbed her hands together.

"How do you talk to a shaman?"

"The trick is not to see a shaman the way he comes out of the dark or in a dream," said Greasie. "Suppose he was at the window there, right now, I'll bet he would want us to see him as a bear?"

"Yes, he was a bear." Mildred seemed surprised.

"Well, there's one way to trick a shaman," she said as she leaned back to the foot of the bed. "Pretend that he's just a boy who showed his little brute at the dinner table, so you say to him, 'Funday, listen here, put that little thing away before the butcher cuts it up for sausage,' and that works because a shaman has sex on the brain, that's how he gets around in our dreams. So, if you cut his brute off you cut the bear down to size."

"I've never thought like that before."

"You've never been on a reservation before either," said Greasie. The bed creaked when she laughed. "Try the brute removal some time, you'll see for yourself."

"But there were other animals."

"What kind?"

"Crows, owls, cats, and a huge snake," she cried.

"There, there, you can talk to the priest tomorrow," said Greasie. She touched Mildred on the cheeks once more. Lightning flashed but the storm had ended. "Crows, owls, and cats are the shaman, but you brought the snake with you on the train."

Mildred took a primrose to bed and when the animals and birds appeared in her dreams later that night she touched them once on the head; the five petals transformed them into clean white moths. She inhaled the sunrise with the pure moths.

Funday appeared at the window once more and when she touched him on the head he lost his black hair, he shivered at the window screen.

Little Baron waved into the room as a small bat but he turned to a moth at the foot of the bed.

Father Laurence pressed his white hands, and then his cheek, to the small stained upper pane in the window. Mildred held the primrose high, she waited to touch the priest as she had the bear.   Then, when the little priest danced through the window toward her bed, she swatted him several times on the shoulders with the primrose. The petals broke from the stem and the more she swatted him the more he grew until she could see at her side the dark hair on his wrists and fingers.

"Miss Fairchild, are you all right?"

"Stay away," she screamed several times and beat the space around her bed with the wilted stem of the primrose. "Brute, brute, be gone."

"This is Father Laurence," he called. "The boys are gone."

"What boys?" Mildred was out of bed, behind the

wardrobe near the door. She shivered, wrapped to her
chin in a threadbare blanket. "Brutes at the windows,
brutes on the bed."

"Little Baron and the others," the priest said in a
gentle voice. He searched for the lantern in the dark.
"Greasie Bobolink heard your screams and told me to
look around outside. We wanted you to be comfortable,
this, your first night on the reservation."

"Do you smell bad breath?"

"What breath?"

"Bad breath of death," she whispered.

"No," he said.

"Never mind now."

"Should I light the lantern?"

"No, don't do that," she said from behind the
wardrobe. "Who was that at the windows, who was the
bear out there?" Her voice was weak.

"Little Baron and his friends have a collection of
animal masks," the priest said. "They stood in the
windows with different masks."

"Bears and crows?"

"Yes, and other creatures."

"An owl?"

"Yes, owls, hawks, crows, the birds."

"Snakes?"

"That must be a new one."

"Who was the snake?"

"Miss Fairchild, there is no place you could be more
secure than on this reservation," he lectured. "No one
here will harm you. What has happened to you is what
happens to all of us from time to time, we call it love
burns from the tricksters."

"Funday, was he there at the window?"

"No, he never wears masks," the priest said. "He
walks around in a blanket burnoose to hide the hideous
scars from a burn on his cheek and neck."

"But he was there," she insisted.

"Miss Fairchild, would you like to walk with me around the village?"

He continued talking before she could answer. Her first answer would have been negative, but the more she listened the better she felt about his invitation. "This is the most beautiful time of the night, the thunderstorm has passed, silent lightning on the horizon, the air is clean and clear. The earth must have been like this at creation, at the first light."

"Thank you. . . ."

"The fresh air will do you good," he said before she could change her mind. "There is nothing to fear on the reservation, not even the shaman."

Greasie lived in a corner room on the second floor of the hotel. From there, she could see the government school, the mission, the pond below the meadow, the hospital, and the sacred mount in the distance. She could see them down on the road, the moon was bright, and later she heard their voices from the mount.

Mildred stopped beside the road and reached into her pocket. "Father Laurence, this is a silly thing, but I want you to see a picture of my father."

"I would be delighted." He turned the small photographs to the best light. She watched mosquitoes circle the moist clouds from his breath as he admired her father.

"My father hates Catholics," she said with her head down. "He warned me. Does that trouble you, that so many people hate you?" She looked at the picture of her father on the porch.

"Do you have an answer?"

"Where are we going?"

"There is a special place at the top of the hill," he said and pointed to the mount behind a stand of white pine trees. She turned to swat several mosquitoes on her neck and then on her ankles.

"Whose house is that?"

"Colonel Clement Beaulieu."

"The mosquitoes wait for my breath," she complained.

"There are no mosquitoes on the mount." He brushed his arms and neck. He heard animals in the distance. Lightning burned in the thunder clouds.

"One bit me on the forehead."

Father Laurence smiled and pointed to the mount. Mildred led the way on a narrow path through several bands of trees. First the birch and poplar and then the white pine. The grass was moist. She shivered under the pine closer to the mount, sleeves were wetted, and her leather shoes were soaked. The wet cotton held to her breasts.

The mount, a natural meadow in the white pine, was covered with sweet clover. Mildred turned in circles, her arms extended, and the moon bounced over the branches. She twirled like a child until she lost her balance and tumbled on her side into the clover. She rolled over on her back.

"This is the mount." The priest was possessed on the mount.

"When I was a child my mother put clover in my pillow at night," she said and touched the moon in the white pine. "She told me that the blossoms would make my dreams sweeter. No bad breath in the clover."

"You could do that here."

"This is a beautiful place," she said and turned over on her stomach, her chin in her hands. She had not noticed that the clover was warm, not wet, there was no rain on the mount.

"Naanabozho, the trickster, was the first to imagine this mount," he said and then sat down next to her in the clover. "The missionaries were the first to take the credit. They named the mount after Saint Columban."

"Never heard of either one," said Mildred.

"Neither had I until one night I came up here to watch a thunderstorm approach," said the priest. "The lightning and rain circled the mount, I could feel the moisture in the air, of course, but not the rain."

"How can that be?"

"Naanabozho, I was told, was transformed into four different animals and birds to protect his sick grandmother who was stranded on the mount during a thunderstorm. The trickster was a bear over there, a crow over on that side of the mount, and an otter and waxwing on the other sides. The four sides of the trickster stopped the rain one night and the thunderbirds never forgot what happened."

"That's fantastic," she said.

"The missionaries said otherwise," said the priest. "There are people who come up here to pick clover, find stones, or cut pieces of bark from the trees on the four sides of mount. The stones and bark are spiritual medicine and heal."

"You wrote about that in your letter," she said. "Do you believe those stories about the trickster, the stones and the rest?"

"Life begins with imagination."

"How did you get that scar on your cheek?"

"I was a child when it happened," he said and rolled back in the clover next to her. "I was chasing a fawn, tripped and fell on a barbed wire fence, nothing more."

"You smile on one side."

Father Laurence imagined that he turned to the side and touched her cool moist shoulder, first with one finger and then with his whole hand. She moved closer and kissed the scar on his right cheek and then drew his head down on her low breasts. He listened to her heart beat and moved his hand across her warm stomach and down her thighs. She opened her legs to his hands. She touched his ear with her tongue and pulled the hair at the back of his neck and then she squeezed the muscles down his back. She tore the cotton from her breasts and he sucked on her nipples.

He imagined how she moaned, writhed in the clover, and forced his hand down on her crotch. He reached inside her panties and pushed two fingers into her wet vagina with a sudden movement. She rolled from side to side on his hand. Then she opened his black trousers and touched his penis. He shot in the clover.

Mildred imagined that the priest whispered his secrets to her on the mount. His breath was clean and sweet and she could feel his smile in her loins. She wore no underwear, her nipples were hard. He touched her ears with his tongue, loosened her hair, and then he rose above her in the light of the moon and made love with her until the doves whistled at dawn. She carried clover blossoms home to her father.

Greasie listened to the voices of the priest and teacher late at the mount and remembered the time when she was seventeen, when Imar Funday caught her on the road one dark night and lured her to the mount where he practiced what he called "animal love with a shaman." She removed her pink bloomers and roamed over the clover on her hands and knees while he circled the mount and leaped from behind trees and mounted her as an animal might. She remembers best the bear, she conceived a child that night with the bear, and from the night with the otter too, but she never forgot the wild mountain goat. Remember the beaver with his sharp teeth at the back of her neck.

163

She would be a bear and roam at night on the mount, under the whole moon. She would flash her silver maw and hold the priest in the clover until first light.

Martha Baer

Mrs. Peacock in the Billiard Room
With the Lead Pipe

A bright air drove across the lawn. Hedges clutched to one another at the edge. It was summer. As the crowd gathered, the lake grew more and more calm, calm as ice, beautiful. Men and women looked out over the sweep of it or hung their heads silently. Some reached down to touch the lake where it crept up and then back on the shore. They felt the wet between their fingers, imagining.

It was there at that lake. It was there that the two young women had been found, floating. There were screams. From the shore, men and women saw the skin white through the water. They saw the bodies, bobbing upward. They saw the folds of polka-dotted dresses playing across the surface. Then, they saw the lake grow smooth and awful.

Later, the group dispersed, coming up from the shore one by one, wondering just how long it was since the skin had stopped absorbing. Richard rubbed his arm. It was dry. Jan passed him without speaking. She hurried away. But none of the onlookers converged at the house to mill on the lawn as they had in the past. Few joined up at the road to discuss it. Because no one knew how it happened. No one knew who could have thrown the two young bodies, senselessly, out there. Or who could have sent them, furious, escaping, running down the long slope of the shore. Who could have urged them, in the silent unwavering evening, to drown themselves, or to swim.

Lenore Peacock hurried toward her car at the top of the drive. She held her purse to her chest. And she held her breath as if to keep down a terrible liquid. It was the last time she would see them, and she knew then that slowly, death by death, the world was emptying. She fumbled for the keys.

Jim Green was the landlord. He had come too in the morning, had come to stand at the lake, to gaze out and feel the loss. His arms hung down. "Such beauties," he thought.

All through that night, Jan Scarlet saw visions. She lay back on the couch, over the figures of woodcutters and trees, over the thick pillows. She saw visions of the young women all over town. She saw them buying wine glasses and china platters. She saw them whispering at the back of the offices. And she saw the bodies—thin arms, bones at the back of the neck—arching and rising up through the water.

Richard phoned Lenore. He felt he had to take action. "Lenore," he said, "did you see them laughing? They were delightful. . . and yet so difficult." But Lenore refused to answer. Richard stared at the dry white hairs of his arms, stone-dry and downy. He said, "Did you see them splashing so joyously?" He looked up. The moon was past the window. The light on the pewter plates was minimal. Richard mustard set his head straight on his great shoulders, and said, to end the call because she wasn't responding, "Perhaps we shall see them swim again tomorrow."

But the following morning only Jim was there. Only Jim ventured back to the end of the hedges where the land sloped down, so slightly, as if respiring, and the grass stood up in the water. Jim stood on the slope, sliding frontward in his shoes. He was quiet. He had left

Jan Scarlet in the bed, sleeping at last, after the long night of unrest. And he came here to watch, to see if any telling ripples were left, to see if souls could last in water.

But it was not just Jim. He looked left. There, behind the cattails and under a hood of shade, standing as tall as himself, was Jonathan. Jonathan was his friend. Jim and Jonathan were old friends, with similar tastes and similar bodies. Both were broad at the top and skimpy at bottom. Jim called to him. "Jonathan!" But his friend didn't hear, and just then it became clear that both had meant to be alone.

Both men stayed, alone on the shore, Jonathan by the cattails and Jim sitting now by the hydrangeas. Jonathan stared out, unmoving, at the water. He had not come to look for waves. He had come to face facts. There were tears in his eyes. The surface was still and black. And all morning, as on any morning, the ripples came and went. The land sloped to its end.

Two women sat in the bright weatherless air of a nation. They sat on chairs slung with canvas. The lawn expanded in green which became yellow where it met the sun. One spoke: "Do you see the azaleas over there?"

"No," said the other. "They are too far. Behind the barn."

"Yes, they are far. And yet it seems likely at least that the azaleas are there."

The other looked out toward the lake. Her arms rested, continuous, pale, so that they had almost no outline under the light, on the arms of the canvas chair. She looked toward the other, intently, through the space between them. "What do you suppose, Sweetest, is the good of likelihood?"

The other looked back, smiling, with a great feeling. "And what do you suppose, Sweetest, I would do without you?"

"Hmm."

"There are moments," the one said, "when I feel there is nothing between us."

"Nothing but the rays of light, swarms of minute insects maybe, a breeze."

"Or nothing at all."

The two women sat for an unlimited length of time. The sun remained bright, and their skin was fair. Their limbs were long and always resting. At the rim of the lawn a white fence disappeared, and two towers, made of rock that was beige or blond, sunk behind the hills.

It was long before she had ever set eyes on the lake that Jan Scarlet had first become acquainted with the girls. In fact, it was as far back as her first days of college. They had come around the corner onto a long hallway, looking around artfully and smiling. They had been peering into classrooms and offices, up through the stairwell, under shelves, staying side by side and yet not once speaking to each other. Jan saw them from the archway at the other end. She stood upright, holding her books to her chest, and watched them. They were lithe and young and beautiful.

Later, she saw them at the lunch hall, under the red decorations for fall. This time, they seemed distant and bewildered. One lifted a peach to her mouth. She held the fruit close to her chin. For a moment she held it, her chin and the peach being fair and similar. Then she turned to the other as if stunned. The peach dropped to the floor. She looked down but did not retrieve it. Suddenly, both stood up with their trays, returned the dirty dishes to their proper place, and left the hall. It was as if the dropping fruit had frightened them beyond all proportion, as if it were a demon omen, or as if it meant something entirely different, something simple and yet so mysterious. Jan Scarlet sat before her lunch tray, curious and worrying.

Of course, at the lake, it was different. With the weather always fine, and she with good reasons now for seeing then, Jan worried less about them. So many years had passed since the lunch hall and since that morning on the quadrangle—"I'm Jan, we have class together"; "Oh," said the women, smiling. Since then, many years had passed, and many instances. The instance of the beach, for one, when Jan had asked them to come with her. "To the beach?" they said in unison. "Yes, we'll take a train there." And they did. They went as friends. Jan brought juice, and they brought chips, and they all laid out on cotton spreads in the center of the sand. And there was the instance when Jan had told them who her favorite painters were. It was then that they'd admired her for it. And she knew, for a while at least, that she would go on.

"There was a war," said one to the other, "that never ended."

"In your dreams, I imagine. Was it ugly?"

"Huge scraps of black iron, houses abandoned and tilted but not yet fallen, glass fixtures split down the middle, women tearing at their hair."

"Men using ropes to climb over walls?" said the other.

"Yes. That too."

They sat by the shed. A huge shadow came down around them. Across the lawn, by the house which was slowly spreading at its base, a drunken man lunged toward the sunlight. His legs were useless to him, and one of his sleeves was torn off at the shoulder. The lawn was yellowed with weeds.

"Sometimes, when I think of the future, all I can see

is animals, a new species of animal, taking over those cities, squatting in all the abandoned homes."

"And where are we then?"

"I don't know. That I can't answer." Now they gazed out toward the lake. It was warm with the dried yellows of the trees thrown over it, like a blanket. It was riding gently up onto the grass. And it curved around the lawn like a bigger hand of a handshake, coming to coves at the sides. Behind them, the drunken man had stumbled to a halt, and he too was eyeing the lake, as if it were entirely tame.

He loved her, it was true, or he loved having her. Jim Green locked up the cellar and turned. It was enough for the day. Jan was waiting. He had a craving to be with her just then, for a lifetime, always with her arms folded up between them so that her elbows were pressed in under his ribs. He slapped his hand against the cellar door, saying good-bye, and started up the stairs.

It was a small building but a sturdy one. It was his third. He leaned up against the car, confidently, having a look at it. A slim brick row house with no trim but a wrought-iron face of a god, or a lion, at its peak. The windows were dark since none of the tenants were home, and it seemed simple, but fine. "Not bad," he said. He drove away.

And Jim was simple too. He was just that way. He had a way of speaking that was plain and correct, and Jan loved him for it. His voice came down from some rocky coast, crashing in its rocky way, though far away, so that it wasn't exactly menacing. And it came down that way often: doing business, making plans, in the mornings, counting pros and cons. "There is a place where we will go tonight," he would say to Jan at breakfast. "The crowd is nice, and the drinks are big, and the band is well in tune.

You will enjoy yourself." His voice came down clear and hard. He had many things to say.

Sometimes, he shouted. "How in all hell do you fucking have the guts to do this?" he shouted once. It was dark. The young woman didn't move. She sat with her legs crossed, her elbows and knees at the corners of her, her breasts round and cold between. Her head was turned, as if listening to him. But she was thinking things of her own. "She was thinking a million different things," Jim explained later to Jan, in his plain tone.

"But she is *good*," said Jan, "they both are. So giving and so agreeable."

Jim said, in his plain tone, "They are good. But they are no good for a man."

And sometimes, he shouted louder, as on the lawn: "I could put it up you a thousand times! But I won't! I don't have time for your goddamn 'maybes'! There are women who know when they've seen what's best!"

Jim pulled into a space on Edgar, putting it into first to keep the car from rolling down the long hill to the gravel works. The huge levers and sixteen gears were coming to a halt over the pyramids of blue dust. Jan was waiting on the steps. Jim went to her. He strode over. He took her, in his arms. The duplex, which was his, his first, peaked up behind them against the dappled windows of a highrise and against the rusty sky. Jan Scarlet was dressed for fall. In her brownish knits and plaids, she seemed to fit the setting of the duplex, like a mammal in a habitat, like a native. She fit, neatly, the picture of the duplex, which was Jim's. It was his own. He took her in his arms.

"Should we go for a drink at the lake tonight?" asked Jan, since they'd all become friends when there was enough distance between them. Jim wasn't angry with the young women now, now that Jan was so loving and reliable, filling the space where they escaped him. "Do you mind?" Jan asked him.

"It's fine. We are all friends now," Jim said, beholding her against the pretty duplex. "Besides," he said, "the lake is the right place for evening."

"And what about the fire?" said one.

"Yes. It exploded colored cinders."

"You mean fireworks. *Fireworks* made patterns in the sky. But I was asking about the *fire*."

"Regardless. Inapplicable. There were sparks."

"Oh but not really. Not green, not dusty *rose!*"

"No," she said beaming, "just joking."

They sat on the lawn. A small speedboat mowed across the lake, leaving a trail of circular oils. They watched, motionless, and yet pleased.

"No, but what if I *had* been sleeping and the house when up? What if I *had* rolled over and seen the bottles of chemicals combusting?"

"I would crawl down to the foot of the bed," said the other, "making signals of cool air. Frantic, hysterical, happy or perhaps afraid, I would scream. 'Out! Surround it! To the lake!'"

The lake eased downward. The boat was gone. A great drawbridge appeared at the last two hills. the young women, dressed in their black and white dresses, leaned back, at last, with relief.

Since the beginning, Richard Mustard had cared for them. It was one of the things, he felt, he could afford to do. So when the time came, he looked in on them. They were placid and happy. They were pretty and kempt. They were on the lawn. So, he thought, just then there was nothing to concern him, he would let them be young as they pleased, and he went home.

Richard went home that day, and many days, to the towers. Verticals of terraces lined the backs like bone. Concrete footpaths looped around the shrubbery. The lobbies were rimmed with chipping tiles and figurines. Richard rode up to seventeen, his home. There he poured gin and considered things. He considered his concern for the girls as a magnanimous thing. And he was satisfied.

Around the room, the golden theme of the furnishings thrived. Bird-patterns in the sofa, gold leaves, brass book ends, autumn-print paper goods, key issues of key journals yellowing in the glow of his history: Richard loved his home. With the gin poured, he went to a chair he loved, past the dark portraits of his friends in golden frames, past the trophies, to the large TV. He sat. He had been, and was forever by name, the Colonel.

But later, the girls became worrisome. He went to see them often. And as they became more and more obstinate, unmanageable, the challenge grew greater, until, in the thick of it, Richard's mandate to care for them seemed almost as serious as certain missions in the past. It was his duty (yet again, so many duties, it seemed, he had had) to see that the girls had the proper lives. It was his duty to their father.

"Yes, he was a fine man," said Richard to the girls. "And he was a fine friend. In peace and in combat. We spent many years together."

The two women listened attentively, looking up at Richard's good form. And then Richard said, to end the conversation at the time when it was just right to end it, "Oh yes, I am true to his name."

It was in the fellow's last few years that he had called on the Colonel. "Richard," he had said, "I ask you." And Richard sat by the bed, amid the smells of sickness and toast, listening with care, challenged. He was challenged by the years of challenge to be matched. He had a record of victories, small and large, to beat. And he was, always, ready for more. "Richard," said the dying man, "I ask you one thing more. . . . My daughters, Richard, my daughters. . . ." The room was silent and clean. Richard, the Colonel, sat barrel-chested, upright by the bed, episodes of brashness, audacity, having grown dense on his shoulders. He nodded, thick-necked, noble. "Yes," he said pledging, "your daughters."

So when the time came, and he had tracked them down (first in their dormrooms at college, then in their flat that was Jim's on the hill), the Colonel took on the task of it, of loving. And he did, he admired their assets, he pondered their failings. The visits were difficult and rewarding. The job was tricky and important. And Richard, always loyal, humorless, was true to it.

In the evening, the gold theme became an amber one. Richard leafed through magazines. The melting light was a pleasure to him, but still something disturbed him. Still, it seemed there was a thing he was not fulfilling. And he was not himself, he was not restful. So, stacking up the significant issues and turning off the brass lamp that was shaped like an airplane with the bulb in its nose, he went to the phone. He felt a need for consultation, for negotiation of a plan. He felt the girls were not well, not right, and it was time for a plan to aid them. It was time they took on a project, something at which they would excel. Richard knew. He knew the father would have wanted, finally, excellence.

And it was the time too, that hour, that he often called Lenore. It rang. He and Lenore would discuss, hash out, decide. She was a woman, delicate with matters of psychology, though bold, admirably bold. It rang. Lenore did not answer. And this was odd. This was the hour when Richard always called her, and always Mrs. Peacock was there. Always, then, matters were solved with her, matters of friendship, matters of timing, matters of pride. Richard hung up the phone. He thought, Where could she be at this hour?

Afterwards, when he had tried to call Jan Scarlet, a young friend of the young girls, and found that she too wasn't home, Richard sat with the matter alone. He set his mind to it, visions of the dead father in combat reminding him. There were jobs they could do, interests to pursue, achievements, goals. He would help them choose some. Now, he would insist. There could be no more discussion or trouble about it.

Richard looked toward the window and strode over. He sighed. The city was quivering against the night, sparkling below. It spread out, in an orderly fashion, toward its own perimeter and toward the wild, unused lands. And then, suddenly, Richard noticed out there, past the last hatch of the grid, a small blot, a going black shimmering thing, a patch or a gap, like a rare jewel, or like a danger zone. It was the lake. Richard knew it. He knew the two girls sat beside it. And as he stared down from his tower at the facile map of the ground, he remembered. He breathed. He remembered what he had learned a hundred times. There was always some last solution.

The two women were alone on the lawn. One spoke: "What's more, in the light, I find myself floating. I dance in my station, completely autonomous." The lawn was enormous, hilly and flat, so huge one could see nothing beyond it. And in fact, they were dancing, all over the place.

"It's love," said the other. They sat down on the wood-slatted chairs, resting their arms on the blue designs. "And when it's love, the forest always escapes you. You can see nothing but lawn."

"It's love or it's chance, or it could be even that we're sisters, bound somehow." They held hands, smiling, over the blue designs.

"Somehow," said the one, staring out over the water, "when I bound up the stairs of a courthouse, or a cellar, I believe I am actually scaling a wall. And when I reach the top floor, or the height that I'd leapt toward, I find that in fact I was, I was scaling. My hands and feet are fast against the coarse vertical, gripping the windworn stone, high up, where it has withstood the pressure of the storms, the alacrity of a passionate air."

"Yes," said the other. "Perhaps there is just a passionate air between us, a storm, picking up the dust where we stand." They stood. Their arms were wrapped about each other. The lawn was on all sides. A wind came.

"Storm on a human scale, or a human, scaling a wall!" said the one, shouting now over the whistle riding between them, the funnel of wind running under them through the gap where only their necks didn't meet. She shouted: "The lake! Look!"

The lake was tortuous, seething. The storm had knocked it sideways, out over its rim, and water teemed on past the countryside. Water crossed over the tiers of farms, blacking out signposts, wrecking the wires. It flooded past houses, covering the rocks and natural protrusions, erasing everything. The women hid their eyes in each other. They held each other up against the storm. They hovered on the island of lawn.

In the morning, Lenore awoke as usual. The storm had passed, but a gray mood still lingered in the pantry. Lenore washed and did her morning things, as if last night had never happened, as if last night, like everything she'd ever done before, had been accounted for. Each morning thing she did was done openly, counted, justified, as if she had never had a thought to be ashamed of. The hanging up of nightclothes, feeding of the birds, the cutting of a grapefruit for breakfast, and pinning the hair in a bun: She was guiltless. She spoke benignly to the birds. She stood firmly on her principles, upright, tall. And when she was ready she went off to work at the bank, as usual, with purpose and with a great morality.

"Good morning, Mrs. Peacock, good morning."

She passed the urn of dried stalks, passed the bubbler and the mailgirl. The sunlight grew stronger as she advanced deeper into the bank, and the windows at the rear wall brightened with the hour. The storm had all but not occurred, and from her office, Lenore could see the perfect weather coming on. She phoned the Colonel.

Richard was relieved. Lenore's voice seemed to make him suddenly spirited, as if the lull of morning had sparked up at the touch of wires. He explained in this sudden, spirited way that he had tried to reach her last night at the usual hour, that he had had a matter on his mind, that he had yearned for an expedient solution. "It was the girls," he said. "I have a responsibility."

"Oh, Richard, yes, last night," said Lenore. "I had stepped out unexpectedly." There was a pause. A dump truck passed at street level. Lenore looked down into its dusty rubble. "Yes, I stepped out," she said. "Children down the block. They were misbehaving, running on a neighbor's lawn."

Richard listened. "I see," he said.

"Yes, I spoke to them firmly but with reason," she said. "I explained the implications. It was dusk. They understood. In the end they thanked me for the warning, and I saw that they lawn was not damaged. They ran off to play in the park."

Richard was relieved. He was jovial. Lenore had been a dependable friend, like a comrade or a house. She had been wise and simple and beautifully built. She had worn neatly cut dresses that narrowed at the knees, and heels that tipped back her shoulders and made her astoundingly tall. Her jewels were very few but fine, and

Richard equated their glimmer with a sure, shining character. He noted the gold settings of her brooches. He admired the plain green stones. And he spoke to her intimately, without hesitation. There had never been a sense of any romance between them.

"Yes, it's the girls," said Richard, recalling again the challenge and feeling courage, since now, with Lenore on the wire, he knew there would be a solution. "Yes, it's that they're lazy, Lenore. They're careless. They're pretty enough, and light-hearted, but I've discovered, Lenore, they're—they're uncommitted!"

Lenore stood, looking out, holding a tissue between her hand and the phone. She saw a string of pedestrians progressing along the opposite sidewalk. She saw their even paces, attache cases, lunch bags. She admired their promptness and their gravity. "Yes, the girls," she said, distracted. "They're like that."

"Do you know them?" asked the Colonel, surprised and with a sense that this was auspicious. He might as well leave the thing in her good hands and call it finished. He had as good as done his job.

"Yes, well, no," Lenore said, turning suddenly from the window. The pedestrians were gone, and she stared now at the office walls. "Well, not exactly, not well." She raised her voice, as if to cancel, by shouting, what she'd already said.

"But you know them? Then you must help."

"No, Richard, I don't know them. It was nothing really. They worked for me at one time. They were clerks." Down the hall clerks were tapping and clicking the office machines. Clerks were calling long distance, filling out cards. They were chatty yet meticulous. "But they didn't work out as clerks!"

"They didn't?"

"No, no they didn't." Lenore raised the tissue to her brow. She faced outward, gazing. There was tension in her arms. "It was nothing, really."

"What do you mean, 'It was nothing'?" said Richard. He got up from the golden sofa, growing agitated. He had thought it such a bright idea. He had thought she'd get them jobs. He'd even seen them both as clerks, perfecting skills, excelling!

"Richard, really. We must discuss this later."

"I have my word to keep, Lenore, and I need this information. Tell me what it is that they can't do!"

Lenore stepped backwards, suddenly becoming unsteady at the elegant points of her high-heeled shoes. She pitched backward, taking hold of the desk, adjusting her pose so that it seemed she was merely leaning there. But in fact she was backed up against her integrity. There was no way of sneaking behind it. There was nothing to do but to stand up in her status, to *account* for her actions. She raised a hand to the back of her head. Still, the bun was small and intact. "Alright, Richard," she said.

Richard softly on the other end: "It's a thing I must know about."

"Yes, Richard, but not a significant thing really. I mean to say, it was not a specific thing they had done, not a fashion in which they weren't adequate. It was, in fact, Richard—well, plainly, Richard—I just did not *like* them."

"I beg your pardon?"

"Yes, Richard, I didn't like them. It's true I had no grounds for it really, that it wasn't just. But Richard, they annoyed me!"

"I don't understand, Lenore, I don't see it. You must have had *reason*."

Lenore was silent a moment, inhaling, taking in the breath that would be her confession. All around her, she felt objects grow solid and the air become cramped with her own honesty. There was tightness in her lungs. "No, I had no reasons," she said, exhaling. She looked down. She was diminishing. The great broad desk filled the room behind her. And then she said, in a tiny voice that did not suit her, "I had only suspicions."

"What do you mean?"

"I mean I caught them doing things, certain things. There were no grounds, really, for accusation."

"What things, Lenore?" Richard was distrustful. He was slouching on the sofa.

"Things, Richard. I can't explain to you precisely. You see, Richard, I felt those girls were flighty, somehow, trivial. Not that they didn't accomplish things, they did their work, they did it to a tee. But then at times I caught them doing things, things that seemed—what?—silly." She began to pace the floor. She was waving the tissue, uncontrollably, in front of her. "I caught them dawdling, for example. I caught them once, holding hands. And then, at one time, I found that they were playing games. Not games exactly, but collecting things. On their desks! Whole scenes! Little panoramas made of figurines, small glass ponies, groups of tiny colored vials, toy boats, marbles!" Lenore's voice grew high and unsteady. Her speech escaped her rapidly.

"I see," he said attentively.

"Yes, you see. It was the things they did, not the things that they did wrong." She whispered: "There was something so terribly ominous about them."

"There was."

Lenore paused. She stood still, straightening her spine, and a huge relief came over her, a sense of freshness, a new size. Now, she felt, she could say anything at all. "And once, Richard, I even caught them kissing. It was nothing sordid, of course, nothing I couldn't tell you of right here on this phone. But there was something horribly frivolous about it, something foolish, Richard, something—silly."

"I see."

"No, Richard, I suppose you think that I was hard, that still I had no grounds to let them go." She spoke calmly now. She raised her hand to her head. Her hair was still neat against it. She felt the small round bun. And she felt she was herself again. She said, "I simply didn't like them, Richard. I couldn't bear their girlishness, their strange laughter. I couldn't *take* their conversations. I'll tell you, Richard, and this is all: In the end, I despised them."

Richard's head dropped to his hands. Around him, the beloved home grew blank and insignificant. The needless cushions faded into the sofa. Certificates of achievement turned white on the walls. "Lenore," he said, "I have a responsibility."

She said nothing.

"Lenore," he said. The phone slipped down to his jawbone. "Please, meet me at one."

She said, "Yes, I will."

"It's not that I don't remember our past, it's more that I don't know what it felt like to live it. I remember only what was said about it." It was dark. The lawn was like a great tank of water, with no cracks and no openings. The two women were floating in it. Only now and then, a glow would brush across the grass, as if the water were lit from under. "I remember the crisp twin beds, the weary father, the Christmases. I remember the day we met, the school yard and the statue of a woman, naked on a rock. And I remember the strong man who wanted you—that was later—and the mousy woman at a picnic. I can remember that we remarked on it."

"But the mousy woman wasn't there," said the other. "She was elsewhere, painting seascapes."

"Yes, but you had asked, 'Where is she?' And you mentioned that she should be. You said, 'She should have come along and painted all of us, in a group, drinking.'"

The moon came out. A green glow came down upon their faces. The young women gazed out at the lake, which was one with the grass. They spoke in tones that ended, that broke feebly against the expanse and the huge teal dimness. They wept.

"I remember only the skin of things, the tiniest portions. I remember what you said. 'Once,' you said, 'there was a doll house, wrapped in sheets, under the tree. Beside it stood a large box, full of furnishings. Sturdy little armchairs, dust-ruffles for the beds, a crib, and a porch swing. You had never been so overjoyed.'"

"That's true. That's what I told you," said the other. She looked out across the blue lawn, as if in its glimmer she could read the future.

"Yes. I remember the whole story. But I can't remember Christmas. I can't remember it." The young woman sat back, stiffening, gripping the cold frame of the lawn chair. She felt herself falling back. She was scared. And the lake was moving toward them, gradually, with the night tide.

"I'm afraid," said one to the other.

"We'll escape," said the other.

"But where will we go?"

The lake came toward them, folding over, steadily, a liquid that was heavy and opaque, viscous, like a poison. The lawn chairs were tipping toward the ground.

"We'll go to a place we've never been before. We'll go to town. It will be safe there. The men will let us in their homes. They'll feed us and cover us with blankets."

"But once, we *were* covered with blankets. You said so: A mohair so fine you could barely detect it. You said, 'You don't know it, but there's wool there. From out necks to our toes. Hold me tightly, and we'll imagine it!'"

"And we did."

"And there was." They held on. They leaned forward, keeping the chairs from falling all the way. And they spoke, keeping track of each other.

"And once I said, 'It's morning. Now we both have

jobs. We work as clerks,' I said. 'There are two blue sportscars in the road, each of which we'll drive to work, and the rumble of motors will ring across the water, making waves.'"

"And we did."

"There were."

"We drove at windspeed all around the county, dodging bunnies and rounding curves. We drove a full lap around the lake, passed the house of the monarchs and every Arab embassy. Embassies lined the route for miles with simulated deserts in between and flags of every possible design. And just then, when you waved at the last Persian child, we arrived."

"We did?"

"We did. You said, 'Here's our place of work.'"

"It was."

"It was a great stone bank with four domes. We parked and straightened our skirts. Money was stacked in the lot. Money was packed in boxes at the rear. There was money on the stairs."

"There was?"

"You said so."

The women grew silent. They watched the dawn shaping the lake as if morning were a story of history. They felt the chairs stand upright beneath them. And they imagined the jobs they might have had, the lives they might have led if only they had thought of them sooner.

All night long, Jonathan had been hidden in the bushes. He was chilled to the bone. He was nearly senseless with fatigue and with desire. Through the leaves and the fistfuls of rhododendron flowers that were magnified at the edge of his sight like pink thumbs on the lens of a camera, he could see the two girls. He saw them in the distance, their black dresses moving now and then in the breeze, their faces turning toward one another and then toward the lake. He saw every move they made.

When the sun was full up in the east, Jonathan at last got up from the ground. The front of his shirt was damp and creased where his stomach had been pressed to the dirt. It was time to go home and change his clothes. So squatting down and peering one last time through the leaves, Jonathan Plum said good-bye. He sighed. A warm flush came to his face as if his very blood were vowing to stay, spreading to his head and hands in an urge to hold this territory. His feet seemed to sink into the land.

At the bank, Jonathan was clean but distant. He looked away at every pause in the discussions. He punched in numbers automatically. He was quick at his work when he did it, but when the lunch hour came, and the streets widened with activity, Jonathan became sluggish. He dragged slowly through the rush of lunchers. He gazed blankly at the pastry shops, stopping for long intervals, until the hour had passed hours ago. When, finally, he returned to his desk at the west wall of the bank, his face was so dazed and fatigued that it seemed he didn't, in fact, belong there. All around him, clerks were picking up that last-hour speed. Lenders and saver grew restless in lines that ran sideways, askew. Jonathan sat down, disoriented. His eyes bulged with the nervous craving for something miles away. He grew feverish. He would do anything to have them. He would die.

"Mr. Plum!"

Jonathan looked up. He reached out a hand, in his anxiety, and grabbed hold of his calculator, pressing all the buttons at once. "Mrs. Peacock!"

"What is it, Mr. Plum? Are you sick? Where's your worksheet?"

And suddenly Jonathan's posture changed. An

arrow shot up through his neck, drawing his whole head back, so that his jaw was strangely craning forward. Mrs. Peacock laid her hand gently on his, so that the buttons for numbers and for arithmetic operations were now pressed all at once and doubly.

"Mr. Plum," said Lenore softly.

But Jonathan's pose did not change. His mouth was wet and tense. His lips were pulled up unnaturally, showing his incisors, like the lips of a dangerous dog. And his temples turned a watery blue. In his mind were a million things, more things that he could ever untangle. Instead, he whispered hoarsely, "Everything is fine!"

That night, as he walked down the steps from his room and along the empty street, past the noses of new trucks lined up at the edge of the sales lot, as he headed again to the rhododendrons, Jonathan stared at his hands. He hated them. Within him, the struggle of lust against dignity grew murderous. He walked stiffly, a sickness growing at each step. He went, again, in the aching cold night, to watch them, to pine. And as he went, he hated going. The fight rose in his neck. The night was ugly and alluring. He arrived at the flowering bushes. They were luscious and hideous. He loved them, and yet he despised this way that he was.

But it was not Jonathan.

"Who is it?" They sat on the lawn. The sky of the nation was blue and bigger than they could ever see. "How lovely," they said. "It could be a visitor."

But it was not Jonathan. It was Jan. The two women looked up at the high, peaked house, from which visitors often descended. They looked up at the sharp eaves and the chimneys jutting into the plain sky. They saw the heavy door, symmetrical between the fourteen columns, and the flag pinned up on the western wall. From the doors, the stone steps spread as they descended, becoming so broad at the bottom that it seemed some essence of house might flood down them, spilling out across the entire lawn. But it was Jan that came down them. She paused at the top, eyeing the scene from above. Then she came down, onto the lawn and onto the soft patch they had found on it.

Jan slid her hand along the banister. She wore plaid slacks and a man's shirt that was dabbed with random colors. It was messy. She was an artist. When she was several yards away from them, she stopped. She made a frame with her fingers and composed them in it. She held up her thumb at arm's length and checked the proportions. She must have been planning a canvas.

The two women were smiling, entertained. They watched Jan's actions as if they were motions of great skill. And then Jan sat down on the grass between them. Her smock draped over her knees, and she looked up, beaming. "I am so happy to see you," she said. "I've been dying to come tell you about my new paintings." And she was. She knew her friends were smart and artistic though they never painted or wrote things down. She knew they had many deep and contradicting feelings. They had, she knew, a sensibility. And she wanted in fact to have it as her own.

The young women looked over the top of her head. The lake was rippling emphatically, tripping up on its shores. But they could detect to pattern of waves across it. They smiled and looked down at her.

Jan grew restless. She pulled up bits of grass and pinched her knuckles and rolled in tiny rolls the tails of her shirt. When they looked at her, she grew uncertain. She could find no agreement in their eyes, no flash of the past or preestablished confirmation. Everything they looked upon shrank to presumption.

"I *mean*," Jan said, "you'd understand my inspiration."

"Oh. Inspiration," said the one. Still they looked down at her, blankly, smiling.

"Yes, inspiration. You know the feeling. Yes, my hands began to quiver, I was hot, my whole body was involved in it. I was up there, all morning, in my attic studio, Jim was gone, and I was completely alone, and yet so full of passion. I couldn't stop! It was beautiful!" Jan stopped. She waited to see their emotions, the gasp of excitement, the flush of their empathy. She felt they were so close to her, there on the patch of grass, under a glorious sun, feeling the most subtle of feelings.

The young women looked up again at the lake. They must have been thinking. Jan could see in their eyes a breadth of comprehension as broad as the lawn. She wanted to see the lake with them and think what they thought when they saw. She spoke to them, calling out, it seemed, from a distance. "But do you see what I mean—about painting?"

"Well, no," said the one. "Not for certain."

"But you must! Who else would understand? That moment of sheer inspiration, shivers going up your spine. Beads of sweat forming!" Jan raised her voice, making motions full of gesture with her hands, gestures of greatness, gestures of truth. How could she convince them? How could she explain that she was one of them, gazing out at the hills, feeling every ripple in the scene? She too was troubled and riddles with subtleties! "I was exhausted," she said in her most persuasive tone, her voice escaping through the taut opening of her throat. "I was exhausted. I was fulfilled. Think of it!"

The two women sat in canvas chairs. One swung her feet, her heels barely brushing across the lawn. Behind them, the house was humming like a large machine, the whole family busy back and forth with summer chores. In front, the lake was black and shimmering like a vast hot parking lot. "I *am* thinking of it," said the one.

"And I am thinking," said the other, "of a house with tall open windows, but no breeze blowing, and no one home but myself. I walk down a long hallway. The walls look the same, as if they were the only walls I'd ever seen. There is a worn ocher couch in the far room. I sit in it. But I don't relax. Nothing in my muscles slackens. I look at the tilting lamp, the dirty bowl full of nails and screws. Then I tap my finger against my knee, but this doesn't please me. It is only a tapping without a want or will. The tapping is completely deserted."

Jan looked at her with a face of injury, like a punished child's or a mother's. Her torso seemed to draw back, in her anger, to depart from them. "You're not listening," she said quietly, distinguishing herself and growing stronger. "I was talking about painting!" she said loudly, feeling, suddenly, a certain clarity in the scene. Her whole scope seemed to right itself, to sit up pert in her mind, and the scene fell into two-point perspective, the trees being smaller than the house, the fence posts going shorter with the distance. "You're not listening!"

"We are."

But Jan didn't hear. She was suddenly thrilled by the new keenness of her focus. She looked at the women in front of her, and she looked at the lake. She saw that the chairs were but sixteen paces from the shore, the shore was some ninety-eight from the house, and she was but a half-step from where they were. She saw the dotted dresses of her friends, the limp collars, and the place where one's zipper was pulling apart at the seam. She saw the many ends of their long hair and the precise angles of their noses. "You don't care a hoot, do you?" Jan said.

"We do."

"We care, but sometimes, we don't."

Jan stared at them, amazed. She saw the breadth of their gazes, and she knew then that the breadth was merely emptiness.

"Sometimes, the day is brighter than we ever expected. The grass seems all ablaze, and just behind our eyes we feel a small round pain. All through the day, this pain is inflating, growing outward like an enormous sphere. We look around and everywhere the sphere is surrounding us. We see a man. He is far away, walking slowly across the lawn. Each step he takes is heavy and pounding, filled with this pain. Later, he tells us he is a healthy man and of a happy frame of mind. We find it so hard to believe. We are simply amazed. And then the great sphere shrivels up to nothing."

Jan cried out, "So what! So what does that mean!"

But it seemed they'd forgotten. They looked at her, low-lidded, imagining apologies. Jan stood. Her fingers were spread fiercely at her sides. Two veins in her neck, from her ears to her collar, were showing. She shouted. "You're insane!" she said. "The two of you! And you have no idea what it means to be a friend!"

In the city, businesses ran like clockwork. Colonel Mustard passed through the glass doors of the hotel dining room. He strode through the lobby which was pretty and shiny. He passed the brass sconces and the paintings of angels on the wall, and he stepped out into the shiny air. In the streets, the trucks rumbled and stopped at traffic lights. Small men in shirtsleeves ran past, picking up and delivering. The Colonel took a long easy breath. He was pleased.

Richard was pleased with the outcome of their meeting. He was glad at the recollection of his friend, Lenore, her neck so long, her hand so comfortably holding the stem of her glass. She had been practical, daring, aiming so boldly at the crux of his troubles. He had watched her pointing out options, pressing her fingers into the tablecloth, leaving vague pockets in the white damask to show from what angles he might take care of the girls. And Lenore had reminded him, just by her manner, that all things were a matter of strategy. Every obstacle, every project, he'd remembered, was merely a matter of making a plan.

Now the wine was in his forehead. He smiled. He passed down the avenue turning left on the boulevard, past the statue of the battle of Gunn. He made straight for the lake, with a march in his step, with a rhythm of purpose, or of a hooved animal. When he arrived, the light was tending downward. The wine was behind his ears. He stood at the top of the broad stone steps, looking down on the lake and the girls. The girls were some nineteen paces from the shore, and the landing where he stood, inspecting, was higher than it had ever been before.

"Ahoy!" Richard shouted from the top.

The young women smiled and waved. In answer they shouted, "Ahoy!"

Richard came down the steps and strode, confidently, toward them. He wore a large gray sweater-vest with a shortsleeved shirt underneath that was of a sheer but quality cotton blend. He wore large heavy oxfords that were hardy enough for safari men. They had deep treads on the undersides that imprinted the lawn with a most distinctive pattern. Weeks later, in the middle of the night, Jan Scarlet would still know that the Colonel had been there.

Richard moved in front of them, between the lake and their chairs. He said nothing for a moment, as he aligned himself, having a look at them. Behind him, the lake seemed to lower itself in response to his size, as if bowing down to him, as if it would do whatever it was told.

Looking up at him, the girls noticed the fine white sideburns and smiled. "Well, hello," said the one, in greeting. Then they both looked down at their shoes. They followed the laces with their eyes. The grass came up around their soles. "How nice that you've come. Now we can all watch the day end together."

The Colonel, however, had not come to watch the day end. That was nothing to him. Coming was merely a part of his strategy. And there was more. He stepped toward them. His footprints lay like two striped bass, caught, on the deck of a boat. "No," he said. "Actually, I have come to discuss certain matters."

The women looked up. They looked all around them, as if the matter might be standing there. They looked toward the tool shed and the rocks. They looked down toward the tiny marina where seven orange sails swayed gently back and forth. "Boats?" said the one, alarmed. "Is it something to do with the boats?"

The Colonel turned around since, in his discussion, he hoped to be thorough, to check every reference, to curb any misunderstandings. The boats were out on the water, moving in circles and serpentines. "No," he said, "not the boats. Now listen here. I've come to discuss certain matters, matters you are not to take lightly." The light was siphoning off the lawn, beginning now to drain off the edge of the west. Richard began pacing up and down very slowly. "It all started forty-two years ago," he said. "It was early morning, and we were in a tent. We were squatting down, eating beans, potatoes, sausages. Your father ate everything on his plate." Richard turned and looked at the girls. "Now," he said, "when he was finished, he put down his fork, and he stood up, and he said to me, 'Richard, we must never stop.' He said, 'Our duty, Richard, is to do what we are capable of doing, to the very *best* of our ability.'"

The young women listened to him attentively. It was a story they had never heard.

"Do you see?" asked Richard with gravity, and with his large chin lowered into the white collar.

The women nodded. They did. They saw the tall father hunching in the tent. They saw the earthenware plate he held with its green glazed surface. And they saw the strings of red beads, attached to the tent supports, hanging down around him.

"Well," said Richard, "it is time. You have sat here long enough." There was a softening of his voice, a strain of apology, and he began again to pace, looking at the ground. His hands were in his pockets. He said, "You, as humans, must not be wasted."

The young women watched him. They could smell the waste of the lake coming up in the breeze. They smelled the fish and the wet dirt of the shore. They were confused.

"Now, I have a plan," said Richard, "to engage you. Some projects," he added, "you will take on." He took a long breath. He was prepared to be clear-headed yet gentle. "First, you must move back to the flat on the hill. You can take all your things, your dresses, your towels, and you can buy some practical furnishings. Then you must work at the bank. Mrs. Peacock has agreed to rehire you. The pay will be low and the hours will be long, but it will be something of which you are capable." Richard stopped again. Now he looked at them squarely. He could feel, rising in his broad chest, his own magnanimity. "It is the life, finally, your father would have wanted."

Now the young women looked out at the darkening mountains. They could see the fifteen brick houses lining the newest road. To the east, a blackness was covering the plain. And along the shore the lake was empty, except for the six bits of paper and wood, floating.

Richard waited. "Well?" he said.

The young women looked across the lawn, one way and then another. It was not their home.

Richard repeated, "Well?" He said, "I have a responsibility. Do you understand?"

But they were silent.

"Do you understand?" he said, raising his voice just slightly.

The women looked up at him wide-eyed. They wondered about the flat on the hill, whether it was stark or homey. They wondered if the streets were busy or slow. They couldn't remember. They had tears in their eyes.

"Speak up then!"

They were silent.

Richard took his hands from his pockets and pressed his ten fingers against his brow. The wine was everywhere. He was enraged. "I have had enough of the both of you! You must do what I tell you," he shouted, "or you'll be sorry!"

Later, Jim went down to the lake with Jan. "You told me yourself," he said, "that they were kind. You have no reason to change your opinion."

Jan was silent and unresponsive. Only now and then, she blew a quick breath of exasperation through her nose. She wore her oldest clothes.

Jim said, "Come now."

As they reached the big house, Jan began to clutch her purse to her chest so tightly it seemed she might fit in it. It seemed she was ready to insist on going home. But she didn't. She shuffled along the flagstone porch that rounded the house toward the rear.

At the landing, Jim took her by the arm. He was grinning. Something in the night air, and in the hardness of her arm, was, to him, intriguing. He thought of the three of them quarreling. He was on the sidelines, admiring his own disinterest. And the small thought was there, within him, that someone always got the spoils.

At the shore, the water seemed to be bubbling. The two women could see the flecks of light appear, drift, float up against the rocks, and then extinguish. But the bubbles seemed to come at random. The women were bored. They turned and looked up toward the house. "Oh," said the one, "there are people coming." And there were. The young women saw Jim and Jan descending. They saw the two disparate figures, one so tall with long arms and full shoulders, one so stiff and little. And Jim was stopping at every third step, turning around to speak to Jan three steps above him, turning the large torso that seemed to be wrapped so tightly at the waist. When they reached the bottom, Jim pointed and told her something. He said, perhaps, "Go now." And then he ran back up the stairs, swung open the double doors and went inside.

Jan didn't move. She didn't shout out, "Hello there, we're visiting." She stood, looking at the ground.

The young women whispered. "Do you suppose he's making her come here forcibly?"

"Or do you think he's bringing her a gift, and she's feeling shy?"

"Or it could be she's feeling nothing. She's entirely numb. And he's planning a shock to awake her."

When Jim returned he was holding four glasses in one hand, the stems between his fingers. In the other hand was a bottle of scotch. "Hello," he said, calling out, in his unmistaken tone. Behind his voice, the rocky coast was teeming. "It is time for cocktails."

The women laughed. They said, "How nice." Jan stood behind them.

And it was just then that the sun had gone down. It was then that any motion, the breath of any living thing, was veering inward. It was the hour when sounds began coming closer, sounds of water, sounds of voices, and the lawn was broadening away. To the left, the shed was withdrawing. The hydrangeas were fading to violet and receding. The hedges were turning to gray. Jim set the bottle down in the grass. He spoke, in his plain tone, as he turned the glasses upright. He said, "We will drink it neat tonight." His voice was loud and close.

But still, Jan stood clenched outside them. She was

disgusted. To her, the drink was nothing. She watched them, but she didn't care. She watched the one take her afghan from her knees and spread it on the ground. She watched the three of them sit down at the corners. Jim poured. And she looked at the two young women, sitting up cross-legged lit witless pups, or like infants. They were easy. She despised them.

"Okay, Love, have a drink now," Jim said. He held out a glass to her as a sign. Jan trusted him. Then he turned to the women, lifting up his own glass. "Jan has some things to say."

Jan moved inward. The afghan was dimming into the lawn, and Jan could barely distinguish its edges, as she bent, trying to find a place on it. Then the weave appeared, fuzzy and spotted. The faces came up around her.

"Don't you?" Jim said.

She shifted her seat closer to him. She cleared her throat. "No," she said.

Jim smiled. He was lying sideways, propped on his elbow, his legs stretched out behind her, and he nudged Jan's buttocks with his knee. "Go ahead now," he said, bending the knee and turning it upward, so that his hips faced up toward the big night.

Jan waited for him to nudge her again. He didn't. She said, "No. There is nothing to be said."

The women were listening closely. One spoke: "But hardly," she said. "I mean, I was just thinking of saying myself that one could say nothing or one could say something else."

Jan stared at her. The woman thought she was funny. Jan hated her.

"The saying," the one woman went on, "seems to be infinite. It seems to extend, like an endless array of discrete things—little trinkets, dried grass, popcorn, autumn leaves. We, it seems, are merely rolling in it. And when we stand up and shake it off our clothes, it remains there, all spread out, endlessly."

Jim listened to her and watched her lips move. He was amused. She was missing the point, and yet still she was enchanting.

The woman continued: "Oh, not that one wouldn't sometimes get tired of it, Jan, if the prattle went on and on, if, say, on a night like this one, a calm but varied voice kept blowing through the grass, touching on subjects like boats and stones, trying out ideas endlessly. Oh, no. I understand: One sometimes becomes utterly exhausted."

The two women now turned to Jim. Their faces were lifted and optimistic. They smiled at him, waiting to see if they'd soothed his friend. But Jan stared at the ground.

Jim was fingering the afghan. He smiled back at them with a huge strength in his eyes, as if with his eyes he were driving a semi. Jan's back, which was now in the corner of his sight, appeared merely as a dark spot, like a shadow or a wall. He looked past her. He looked at the two of them. They were weak and yet graceful. They were flighty and trifling, and yet they were long-necked, fleshly. They were full-breasted. He could see through their dresses. One of them was turned slightly sideways so that he could see, hazy through the fabric, the heavy cupped underside of her, as if his hand were already holding it. His eyes were on her nipple, but it seemed, instead, he had his tongue there.

"Well," said one of the girls, turning now toward the lake and looking outward. "Maybe we should all be very quiet tonight, and just watch, watch how dark the night grows."

Eventually, Jan looked up. She looked up to check on things, to see if they were looking at her. But instead she saw other things. They were things she couldn't believe. At one time her focus had sharpened, her vision of her friends had cleared, but now it was as if a whole new layer were peeling back, like a curtain, revealing even more. Jan lurched, undetectably, backward. She was amazed. She was ill. She saw the women's shoulders nearly bared. She saw their legs outstretched. She saw their chins craned forward, both of them, so their necks looked long and yearning. And she saw the mouths, half open, as if in a moment their tongues would come out to beckon him. She turned, suddenly, to Jim. He was perspiring. She saw his fingers creeping across the afghan, as if he couldn't stop them. She saw a wetness dripping at the corner of his lips. All around her, the lawn was black and humid.

She muttered, nearly hissing, "You've had it all planned, haven't you? You think I'm stupid. You think you'll shatter my illusions! You slime!" And suddenly Jan stood up. She stood up, and she ran. She ran weakly, stumbling over the huge dark lawn. She pressed her tiny hands against her temples. Running, she pressed them in her eyes. Once, she fell, and rising, leaving the pieces of grass stuck on her palms, leaving the stinging in her knees to run all through her, she began to cry. A terrible moaning came up in her. She ran past the house. She ran, gaining speed, onto the drive. And then she drove, dangerously, through the town. And in her tiny, shaking hands, she felt a great hot power growing.

Jim watched her until she disappeared behind the house. He saw her stumble on a rake that was leaning up against it. "She'll be fine," he said.

The two women sat up straight and stiff. They were startled. One put her hand to her brow and shook her head. "Will she?"

"Was that anger?" asked the other. "Was that jealousy?"

"Something we did," they said. Their voices were high and weary. "To her, it seems, something we did had a meaning."

One of them bent at the middle and held both of her shoes. The other one looked at her knees. The knees seemed far away. She said, "Sometimes, I reach up into the air, thinking there is a cord up there, which, if I pull it, will make the scene change." Her voice went higher and higher, escaping her. She was crying. "I wave my hand around, all around, trying to find it, but there's no cord there, anywhere!"

Meanwhile, Jim was watching over them. The night was darkening still, just as he'd expected. The ground was spreading, flat and luxurious, spacious, and yet somehow perfectly isolated. He figured, eventually, they'd excuse themselves.

And they did. The women sipped their liquor until the crying burned away. It seemed, over the heat of it, their sobs evaporated. The one at last let go of her shoes and sat back. The other looked away from her knees and out at the lake which, just then, was motionless.

Jim watched them, rocking, drinking. He watched their necks relaxing, their limbs unfurling. He moved, inward. He thought of wiping the tears away. He thought of his fingers sliding over their faces. He said, softly, soothing them, "Come on. Drink up." He felt his ribs and his underarm growing warm against the afghan. "That's it. Drink up." And he thought of his hands, both hands at once, sliding.

Jan paced across the front room of the duplex. There were no lights on. Occasionally, she picked up a book or a wrench or a piece of pipe from the tool table. She would hold it there for a minute, in the dark, in her new, powerful palms. And then she would let it drop, smack, on the bare wood floor.

When Jim arrived, she stood in the doorway, furious. He tried to pass her. He grabbed her wrist and threw it down against her side. She shouted. "You did it to them, didn't you?"

Jim stamped to the bedroom and thin-lipped, silent, began to take off his clothes. He unbuttoned his shirt and tore it off him. It was clean-smelling and unwrinkled.

"You did, didn't you? You did it to both of them!"

But Jim didn't answer. He wasn't listening. He was lying flat on the bed, his chest heaving.

"They let you this time. They let you do it to them, didn't they!"

But Jim didn't hear. He didn't care. He was lying there, his fists clenched on his stomach. Around him, the room was dim and ordinary. Then he felt a heat creep across his brow and around his eyes. He felt a cramping in his hands, which were tense and dry. And he muttered, "Cunts. Next time."

The Colonel phoned Lenore. "No, no," she said. "I was just taking lunch. Not at all." She was gazing out the rear window of the bank, watching the policemen on the corner, telling jokes and stories. Behind her, the pâté and boiled eggs were half-eaten on her desk. She turned from the window. "I see," she said. "No, I'm not surprised."

Later, when the Colonel had begged to meet her and she'd agreed, and the long curtains were drawn across the windows, Lenore sat down in the corner chair. The afternoon light glowed through the drapes, turning the whole room strangely yellow. Lenore sat in the corner chair, her ankles crossed, her heels higher than ever. She picked five loose hairs from her dress at her knees. And she eyed the long silk rope that hung, harmless, alongside the curtains.

When, finally, she went back to her desk, she straightened her dress so that the zipper hung like a plumb line behind her and the bodice no longer buckled under her arm. The dress was a dark textured weave with threads of pale blue running through it. She lined up the clasp of her pearls with its zipper. She straightened the rings on her fingers. She spoke softly to herself. "Lenore," she said, "men and women are depending on you, to help them build homes, to educate their young ones, to grow." She said, "There is no time to be wasted."

Then she sat down, pulling a large stack of files to the clean space in front of her. She looked at the writing on them in her own earnest hand. But there was something repellent in everything. Her script was tipped too far to the left. The desk was too broad. The eggs smelled inhuman. Lenore forced her eyes to the page, and she began transcribing, leaning into the new forms, filling in figures, marking checks and stars. Page after page she completed, resourceful, determined. She ignored the plate of pâté. And when she had started the last seven sheets, she spoke again. Softly to herself she spoke: "Richard, this is not something, I'm sorry, that I'll be concerned with."

Again, that night, Jonathan went to the bushes. He couldn't bear it. He had tried to stay away, but the nighttimes reminded him, always.

This time, he brought a blanket. Behind the rhododendrons, where the shrubs formed a rear wall and the branches overhead formed a roof, the ground was softened and damp. Twigs and dead leaves were broken into tiny pieces like piled flakes, a fine mulch. Jonathan Plum lay down. He lay on his side and looked out.

They were there. They were sitting in the lawn chairs, their heads tipped back to see the stars, their necks blue in the night light. Their arms were bare and slender on the arms of the chairs. Their breasts were enormous.

Jonathan breathed deeply. There was a pain in the back of his throat. He felt he needed to cough or to drink huge quantities of a thick, sweet substance. He breathed again. There was a noise in his lungs. He ran his hand lightly down his face and then down his own tight neck.

For days, Jim said nothing to her. "Please," Jan would say, "let's talk it over. You know in time I'll forgive you." At night they lay side by side without touching each other.

Eventually, he would answer her curtly. "Where are you going?" she asked him every evening.

"I am going to meet my friend Jonathan," he said, pulling on his jacket. And that was all. She watched him as he went down the back stairs. He didn't check the banisters or the gas meter. He didn't put the lids back on the garbage cans. He went straight for the car.

And every night Jan was alone. She was bitter. She didn't make dinner. She would wander from room to room, scratching the black marks on the walls, pulling the snags in the bedspread, the drapes. Sometimes, she would wander up to her attic studio and stare at the unfinished canvases. But she was uninspired. She thought of the young women speaking. "Inspiration?" they had said. And sometimes, she picked up a small knife from the table. She eyed a blot of red paint on her palette. She felt a terrible passion.

But, in fact, Jim did not go to see Jonathan. Instead, he went to the bar, alone. He sat on the far barstool, the one by the door and the stuffed paw of a bear. He fingered the claws absentmindedly, and he drank eight shots of whiskey. Night after night, he sat there, slouching. His shoulders came forward, as if to hide a stain on his clean broad chest. He tapped the claws or ran his hands through the dead fur. And always, he thought, he made plans. He thought of how he would sneak up, how he would take hold of an arm or a wrist. He would show them what it was to be scared. And when they were quaking and willing, sobbing probably, and bent at the waist so that their dresses fell away at the shoulders, then he would show them what it was they'd missed.

The Colonel shouted on the third day, "Then where is she!"

"Pardon me, Sir, but I told you. She didn't say. She only told me to take down the name!"

Richard hung up the phone. It was five o'clock and still no sign of Lenore. For three days, he had tried to reach her, but now, just in his hour of need, she had disappeared. Richard strode to the window. He put his hands on the sill, between the ashtray and the brass statue of a hawk. He was ashamed. Where had she gone for three days? Why did she leave him? To mock him? To prove that his duty, for once, was too much? Did she think she would show him that this mission, this petty one, so harmless, domestic, was one he couldn't take on alone?

Below him, the city spread out like a model or like a scrap of gold lamé. The streetlights were just coming on. The windows were showing up bright white or amber, and carlights were moving through the streets like mice with white noses. It all seemed so small. Richard shook his head, weak with disgrace, exhausted. He was failing. Out there the city was tame and calm with evening. The buildings would fit in the palms of his hands. And yet, he was failing.

Again, he rang. This time, he phoned her at home, thinking she may have at least come back for dinner. The ringing began. He waited. He threw back his shoulders, holding the phone firmly to his ear, feeling again slightly hopeful. But it rang. It rang again and again. And in the silences or the faint humming between the high long sounds, Richard thought he heard awful, muffled laughter, a sickening, airy laughter that was meant only for him. He slammed down the phone. Why did he bother? What did he want of her? Why did he imagine himself so helpless alone?

The tiny lights were pricking the window. The sky

was growing red and gray. Richard strode over. Now, the city seemed all packed in together, streets and buildings clutching one another, timid, under the great height. Brittle strands of steel and light criss-crossed jaggedly. Richard was indignant. He thought of all the things he'd done before, the heroic deeds, the victories. He thought of running across open fields, advancing. And he looked out toward the edge of town, the open spaces, the lawns. He looked hard at the lake. No, he thought, this is simple. He moved his face up to the glass. He held the neck of the hawk. No *this*, he thought, will not stop me.

At the lake, the women sat on canvas chairs that slowly became damp underneath them. Suddenly, they were afraid of the dark.

"Scared of the dark itself," said the other. "As if it were a thing of substance, of objects, angles, corners, thin sheets of a dark mineral, invisible things we could never name."

They paused. They felt their elbows knock once or twice against the wooden arms of the chairs. They looked out across the lake at the two towers sharp as knifepoints at their peaks. They looked at the dark heaving of the hills.

"Perhaps we *should* move to town," said the one. "Then at night we could light candles or open the oven door so that the bulb would go on and the light shine out from its hollow."

"But then what? Then what? Then the tables and chairs might be visible, the collection of painted eggs, the shells, but only the outlines would be clear. Still, there would be darkness, something or nothing inside. And still, outside the walls of the flat, still there would be a monstrous, unimaginable world."

"Yes," said the one. She was silent. She could see the

icy surface of the lake, but it was underneath, the depth, that scared her. She spoke: "And then at any minute, a man might appear, a delivery man or a neighbor. Our necks would stiffen. And when we went to the door, he might start telling us things, things we couldn't believe. 'Quickly,' he might say, 'a child has been wounded in your yard.' Or, 'Come now, there's a fire down below. You must evacuate immediately!' Or he might speak very softly, urgent, 'Every woman under forty who lives in this house will die of a disease of the organs.'"

They stopped. They looked west. The new houses were all still vacant. They looked down at their shoes. The leather was soaked with dew. There seemed to be nowhere to go.

It was later than usual. Jan Scarlet sat on the back steps, overlooking the empty parking spaces. Jim had not come home to change his clothes. Jan sat with her legs folded close to her, and with nothing to do with her hands. It could be he was still fixing shingles at the threeplex on Eighty-third, or perhaps the car had broken down as he'd come through town on his way, or maybe he had gone straight to the bars. Jan had her hands on her knees. She listened, continually, for a motor.

Later, she began picking little splinters of wood from the steps. She felt for the rough spots. She grabbed hold of a loose point. She peeled up the tiny shards, as if there were a skilled and proper way to do it. She pretended this was her craft. But only more time passed.

She looked up. The pavement was gray, like a hollow, lit by a small light. Then, gradually, she knew. She knew Jim wasn't late on the job or stranded at a gas station. She knew he was deliberately staying away. He was at the bar, drunk and mocking her. Or he was off with Jonathan, telling jokes. Or he was there, out there on the big, filthy lawn, doing it again.

She got up and flung open the back door. The stairs were dark. The banister was dull and unpainted. She stamped past the work table that smelled of oil. And, in all her clothes, her hair uncombed, her fists perspiring, she got into the bed.

Finally, Jim came. It had been hours. But Jan was still awake, facing the wall. She heard him breathing unevenly as he took off his clothes. She felt him getting under the sheets. She felt a tremendous heat, as if a steam were pouring off his skin, filling all the spaces underneath. And then she thought she felt the bed, just the outer casing of the mattress, begin to quiver.

He did it, she thought. He did it so much it made him shiver. Where else could he have been all this time? Jan curled away from him and cupped her hands around her face to keep the noises in her throat from sounding. She bit down on the butt of her palm. And them, she thought, they did it to him. They put their hands all over him. And then they let him loose. They sent him back, limp, like a spent man or a dead sparrow.

Jan couldn't lie there any longer. The heat of him was impossible. Still, she had on all her clothes, and her shoes were nearby in the corner. She knew the town was big and emptied. The streets spanned miles, dark and quiet. And she knew that no one, in all those sleeping houses, would hear her car racing past them.

The Colonel sat up in his bed. All this time, he had felt determined, and yet he had not thought of a solution. And then he turned on the light. He stood up at attention. He flattened the front of his pajamas. And he smoothed back his hair. The horns of the ramhead threw shadows up toward the ceiling. The lamp shade was a deep, soft gold. And the walnut dresser from Germany had more drawers than he could ever use. But now he clasped his hands together and set his jaw, as if he knew precisely what to do. He bent down carefully, holding the rim of the nightstand. He kneeled on one knee. And he began searching for something in the corner of the lowest drawer. He shoved aside the unused socks and underwear, the shaving brush, the Russian hat, and he felt all the way to the rear.

Jonathan whispered over and over to himself: "Not tonight, not tonight. . . ." He sat at the small kitchen table, his hands around a mug of tea, making this resolution. He was testing himself, not to see if he could give them up entirely, but simply to see if this once, he could show a measure of control. "Come, John, just once, stay home."

For a while, he held on, sitting. In front of him, the stove, the soiled cupboard, and the greasy photo of a baseball team were things that he could fix on. He stared at the empty egg carton as if it would teach him stay.

But it was not long. It was not long before the heat started, and the ugliness of the dim kitchen, the lidless kettle, filled him with a mixed desire. It was tender and selfless. It was brutish and murderous. He stared at the curves of the milk pitcher. The ladle and the long blunt spatula seemed slowly to come alive. And he felt, as he reached to keep the cutting knife from snaking across the counter, his cheeks and hands begin to swell. A hideous groan came out of him. He stood and grabbed up his raincoat. And he left the chair, fallen on its side.

Jan was back in bed. Her eyes were wide open, her body straight and still, as if frozen. Jim lay beside her, sleeping fitfully. At intervals, he made loud mumbled sounds, sounds of surprise or of a horrible fight. Without

moving, without a single twitch of the frozen limbs, Jan
spoke. She spoke calmly, as if Jim could hear. "We will
go to see them in the morning," she said. Coldly, she said,
"We will forgive them."

It was nearly dawn. All around the lawn, the hedges
were heavy with stillness. Behind the shed, the azaleas
glistened with dew. No birds hopped in the grass. And
at the far side of the lake, just below the freeway at the
base of the hills, a fine gray streak appeared across the
water.

The house was vague and imposing. On top, the
many planes of the roof varied in shade. Some were
nearly black, and some were merely dim, like the sky. No
breeze rustled in the flag. But on the landing, there was
one lean dark shadow that seemed, just slightly, to stir. It
may have been the shadow of one of the porch columns,
thrown against the house. Or it may have been simply a
ladder, or a long plank, in the dark, leaning there. Or
perhaps it was the figure of a man, very slender, or a
woman, tall, in a straight dress, on high heels, with her
hair pulled tightly against her head. But it stirred only
once, and then it was gone. In the center of the lawn, the
canvas chairs were empty.

The Colonel was back in bed, the strapping torso
curled like a small child's. The pillow was gathered up
in his arms, pressed against his chest and face. On the
floor by the bed, everything was thrown in a heap: the
heavy shoes, the wool trousers, the overcoat.

Suddenly, the phone rang. The Colonel jolted
upright, his lungs filled to bursting, unable to exhale.
"What? Lenore? It's you?" He listened to her strained

voice coming over the wires. He could not understand
her. She was sobbing. "What? Meet you? I can't meet
you. Where? Not at the lake, Lenore. We must not meet
at the lake!" There was a click. The voice was gone.

"Why now?" Jim shouted. He was naked. From his
waist to his brow, his body was flushed. "Why do you
insist like that? I don't *want* to go to the lake!"

Jan was fully dressed, though the sun had not yet
risen. Coldly, without a gesture, without, it seemed, a
tone in her voice, she spoke. "You will come with me,"
she said. "I want you to see your young friends now,
right now."

Jim felt the back of his head. It was burning. He
turned away from her. "Why do you do this to me! What
are you thinking, Jan? I didn't touch them! I didn't *do* it!"

Jan didn't move. Her hands were in her jacket
pockets. Her spine was straight with resolution. "We'll
just go see them," she said. "We'll talk it over." Her face
was firm as a mask.

And that day, the dawn came on ever so slowly. It
seemed hours until the first clump of flower had hue. The
stillness lay heavy on the hedges, the shed. The grass
stood up in the water. Out beyond the lake, there were no
shadows cast by the towers, no cars on the road. There
was only the sheer gauze of gray. The lawn seemed
smaller than before, confined by the guarding quiet, the
low sky. At the edge, which was closer, the grass sparkled
dimly. In the center, the canvas chairs were empty.

A car came slowly up the drive. Its motor was
barely heard. Its headlights came briefly across the lawn,
nicking the back of the chair which stood, empty, on the

right. Then the faint hum died away, and there was a pause.

Jim and Jan took the long way, coming around the house through the wet yard. Lenore and the Colonel were already there. Jan saw the empty chairs, the small knobs at the tops of the back supports, the limp canvas. She saw, through the gap between the sagging chairbacks and the seats, a small piece of the hills. Jim brushed past a wet hydrangea. He noticed, as he came past the house beside Jan, that the lawn, which had been warm and familiar, was now only a broad gray space. But nobody noticed Jonathan, hidden in the bushes, weeping.

At first, only a faint slapping was heard. Lenore Peacock felt for her bun and turned away. It looked as if Colonel Mustard were smiling. But, soon, there were screams, laughter. There was splashing and excited cries that started high and then bubbled under. Jim Green looked out, his shoulders tending, gently, downward. His face was calm. Jan Scarlet saw a new hope in everything.

Out, far across the water, two young women were swimming. They were kicking and diving, playing games. They were laughing and shouting and swinging their legs through the cool depth. They were swimming circles around each other and then linking arms, going under, and coming up out of breath, floating. Now and then, over the surface of the water, great arches of droplets flew upward, and they hung there for an instant, shining.

Misha

The Koi

Spinne pressed his palm flat against the greased glass. He pressed, no result, pressed again, nothing. This time the force of his shove was like a birth contraction, glass falling soundlessly around him, icicle gashes flowing down his arms; new orifices springing out in a flash of water and light. Chips of tourmaline carved the static air in the back of his brain. His teacher, Tomo Adiba, cursed his soul. Spinne's mind twisted into focus with a staccato strobe, a shower of koi. Tomo tossed them out of the shop, red and white fins stroking the air.

"You stupit cop. You didn't feel through it!" Tomo hurried the fish into coldsax, screaming at Spinne. "You fucked it up!" Spinne selected a fish for himself, put it in the coldsax, and drawing on his black jacket, zipped it into the carapace of stiff leather. It was a white fish, with a red spot on its head.

Tomo ran out a second before the alarms began to ring. Heat sinks flew at Spinne like hot beetles. He rounded a corner and ran full into a scatter of Blakratz, some hired gang for a corporate flunky, strictly illegal.

"Halt!" the barrels all raised in a mechanized swing to fire.

The holy fish fell out of the jacket onto the ground, its fins waving feebly in the drowning air.

All eyes snapped to it, and Spinne, a professional,

sailed tong gas straight out into them, a cloaking and anesthetizing curtain. There was a scattering of orange fire, but Spinne was already rolling away from where he had been, his cut hands snagging on the street scurf. His visor pulled into its axolotl mask, sealing out the gas. He grabbed for the koi but another hand, smaller, browner, snatched it and was gone before he could spring to his feet.

"My soul!" he screamed after the retreating figure. He followed footsteps like a hound follows scent, but quickly lost them in the twists and turns of Makiver 4-1: the warehouse and wharf section of this filthy city.

At Tomo's, black market and temple gardens, the fish slid by like smooth rays of sunlight, orange and yellow in the swirling water of the pond. These koi, sold as soul keepers for the Fisheaters, would bring him good money. This cult was a very lucrative one for the stealer of koi. As he tossed the green pellets to the fish, he looked over his shoulder at the cop, Spinne, sitting motionless by the pond. Tomo was irritated. He had used the cop, now he wanted him to be gone. Tomo wanted his rice, his ginger, and his tea.

"What are you doing? Waiting to die?"

Spinne didn't answer. The koi pulled his eyes like a needle pulls a thread. Tomo was suddenly furious. Of course he owed the big money he would get and his life to this cop with the sullen face.

"Here," Tomo plunged his arm into the water and pulled out another of the red and white carp. "Here stupit, I shouldn't do this, but take this new fish and go."

Spinne just stared at it. "I put my soul into Ebisu."

"Ebisu?" The god of luck.

"My lucky fish," Spinne nodded.

Tomo cursed under his breath again, but shuddered when Spinne put those black opaque eyes back on him.

Spinne was like some sharp muzzled predatory animal, and a cop.

"Your fish is still alive," said Tomo, rising and putting on the tea. "It's up to you to go and find him then."

Spinne stared at Tomo. He had put his black wasp of pain safely away in a bottle of morphine where it buzzed harmlessly in the back of his mind. "How do I do that?"

"In here," Tomo rapped one rice-white hand against his chest. "Your feelings will guide you. You are a Fisheater now, and your soul is liberated from your own flesh. You can do many things that you couldn't do before. So go. Go away now." Tomo picked up a rice cake and waved Spinne away with it.

Spinne stretched his long spider legs from the pond and strode out in search of his soul. He was sorry. Sorry he had ever heard of the Fisheaters. Sorry he had put his soul in a fish to keep it pure.

Nika put the red-hatted koi in a white enamel bucket with two other fish and then headed out to the Mer. The underwater "temple" of the Vernaz Fish Cult was a little different than the Japanese gardens of the Fisheaters. Vernaz was a fish cult in a whole other light. Outside the entrance of the Mer, there was a barker in a merman suit. He was swinging a fish cane and shouting, "Come on. Come on in and have fun. Fun with fish."

Nika's lips moved in a soundless curse as she watched the scaled man fiashing like gems in the neon. He saw her and sneered, jerking his thumb to the side entrance.

Inside five adepts moved around the bucket oohing and aahing over the fish.

"Just look at those fish!!" they squealed.

"Nika always brings the best fish."

The metallic scales gleamed in the sodium lights like a jewelers catch.

Swedish fish poured like a rainbow of syrup into Nika's pockets. Sweets, and toys; an orange jade fish pendant with "Mer" carved on it went around her neck.

"Look at this one!" A blonde in shining green satin pulled out Ebisu and held him up to the light.

"He's too sweet," a redhead said, her white teeth fiashing like a fox.

"Yes, more than for eating." A third pressed the fish between her breasts and giggled. She then reluctantly dropped the fish into the bucket with a gentle plash. Nika looked up. Huge fish circled the underwater dome, captive sharks and gunmetal wolf eels with gnashing jaws. The fioors were full of "Mermaids" with fish dildos and clientele slimy with sweat and fish oil. Nika poured the bucket into the alabaster fountain in the center of the room, and held out her hand for the three credits.

Pocketing them, she spat into a silken cushion, and hurried out of the stew with jerky steps. She headed back toward the place where she had captured the red lionheaded koi. Perhaps there were more taken in the bust on the fish shop. She had an idea—Tomo probably was in on it.

Spinne put all his powers of memory and observation to work, all that the years on the force had taught him. The sugary web he wove for the return of the fish thief was sure to work. Back on that street.

He wore his leather coveralls and soft boots, just waiting, in typical gumshoe immobility, for the inevitable prey, jiggling just the lightest of lines he had strung across the alleyways. Gossamer strands of electric eye impulse signaled the movement of a thief on the edge of his beat.

The tan clouds rolled over the arc of the skyrise. Brittle shards of glass gleamed dully under his feet. Little torn tin chips of sound cried out their consumer commercials. Spinne crushed his heel into a humming gum wrapper to silence it. The lateness of the hour, the underwater shimmers of the tremendous heat of the factories, made the huge ducts warble and sway in the brown sunlight. Pigeons, swimming through the air like schools of small silver fish, mesmerized Spinne's eyes, black and insectlike behind the gleaming shades.

The shrill whine of the broken circuit made Spinne leap forward on his arachnid legs, two Blakratz caught in the electric web sparked with pops and sweat of fear.

"It's a fucking cop!" the tall one shouted.

The other one, fast as a small coiled snake, struck out with a 12-inch steel spike. The point of it sliced away part of the coverall on Spinne's thigh. In anger and frustration, Spinne spun around and down, his chrome barrel reflecting the sky, the double flash of powder and sunlight signaling the red flowering of the Blakratz death. He knew the thief would follow, where there's smoke....

Sticky with blood, Spinne finished dragging the bodies to the spot for pickup, and reset his electronic grid, hoping that the prey would arrive before the flies did.

He hadn't long. Looking up through the bottom of the grey length of staircase, the metallic pinging of a stealthy descent met his ear. Cat curious at shots perhaps? The sound of metal on tubular metal ran a chill down his back. Something steadied itself on the handrail. Spinne edged back further into the darkness.

Nika hopped down the last step, and turned in a nervous flash to meet Spinne's black-gloved hand clamping her shoulder. The brown hands coming up to hold his thrilled him with self assurance.

"Where is the fish!?" he hissed.

Nika reddened. Some half-strangled snarl escaped from her lips.

215

Spinne relaxed, then slammed her head hard three times against the metal rail. He put his elbow between her shoulders, his glove tangled in her hair pulled her up again. He wiped his palm hard against her face, bringing out the bright blood. He took a ragged breath. "Where?"

Pain flamed in her eyes and her bloody jaws snarled. Spinne, trembling with tarantula fury, put the cold to her temple. He could see her green eyes burrowing away like a flurry of badgers into her pain. No, wait. He closed his eyes in concentration. That wasn't the right question for this street ferret.

"How much?"

"30!" A triumphant snap.

He winced, letting the credit bounce and spin on the asphalt.

She snapped the jade fish from her neck and slapped it in his hand.

He held it up slowly while she fingered the silver. "Vernaz!" He spat, angrily.

Nika nodded and he dropped her like an old boot. She fell to one knee, watching the cop race the night. She smiled a leather smile, and trotted unsteadily after him.

Outside the Mer, Spinne hovered in the lengthening shadows of the day. The Barker, glancing at him, couldn't see the badge. "Hey, hey there! Say, what are you doing with your hands in your pockets, fella? Come on in where you can have some real fun." Strains of Sakamoto lured Spinne closer.

"Holy Mackerel. . ." the barker saw the badge.

Spinne smiled, held up his hands, palms out. "No trouble?"

"No trouble at all," repeated the Barker nervously twisting his fish tie in the low sun.

Spinne wrinkled his nose at the smell of the wharf as he slowly descended the tube to the underwater house of horror.

Nika slid in the side door.

216

Inside, Spinne was met by a red-haired "Mermaid" in a slick rubber costume.

"I'm looking for a fish," he said.

"Oh?" The red-haired maid smiled and pursed her lips.

"A particular fish," Spinne leaned his face close to her thick red lips. He saw her orange eyes grow hard as she caught sight of his badge.

"We don't want any trouble," she grimaced.

"No, no trouble." Spinne wagged his dark head agreeably. "Consider me a- a- customer."

A great wave of laughter and wild splashing came from the central fountain, where Spinne, suddenly struck with horror, saw a woman raising up his Ebisu to perform sexual acts.

Spinne leapt forward firing his .38 wildly. The fountain lights shut down. Shots and screams mixed blood with water and semen. Spinne stopped shooting, thinking of the sharks and the glass walls.

He remembered Tomo's way. Put the gun to bed. Like running through water, he waded through the wet thrashing bodies of Mer clientele. He saw the thief darting past, with something white and red under her arm. He followed her.

The barker had gone. Nika stood in the fading orange rays of sun, holding Spinne's soul between her thumb and forefinger. Spinne, remembering the words of his teacher Tomo, moved slowly. Toward his soul drowning quietly in a young woman's hand.

Conger Beasley, Jr.

Head of a Traveler

Head of a traveler left lying on a loose stone road outside Siena was happened upon by an Italian pharmacist. He stopped the car, got out and examined it. The shock sent his heart sculling to his throat. The face was his, the features a facsimile of his own. Someone had severed the head from the neck of his double and left it for the crows to peck. *Impossibile*! he whispered and gave the head a kick. The head bounced over the hills, through vineyards, all the way to Firenze. The pharmacist got back into the car and returned home. That night he muttered a prayer for the decapitated body of his lonely double.

At the Ponte Vecchio the head bounded over the shops and into the Arno. Face up, it floated downstream. The pharmacist, out fishing with his son, hooked one eye.

The face—a facsimile of his own, dripping weeds, the blue flesh pulped by ravenous fish—grimaced wryly. *Dio mirabile*, the pharmacist whispered. His son upchucked on his shoes. Inserting a stick of dynamite into the lipless mouth, the pharmacist lit the fuse and blasted the features to shreds. Skin, bone, soggy tissue splattered his spectacles. At the instant of detonation he moaned deliriously. Police arrived, a flock of *paparazzi*. The pharmacist experienced a feeling of sexual arousal. His ears bulbed, his nose turned red. "I have thwarted my fate," he declared, "that destiny decreed by a vengeful God that I must die *in absentia* for crimes I did not commit."

The reporters took down his story. The next day a new head lay in the streets.

Conger Beasley, Jr.

Japan Invades America:
A Scenario

A stage, dark and bare, dimly lit by overhead lights, illuminating an interior similar to the entrance of a cave, but with this exception: no bats. To the pulsating sound of minimalistic music, figures crawl across the stage. It is difficult for those in the audience to determine exactly where the figures are coming from. They are definitely not coming from the wings. Even though the figures crawl on all fours, they are obviously human and not some species of animal. They seem to emerge from an opening at the back of the stage. In no fixed or ranked order they emerge, more like a swarm of insects, pouring forth in amazing numbers, wave after ragged wave. The stage brightens; gradually the figures become visible to the audience. The faces are oriental: slant eyes, swarthy cheeks, glossy black hair. Some, like Sumo wrestlers, are clad in modest loincloths; others in expensive robes and silk pyjamas; still others in uniforms and dark business suits. As the music up-tempos, the first wave reaches the edge of the stage, and without pausing—nimbly, with amazing dexterity—they slip off the stage and crawl across the floor of the theatre at the same steady pace toward the first row.

Now comes the interesting part, that peculiar interaction between performer and audience that makes

221

for a memorable evening at the theatre. With scarcely a pause, the first wave crawls into the laps of the people sitting in the first row and over their heads and shoulders and over the backs of their chairs and onto the laps of the people in the next row; and so on, in a steady, relentless march, until almost half the orchestra section is blanketed by the presence of the silent, wiggling figures. The music increases in tempo, a few basic motifs repeated over and over, punctuated by the strident whine of a woodwind instrument.

At this point it is obvious to everyone in the back rows what fate has in store for them. But there is no outcry at this, no panicky leaping to the feet and bolting up the aisles. The rest of the audience calmly awaits the onslaught. Numerous individuals actually reach up and wrap their arms around the orientals who come crawling onto their faces and chests. Women and children, though scrunched down into their seats by the weight of the invaders, still manage to snatch a furtive embrace before being folded up in their chairs.

The tide swells on toward the back rows. Once it reaches the wall, it will pile upon itself like a wave. Higher and higher the wave will mount, not in anger or frustration or any sense of urgency, but calmly and methodically. . .inevitably. And, inevitably, the pressure of that dense mass will squash to messy little bits anyone so unfortunate as to remain underneath.

And yet the prospect evokes no sense of alarm. The people in each row passively await their fate. Hundreds of poignant hand-to-hand grapples occur, with people embracing the full weight of one invader and then letting go bravely to embrace the next. In its curiously stifled intensity, the scene resembles lovers having sex on a cold winter night under a stack of heavy blankets. Audible over the throbbing music is the soft, slushy sound of strangled whispers. The overall effect—and this, really, is the point of the performance—is a kind of riotous silence, a sense of exultant submissiveness. The triumph belongs to the audience as much as it does to the performers. In the face of annihilation, both groups achieve a kind of catharsis. At the end of the performance, applause resounds from somewhere. . .the basement, the rafters, the lobby; desultory clapping by a lone aficionado for whom this spectacle represents a breakthrough into an entirely new form of behavior.

Don Webb

A Tale of the Downturn

In homage to Jane Gallion

Having activated the dishwasher, she wiped the sodden bits of Smurf cereal off the table with the dish sponge. She threw the sponge in the sink hoping for a moment's peace. But no. The bedroom door slammed open and the kids ran out grinning bestially slopping water in all directions. She ran to catch them — to corral them — telling herself she had all day to clean up the various messes. And she would need every minute of it. She picked Bobby up, almost dropped him (greased pig) and carried him into the back bedroom of the double-wide. Tony escaped meanwhile out of the trailer and into the trailer park. Tony was three and he wanted to play with Mr. Belsen's black chow dog. The dog wanted to eat Tony. Mutual desires seldom balance in this world. She gave Bobby a quick swat and told him to get dressed. She ran forward toward the door out into the insects and heat. The dog was barking, its ears back down on its head, stretched to the last inch of the chain. Tony, still dripping, was walkig up to the dog. "Kitty kitty." He had a toy cat that named for him the entire world of four-footed beings. She caught him by his pudgy arms and yanked him back. Tony squealed and began to cry. Every pair of curtains parted, eager for this domestic entertainment.

225

Thank god Mr. Belsen wasn't home. He'd stick his ugly purple head out and tell her to keep her kid away from his dog.

A sociological note: According to Eric Hoffer individuals reduced to poverty or near-poverty from the middle class tend to resent their new status more than those trapped in poverty all their lives. Mr. and Mrs. Daimler qualify as examples. Mr. Daimler "Bob" to his buddies when he had buddies, "Robert" to his underlings when he had underlings and "Bobo" to Anne — lost his executive position in a petroleum multinational due to certain changes in the exploitation/distribution of fossil fuels on this planet. He now works in the food service industry. "May I take your order now?" Bob had known economic security all his life. They had everything on credit. Anne taught English composition at the community college. She lost her position due to "economic restructuring," a consequence of the State's loss of revenue. Unlike Bob she came from a poor family. She won a scholarship to a public university. They met. He was rich. She was pretty. This poor/sad to rich/happy to poor/sad suggests we are three-quarters of the way through the Cinderella. We are not. This is Anne May Daimler *née* Waugh's story.

Bobby had locked her out. He stood inside laughing. Threats didn't work. He could stay inside forever. She appealed to reason. Who will cook for you if I'm locked out? This proved a telling argument. You always have to resort to threats and food. You are dealing with animals. When she got in she wanted to tan his hide. She refrained. She would have to walk down to the Piggly Wiggly today. She wanted to get back in easily. She couldn't take the heat. It had been a hard summer, a hot summer. Hadn't been this dry for 116 years. But you know all that, you read the papers just like I do. She felt she was melting all this summer. There was wax inside of her hollow bones. It was running out — like the grains of sand through the hourglass in that damn soap opera Mrs. Horn listens to every day. Mrs. Horn is hard of hearinng — lost to scarlet fever as a child. The soap opera comes on and the kids want to know why they don't have a TV any more. Especially Bobby, who's five, older and therefore more addicted to the tube.

Getting along without a TV had put a big strain on the evenings. The kids were packed away by eight and Bobo and she amused themselves. You can only play so many board games until you find their novelty runs thin. Conversations are fueled by the day's activities and neither of them had activities that they deemed worthy of discussion. You go to bed early. You sleep a lot. And of course there are books. The library was a mere ten blocks away. She walked to the library twice a week, in the hot sun, melting inside. Getting lighter, ready to blow away.

She came back to herself still holding Tony, who still screamed. She took him to the back bedroom, rocking him in her arms, lullabying. Automatic mommy. She wandered off like that more and more. Her mind was eager to escape this, to go anywhere but here. Tony quieted down and she went on to do the thousand-and-one tasks of domestic maintenance.

She was fixing supper. Tuna Helper *sans* tuna. Bobby, seeing this was an unguarded moment, snatched the jar of grape jelly from the kitchen cabinet. She spotted the motion in her periphery. She turned. Bobby, fearing the worst, dropped the by-now-open jar which sloshed its contents across the linoleum. Bobby fled through the jelly, down the carpeted hall and into the bedroom. Every step he took became a purple foot glyph. She was completely entranced. She thought of Robinson Crusoe finding Friday's footprints.

Robert walked in. And all hell broke loose. As a

worker in the food service industry he had had it pounded into him again and again. All surfaces must be kept clean. Now it was time to pound it into Anne. Not literally. No hitting or slapping. Only yelling, only sarcasm. But each time an argument occurred violence came a little closer to the surface. It scared Anne. It scared Robert a little bit too.

Dinner was silent. The kids were used to silent dinner. Everyone was silent. Anne had to excuse herself from the table. Menses. She came back and began to scrub the carpet spots. Robert told her not to bother, that they'd set. Grape jelly sets fast. And since when was he an expert on stain chemistry? Hostilities renewed. And kept up till both kids were crying and both adults were ashamed.

Anne said she was going on a walk. Robert wanted to protest, but could think of no rational reason why she shouldn't walk. Maybe she would calm down. Maybe he would calm down. Anne hoped he would clear the table while she was gone. Do something. Some sign that peace was still a possibility.

It was a beautiful twilight with Venus glowing brightly in the west. The full moon was beginning to rise large and canteloupy. She headed east toward the moon out of the trailer park. The live oak didn't look so drought-stricken in this light, and the cedar was positively inviting. She paralleled the empty highway. She had walked for a long time, long enough to have forgotten why she was walking, when she saw the creature.

It stood a few feet in front of her — outlined by the moon. He, obviously a he, was built like a man. Reddish-brown fur covered his body. He was at least seven feet tall and his purple eyes almost glowed. There was a strong smell, a biting musk.

They stood watching each other for almost a minute. Then he turned and walked away following a deer trail.

She went back to her trailer and picked up the dinner dishes. Bob was washing the kids. They'd gotten into something while she was away. She was glad she didn't know what. It was nice to miss the occasional domestic tragedy.

She was at the library early the next morning. There was heavy dew on the St. Augustine grass. A wet miracle. The librarian came and opened up. The library had a surprisingly large occult and pseudoscience section. A town kook had collected these things for years, the librarian told her. Left them all to us in his will. She checked out everything they had on Bigfoot, even books with only a passing reference. She lugged them home in a faded Gucci bookbag. It took days to find what she was looking for. Research was constantly interrupted by the little monsters. She hid all the books before Bob came home.

The book that told her the most was Jim Brandon's *The Rebirth of Pan*. Brandon talked about Wilhelm Reich's theories, how desire is a force, the life force. How it can be collected in metal boxes. Like trailer homes. Brandon thought that all that life force might bring things into existence, just as her womb had brought Tony and Bobby into existence. The other necessary ingredient was blood. Brandon noted that women in their period are more likely to encounter strange beings than at any other time. She had found what she wanted and carried the sixteen books back to the library.

She walked back to the trailer. Tumult sounded from within and she made up her mind. She would see him again and if he wouldn't carry her off, she'd run along beside.

Jeffrey DeShell

from *In Heaven Everything is Fine*

3 am the characters assemble themselves in the flat Sweet Jane and I share Toulouse-Lautrec brings La Goulue and a couple of cases of champagne Sally comes in with Sweet Jane Frances Farmer Art and Sue Side arrive all talking at once Raoul shows up with a girl I've never seen before and a color tv the girl looks like she just stepped out of a Kirchner painting the tv's a beaut a Sony every time I see Raoul he brings me a color tv I don't know what this means Hey Raoul thanks for the tv want some champagne.

Sweet Jane and Sally go to the Schizophrenic Bourgeoisie to have a drink. Someone puts a quarter in the juke box Sweet Jane starts to dance all by herself. She starts out slow but as the tempo picks up she begins to move self-contained really beautiful. Next song Sally joins in the two of them heating up the men begin to notice. Another quarter hard fast beat the girls really get into the rhythm now the men crowd around to watch. One of the men throws a bill on the floor Sweet Jane undoes a button on her blouse. She moves really well gorgeous and teasing the men holler and whistle another dollar appears on the floor another button is unbuttoned everyone getting into the music now Sally takes the hint begins to tease lifts her t-shirt up and down the men whistle applaud hoot stamp their feet Sweet Jane undoes another button removes her blouse twirls it above her head then liberates her sweet breasts from her sweet bra the men love it an incredible pair of tits really nice. Another quarter in the juke box another dollar on the floor now it's Sally's turn she lifts the cotton up to her nipples slowly painfully slowly the men watch smile laugh applaud stick their hands into their pockets Sally lifts her shirt up to the tips hesitating then quickly over her head the men applaud cheer whistle Sally's nipples are erect. Sweet Jane already has the first button of her jeans undone grinding her hips a thin film of sweat now noticeable on her upper body the music shifts a slow raunchy number Sweet Jane unbuttons another button instantly commands everyone's attention even Sally's now another button Sweet Jane hooks her thumbs in her pants grinds her hips more bills and change appear along with a few interesting suggestions she begins to pull her jeans down now visible brown panties the men going wild screaming laughing leering cajoling over her hips past her thighs the song changes she effortlessly steps out of her jeans. Sally stops dancing as if on cue begins to gather up the money Sweet Jane shows one cheek now the other now both keeps her hand over her crotch completely naked now except for that hand the men fondle themselves laugh drink holler and plead but as the song ends Sally and Sweet Jane run into the bathroom the men laugh slap each other on the back.

CORPSE SEX DAMAGE AWARD

Sacramento
The mother of a man whose body was stolen and

sexually molested by an apprentice embalmer has been awarded $142,500 by a Sacramento Superior Court jury.

The jury deliberated more than seven hours before deciding Wednesday to award Marian Gonzales, 55, the $125,000 in compensatory damages and $17,500 in punitive damages.

Gonzales said during the trial that she suffered severe emotional damage after Mary Greenlee, 23, stole a hearse containing the body of John Mercure, 33, on Dec. 17 of this year.

Greenlee subsequently admitted to police that she had sexual contact with Mercure's corpse and with up to 40 others while she worked at the mortuary.

A letter had been found with the Mercure's body in which Greenlee described her first sexual contact with a corpse, and pleaded for help for her condition.

The letter said, "I've written this with what's left of my broken heart. If you read this, don't hate me. I was once like you. I laughed, I loved, but something went wrong. I give it all to know. But please remember me as I was, not as I am now."

I am angry I am ill and I'm as ugly as sin
My irritability keeps me alive and kicking
I know the meaning of life it doesn't help me a bit
I know beauty and I know a good thing
      when I see it
This is a song from under the floorboards
This is a song from where the wall is cracked
By force of habit
I am an insect
I have to confess I'm proud as hell of that fact

The woman Raoul brought over is sitting in the loveseat I pour a glass of champagne offer it to her Thank you You're welcome I don't believe I've seen you here before what's your name I've never been here before and I don't give my name out to strangers You must have a lot to hide I imagine everyone has a lot to hide very clever woman maybe a bit too clever if you know what I mean but she has the angles the lines the self-awareness the angst just right I will call her Kirchner's Woman.

Sally walking. Sally walking down a street Aspen Colorado. Sally intelligent beautiful unattached. Sally window-shopping American Express Mastercard Visa. Lunchtime five more shopping days till Christmas. Aspen Colorado a pleasant place for holidays snow and white everywhere. Sally tall graceful beautiful anonymous. Aspen Colorado full of beauty a town of perfection. Sally walking down a street Aspen Colorado Christmas shopping something wrong with this picture. Something wrong in the eyes of Carl Peterson age 26 of Denver Colorado. Who decided to die in Sally's arms.

Sally walking. Sally walking in the snow getting slightly hungry spinach salad maybe soup what to buy for Danielle a man walks up to her says hello takes a pistol out of his pocket fires into his own mouth Sally jumps back the man begins to fall Sally tries to catch him too late he falls to the snow blood everywhere. Sally hears a scream puts the stranger's head in her lap begins to cry. Later Sally takes a hot bath fresh clothes hops in her car vague plans of California.

7:00 5 7 "Scruples" (Part 1) (1980) Lindsay Wagner, Barry Bostwick. The young wife of an elderly millionaire opens a Hollywood boutique and with the help of a handsome photographer and a New York fashion designer, soon turns it in to a huge success.

2 8 56 "Real People" Siamese twins, a dog who eats with a fork, and a mother in Argentina who has had thirty-seven children.

It's hot. Maybe past ninety the asphalt streets melt in the sun. They sit naked in a bright room expensive furniture shiny hardwood floors. They have divided the room in half. They stare at each other listen to loud laughter in the next room. The shock of recognition comes they suddenly see nothing but themselves in each other. The woman crosses over to him hands him a shiny black pistol. She leaves the room. He examines the pistol carefully thinks of how incredibly thirsty he is. Later they will make love on the shiny hardwood floors.

Art and Sue Side are sitting on the couch laughing and watching tv Toulouse is sitting watching everybody else Sweet Jane Sally Joe and La Goulue are dancing in the middle of the room Raoul is in another room talking on the phone Frances has had too much to drink is sitting on a chair in the corner staring at the floor I decide to try again Would you like to dance No but I would like another glass of champagne she holds her glass out to me jesus I think I need another cigarette.

Toulouse-Lautrec sits drinking in his studio waiting for La Goulue to arrive. The posters that Toulouse has printed have become great successes in a very short time, bringing wealth and critical acclaim to Lautrec, and instant fame for La Goulue (who is currently in negotiations with one of the major networks for a prime time variety special co-starring either Pat Sajak or John Davidson.)

Toulouse has been commissioned to print a series of six nude portraits of La Goulue for a very large sum of money. La Goulue was supposed to be at Lautrec's studio two hours ago, and he has no idea where she is now.

Toulouse-Lautrec is the city's favorite son right now, he even has had a drink named after him at that prestigious artists' watering hole, The Banker. Toulouse is confused by all this new found fame and fortune, he's not sure exactly what it means. The money is nice, and he feels finally that he's getting the recognition he deserves, after all, he's worked very hard, so what could be wrong? Isn't he living every artist's dream? Why isn't he happy? Toulouse-Lautrec mixes himself another drink and waits.

EXCEPTIONAL

Tall, handsome, athletic, successful, affluent, Ivy League Senior corporation executive, 40, seeks an attractive female in her thirties for a lasting relationship. Interests include the arts, cultural events, gourmet food, fine wines, skiing, tennis, sailing, hiking. Box #5A.

Freaks was a thing I photographed a lot. It was one of the first things I photographed and it had a terrific kind of excitement for me. I just used to adore them. I still do adore some of them. I don't quite mean that they're my best friends but they make me feel a mixture of shame and awe. There's a quality of legend about freaks. Like a person in a fairy tale who stops you and demands you answer a riddle. Most people go through life dreading they'll have a traumatic experience. Freaks were born with trauma. They've already passed their test in life. They're aristocrats.

    Raoul comes into the room When I was in Mexico he begins I knew this Indian who believed the gods were pissed at him and the only way he could stay safe was to constantly surround himself with music he used to sit in the corner of the bar and sing softly to himself and he always had a couple of those five dollar transistor radios around him at all times for when he got tired of singing he wouldn't talk to you unless he trusted you real well I guess he thought you might be an assassin sent by the gods or something to knock him off if and when he did decide to trust you he would turn on all his radios and kind of sing to you you know tell his story in song so he offers me a ride home in his pickup one night got three or four radios turned up pretty loud and he starts singing to me how he used to work in this village making and fixing shoes until the son of one of the gods came down to get his shoes fixed and this son of a god fell in love with him and the father of the kid this god got real pissed you know figuring this guy had corrupted his young son or something and some of the other gods got mad too because this boy's really beautiful and they're jealous I mean here's this gorgeous son of a god in love with a fucking cobbler for chrissakes and this cobbler's got a wife and two kids I mean he don't even like boys so he's got five or six gods just ready to stomp him you know but this one goddess takes pity on him sleeps with him and tells him to get the hell away from his village and that as long as he can hear music he'll be safe that was about twenty years ago he hadn't seen his wife or kids in twenty years so anyway just as I was getting ready to split to come back here the old guy disappears can't find him anywhere they look and look finally find his truck in the bottom of a canyon nobody can figure out how the hell it got down there I mean there's no roads or nothing they find his truck alright but there's no sign of the old Indian but funny thing about the way they found his truck was by ear they heard it about a mile away there were at least a dozen radios surrounding the truck all going full blast.

Nerve gas works quickly, within minutes in a fatal dose. Victims first find their muscles beginning to spasm. They lose control of their bladder and bowels, and finally the muscles of the diaphragm become paralyzed. The victims suffocate.

There are no good antidotes to most chemical weapons, but atropine can reverse the effects of nerve gas. Unfortunately, atropine itself can be lethal if a soldier takes it when he has not gotten a dose of nerve agent.

We're desperate
Get used to it
We're desperate
Get used to it
We're desperate
Get used to it
We're desperate
Get used to it
It's kiss or kill

Kirchner's Woman lights a cigarette hands it to me Toulouse Lautrec is sketching in his sketchbook La Goulue dances over to him whispers something in his ear Lautrec whispers something in reply I'm not your fucking slave La Goulue screams you can't Just order me around any time you feel like it I mean who in the fucking hell do you think you are Lautrec says nothing just sits there quietly this infuriates La Goulue answer me you son-of-a-bitch remember big shit artiste you have me to thank for all your success do you hear me me to thank without me you're nothing but a perverted midget the stories I could tell Lautrec turns red at this remark La Goulue spins on her heels and marches off to the kitchen Frances boozily shakes her head and for some reason follows La Goulue.

I'm sitting in the Dirt Chute trying to get quietly smashed I want to feel I want to feel tragic hard-bitten cynical drunk Irish I sneer but I don't feel any of these things not even drunk. The way my life's been going lately I should feel something sad depressed something I mean I have the right but I just shrug it off no highs or lows just one continuous shrug.

I am not having a good time. This is the place where fifteen year old boys come fresh off the bus. Low ceiling, smell of sweat, amyl nitrate and vaseline. Three seats down a fellow giving a guy a hand job under the bar. The guy beside me drinking a frozen strawberry daquiri. Just another shrug. The silence beyond the scream. Level out shrug it off be cool. It's what you know that makes you go it's what you learn that makes you squirm. The beat indeed goes on. This is my cool funk hipster persona how do you like. It is so hip because all of us cool funk hipsters start the next sentence with the last word of the. Previous research has shown that language determines thought or is it the other way. Around here language seems to be the only gesture left that one can even partially. Understand this everyone's life a series of one misunderstood gesture after. Another brandy please I'm not feeling that clever the boy next to me sad lonely puts a Linda Ronstadt record on the juke box because when one is sad and lonely this is the appropriate music to put on the juke box it's expected even though the music's the thing and nobody cares who played it or why just another wasted gesture. The inevitability of cliché.

Sitting here shrugging it off I'm here because the drinks are cheap. Also, I like the smell of vaseline.

Rusty Hoover

The Freudian Paragraph

Never before she said had she been much interested in her dreams until the night Sigmund Freud appeared in one of them yes Freud and spoke to her. Now, with a bedside cassette machine to record them and extra cassettes and extra batteries and a tall stack of books to interpret them and a stack of magazines with articles that interpret the books that interpret the dreams, Doris's dreams had become an obsession. She began to sleep day and night. What next, thought Arnold. Arnold was Doris's husband. She tried to explain to him how she had actually met Freud in a dream yes Freud saying this is it Arnold this is what we've been waiting for this is going to help us understand what's gone wrong with our marriage. It's going to help our daughter think of your daughter Arnold. Once we understand our dreams we'll understand all our subconscious drives and motives for doing the things we do Arnold, she said. It had all seemed so perfectly natural and naturally perfect while she was dreaming it until she woke up and got up and got dressed and then my God realized and was afraid she would forget it and so scribbled it all down: that Sigmund Freud walked up to her, took the cigar from his mouth with one hand and with the other shook her hand. That's all I wanted to know, said Freud.

Paul Garrison

From Strange Beginnings

Old Moses, boy, he could hit the cover off a fastball with one fist tied between his legs; and on the mound he was a southpaw fully aware of the effects roughness has upon the magnus characteristics of rotating spherical projectiles. But there always seemed to be a splice in his circuits, a flaw in his game, as though Abner Doubleday had plucked one of baseball's finely tuned strings, sending a ripple of difficulties across the bright green turf of Fenway Park.

As interim manager of the 1999 Red Sox, I first saw the boy pitch during a game of championship high school ball in Northampton. That was also the first time I saw his name in print: Moses Fleetwood Washington, Southpaw. 6'2", 190 pounds. Record, 0-8. 4.9 ERA. Even then and despite his figures he was an impressive prospect—the bill of his cap pointing toward the heavens and that graceful rotation of hip and shoulder, the sheer velocity of his fastball and the poetry of his curve. The way he bit into a hotdog between pitches. There was apple pie in that boy. Still, even in his early days there was a faint feeling of imminent danger every time he tipped his cap to the crowd, and you could hear somewhere in the eager smack of his bat every last one of his twisted eccentricities.

The first eight innings went decidedly

243

Northampton's way. Washington was pitching a no-hitter against a group of pimpled freshmen and cripples: The only upperclassman on the opposing team was a lanky righthander who was knocked out in the second inning, and, except for their third baseman, the entire infield suffered from a kind of collective muscle pull which made it easy for the scrappy Northampton lineup to squeeze singles through the wide gaps in between their tender and immovable diamond proper.

Sitting on the bench for eighty-eight minutes while his club banged out nine runs on eleven hits, though, gave old Moses a few too many splinters in the psyche; and, as he trotted out to the mound in the bottom of the ninth leading nine runs to zero, Moses Fleetwood Washington felt the faint slippage of disks somewhere in his frontal lobe. His synapses had failed him. He had beaned seven batters in the temple before anybody understood what had happened. Upon regaining his control, Moses became aware of a curious sagging on the left half of the field. What were typically routine ground balls seemed to pick up speed as they guttered through the legs of Northampton's third baseman. Soon, Moses began to feel more than the products of the mind slipping, for his team had no one healthy in the bullpen. And now, even the players on the right side of the diamond complained that the turf beneath their cleats was giving way.

Frightened and desperate, Moses succeeded in pulling loose the finely sewn seams of the baseball. But even this didn't help his game, and merely made his fingertips bleed into the webbing of his glove. With two outs and the score tied at 9, he began shaking the baseball as though it were one of those glassy Christmas paperweights, hoping feebly to stir up some sort of miniature snowstorm under which he and his teammates could bury themselves until the following spring thaw. Moses concealed the ball in his mit and, pivoting on his right leg, faced each base, all of which supported opposing baserunners waiting for the next pitch. Moses looked in for the sign and, pausing for a few seconds in the stretch position, admired the sizzle and warp of the tobacco-infested center field sod. He entered his wind-up.

Without stopping at the belt, he spun a fastball on the inside part of the plate faster than you can say hey Willie Mays. The bleachers buzzed like vibrators. Moses tossed a fancy spitball that danced across the outside corner for steeeeerike two, and can't ya hear those sleigh bells ring?

At this juncture, the owner of the Sox farm system himself bolted out toward the mound, his blue pin stripes snapping to the rhythm of the crowd. Moses took a bite of his hot dog. "Make him buy your product, boy. Force it down his throat." I dubbed in my own words over the hushed vowel shapes of his dropsical lips. "Give 'im the old supply and demand curve, boy."

Before the umpire could unsquat himself, the owner had left the field, and again the stands hummed. Moses fell to his knees and then on his belly to survey the land. The peat was as smooth and flat as his living room floor. So, taking his place on the pitching mound, Moses wound himself up and fired, splitting home plate into two equal chunks of rubber and splitting the bat into a thousand splinters, some of which sought the blue heat of his own left eye while his right followed the ball in its abandonment of the stratosphere, whereupon, at the apex of its flight, it began rotating on its axis like the other planets. The fans oohed and aahed. The center field stands crept toward the field to get a closer look. Northampton utility players, anticipating the infield fly rule, scampered across the first base line. Hot steam rose from the opposing team's locker room. But just as the ball made its reentry through the clouds, the earth around the mound began to tremble. Just as the runner on third crossed home plate, a fissure snaked between Washington's legs. And just as the ball entered the stadium, inches before its elegiac ending, the miniature quake, like a mother's slap, knocked Moses flush with the universe. It was hard to tell the razzing of the crowd from the cheery-red sounds of the sirens.

Two years later the Sox were in the cellar when we called up Washington fresh out of high school. He pitched a few good games, when the weather was right. But there was that one game against California. Fire and Brimstone. There was Moses, his trajectory too high and his spirits low, sitting on the rubber and eating Cheese Crunchies as the winning run trotted across the plate. I was in the bullpen when Tiny Walker, the pitching coach, told me the whole story.

"From strange beginnings," began Tiny. It seems M.F. Washington's life was destined to be problematic from the outset. He was conceived by unwitting parents in a cleaning closet at Reagan's 1980 Inaugural Ball in Washington, D.C. and, eight months later, plopped prematurely between the fatty yellow cushions of a New York City cab. Mother had planned to have little Moses within the clean white walls of some memorial hospital, but her son's head was much too large and popped screaming into the world, forcing the driver of the cab to pry the boy out with the handle of a fungo bat he kept in the front seat to blacken the eyes of criminals. Reared on Twinkies and breast milk, however, little Moses began to grow big and strong.

On his son's eleventh birthday, Father signed Moses up for Little League. "Moses," said his father, "I'm signing you up for Little League." Moses liked the weight of a baseball mitt on his tiny hand. He liked also the way his black cleats shone in the little light of his Mickey Mantle desk lamp. Father was so proud. And, before long, it was time for the boy's first practice of the season.

Moses did a spit shine on his new black shoes, dancing one of Mother's handtowels across the toes. He tied each lace carefully, double-knotting, tucked the lower crescent of a figure eight into his seat of brown corduroy and, glancing back into the mirror, went off to find his bat and glove.

At the top of the stairway, though, Moses saw that the door to his parents' bedroom was open. But Father is at work, thought the boy, making phone calls. But Mother is at the market. Moses tugged at his jersey as he approached the doorway. He could see a light near the high bed, and he began to sweat. There, in the purple light of the room, was his mother, sitting upright, breasts like rosin bags, her fingers wrapped tightly round the stomach of a Louisville slugger and one stockinged foot dangling in the cat's milk dish. "My bat!" cried little Moses as the cat leapt into the room.

The episode was merely one in a long series, for it was, after all, the boy's *father* who most influenced his fielding. The two often played catch in the backyard while Mother baked meatloaves in the heat of the kitchen.

"He's going to second," Father would cry as papa's little boy raced after a misplayed line drive. But no one was ever there to tag the invisible runner out. Moses would grab his ball and mitt and watch through the living room window as Father's pin stripes played the National Anthem on old Mother's creaking backbone.

From strange beginnings.

On a windy day in Chicago, Moses ran out to the mound like it weren't the seventh game of the goddamn World Series, and you could tell by the way he spewed an imaginary stream of tobacco into the soft Illinois soil that the Red Sox would lose.

The ivied walls of Wrigley Field radiated. It was like playing baseball inside one of Washington's contorted fantasies, though clearly it was the Cubs who were in control. I was sitting comfortably in a corner of the dugout when their first home run jumped over the fence. We were all amazed. There were little Anson Boozler and Jumpin' Joe Bixby fondling their chins with the tips of their gloves. There was Sal Butterworth, the oldest member and back-up catcher of the club, clutching the cup beneath the crotch of his uniform and mumbling pitching signals. And there were Tiny Walker's eyes, big as goose eggs, following the white smear of baseball over the center field scoreboard. It was the first time a team had ever scored off Moses in the first inning. He made five successive pitches, three of which found their ways into the soiled mouths of infield mitts, and two of which sought the murky thoroughfares just beyond the crowded ballpark.

Moses came trotting into the dugout, smiling and blowing bubbles, and waving to his father who was climbing all over a peanut vendor to regain a seat next to Mother. Tiny made a phone call to the bullpen.

"No one there," he shrugged as he hung up the receiver.

"What do you mean `No one there'?" This was the seventh game of the goddamn World Series. I always left the pitching roster up to Tiny, since I knew very little about the position, and it seems he had taken the wrong kinds of precautions. We had used all of our long relievers to get through the first six games and were counting on our short relief ace, Sheldon Maxwell, to clean up in the ninth before Washington's game had a chance to fall apart. There was no one available to pitch for us that early in the game. No one but Moses Fleetwood Washington.

Tiny and I sat on opposite sides of Moses, who squirted mustard onto a cheeseburger from a little plastic tube, and stared out at the waves of cheering fans which rose and fell with the crescendo and decrescendo of the electric organ. Gregor Franks led off with a bunt single and the Chicago media mumbled into microphones. Jose Sanchez shot a single into left field and the Chicago sportscasters in the booths lining the upper deck of the stadium shook their heads in sync. Batting third was Moses, who, although he had his problems on the mound from time to time, had the batting style of a logician—bat back, feet spread, elbows in. Given a pitch to hit, Moses never missed.

"Batter up!" yelled the umpire at the empty on-deck circle as Moses stumbled up the dugout stairs. He insisted on using the same bat he had left out in the rain in Fenway at the beginning of the season, and it was rotting from the inside out toward the tender, molding trademark. Moses dug his cleats into the mud around home plate and took a couple of practice swings with what looked from a distance like a flimsy loaf of enriched white bread.

The first two pitches whizzed past the center of home plate, but the third rebounded off Washington's reaching bat and over the right field fence. Moses had eaten an entire apple by the time he crossed home plate, and tossed the core into the press box past the click click click of glossy magazine photographers. The game was tied, 3-3.

Three outs later, Moses tipped his cap to the sixty-thousand strong and trotted back out to the mound. Six pitches and two outs later, the home plate umpire decided to check the baseball, some of whose seams had been plucked and whose leather casing had been scratched through to the string. There was a conference on the mound. A strip search. And it was decided that Moses should continue, though this time with a brand new baseball. He turned it round in his big hands and contemplated its contours. If only a person could fit inside, he seemed to be thinking as he wheeled a knuckle ball high into the strike zone and watched it fly screaming into the left field wall for a double.

"Take him out?" I asked Tiny.

"We can't," he insisted.

From my position in the dugout I could see Moses shielding his face from the umpire as he quickly, faintly, touched his tongue to the top of the ball as though he were snatching a granule of sugar from a doughnut. The pitch began on the outside portion of the plate, but skipped wildly inward at the batter and just knicked his left earlobe.

"Now?" I asked.

"Later," said Tiny.

Pacing up and down the bench, I could see Washington's parents in the second row behind home plate creating their own miniature wave beneath an afghan of red, white, and blue. A conscientious beer vendor grabbed one of the star-spangled protrusions of yarn, an act punctuated by the sharp sound of bat on ball. Sanchez, the shortstop, got a glove on it to save a run, but the bases were loaded. If you listened carefully you could hear the grumbling digestion processes of Washington's stomach as Tiny walked toward the mound.

They talked and gestured for what seemed like fifteen minutes while the umpires cleaned debris off the field. Then Tiny made a motion. Not toward the bullpen, but toward the stands. Moments later one of the hot dog vendors marched eagerly across the field and sold Moses two Vienna hot dogs with the works. "He said he was hungry," Tiny would report weeks later over beers.

The rest of the game was relatively uneventful from our team's standpoint, although, just after the seventh inning stretch, a U.S. Naval helicopter dropped its long black talons into the infield grass between pitches. But it was no use. Moses simply shook hands with the President, thanked him for being such a concerned fan of the game, and asked the home plate umpire for a new ball.

The last time I saw Moses he was sprawled out on the pitcher's mound drinking Coca-Cola and drawing new game plans into the dirt with the periphery of a genuine World Series game ball. Old Moses, boy, he could hit the cover off a slider with one limb tied behind his neck; and on the mound he was a lefty fully aware of the effects wetness has upon the magnus characteristics of rotating spherical projectiles. But there always seemed to be a splice in his circuits, a flaw in his game, as though Abner Doubleday had plucked one of baseball's finely tuned strings, sending a ripple of difficulties across the bright green turf of Fenway Park. As though every last one of his unfortunate mishaps were nothing more than the product of a collective eccentricity.

Contributors Notes

Curtis White is the author of *Metaphysics in the Midwest* (Sun and Moon) and *Heretical Songs* (Fiction Collective). He is co-director of Fiction Collective Two.

R. M. Berry teaches literary theory and creative writing at Florida State University in Tallahassee, Florida. "The Anatomy of Marcantonio della Torre" is from his novel-in-the-works, *Leonardo Da Vinci Is Dying*, in which the celebrated artist-engineer undergoes a number of ordeals on his deathbed and discovers a 1955 Buick Roadmaster in his back yard.

Stacey Levine was born in St. Louis and lives in Seattle. Her first collection of fiction, *My Horse and Other Stories*, will be published next year (1990) by Sun and Moon Press.

Jeff Duncan's "Spade Work" is from a collection of "historical" fictions. Others deal with Charles Darwin, Ernest Rutherford (co-inventor of the Geiger counter), John Deere, J. Edgar Hoover, Rita Heyworth, Benoit Mendelbrot, Thomas Jefferson and Walter Mondale.

Edward Kleinschmidt has two books of poems, *Magnetism* (The Heyeck Press, 1987) and *First Language* (Juniper Prize, The University of Massachusetts Press). Since 1981 he has taught English and Creative Writing at Santa Clara University.

Constance Pierce is the author of *When Things Get Back to Normal* (ISU/Fiction Collective) and *Phillipe at His Bath* (Adastra). She teaches at Miami University, Oxford, Ohio.

Beverly Brown's fiction has appeared in *The Chicago Review, The Denver Quarterly, Confrontation* and *The Western Humanities Review*. New work is forthcoming in *The Chicago Review*.

David Wong Louie is a resident of Santa Cruz, California, and is presently living in Poughkeepsie, New York, where he teaches at Vassar College. He is a recipient of a grant from the National Endowment for the Arts, and has stories in *Best American Short Stories 1989* and the Asian American literature anthology *Aiiieeeee! 2.*

Jacques Servin is Federation Fellow in writing at Louisiana State University. His work has appeared in *Exquisite Corpse, Mudfish, New Delta Review,* and elsewhere. He is working with Wilson Baldridge on a translation of Michel Deguy's poetry.

Gerald Vizenor teaches literature at the University of California, Santa Cruz. He has written critical essays, narrative histories, short stories, and three novels. *Griever: An American Monkey King in China,* his second novel, won the American Book Award in fiction for 1988. *The Trickster of Liberty,* his most recent novel, was published last year.

Martha Baer has published short fiction in *Fiction, New Observations,* and *Between C & D*. She lives in New York and teaches at The City College.

Misha is the author of a short story collection, *Prayers of Steel,* and a novel, *Red Spider White Web.* She is currently working on a second short fiction collection and a new novel entitled, *Yellowjacket.* She lives at Badger Set, an orchard in Cove, Oregon, with her husband Michael Chocholak, a composer of electroacoustic music.

Conger Beasley, Jr.'s latest book, *Sun Dancers &* *River Demons: Essays on Landscape and Ritual*, will be published in the spring of 1990 by the University of Arkansas Press. He lives in Kansas City, Missouri.

Don Webb has 105 publications stuffed into a small bookshelf, each with a story, poem or article of his in it. Both *Rampike* and *Trucker's USA* are represented.

Jeffrey DeShell was born in the town of government publications, Pueblo, Colorado 81005. His work has recently appeared in *Between C & D, Black Mountain II Review* and *Blatant Artifice*. In 1983 he was awarded a Henfield Transatlantic Review Prize for fiction. He is currently teaching somewhere and working on a new novel.

Rusty Hoover's *Raising the Costs: A Report From Cape Canaveral*, a four-part series on the January '87 opposition to the first flight test of the Trident II nuclear missle, is available from *Downtown* magazine, 151 First Avenue, New York, NY, 10003. He is an editor of *The American Book Review* and lives in Hoboken, New Jersey.

Paul Garrison has recently completed his first collection of short stories, *Mutilations*.